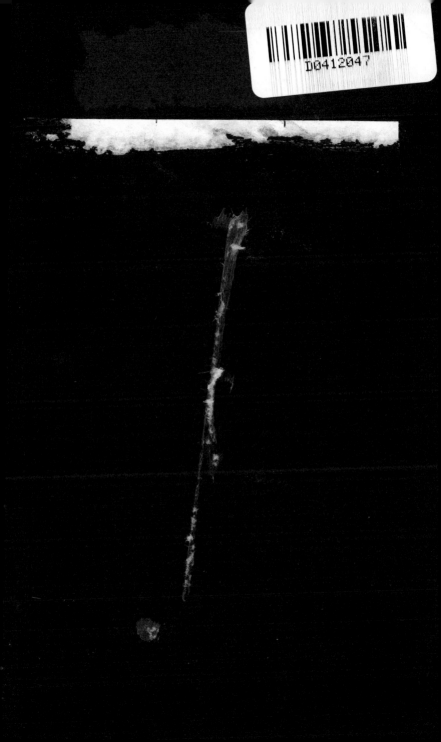

Last Train From Kummersdorf

Leslie Wilson's mother was German and her father was English. She has lived in England, Germany and Hong Kong and now lives in Berkshire with a husband, a cat, and sometimes her younger daughter who is a fashion student. Her elder daughter works for a charity. Leslie Wilson is the author of three novels for adults and has had short stories published and broadcast. Her hobbies are gardening, photography, and Chinese martial arts. She won the 1996 Southern Arts Literature Prize for *The Mountain of Immoderate Desires*.

Last Train From Kummersdorf is partly based on family history. You can find out more about this at:

www.lesliewilson.co.uk

LESLIE WILSON

Last Train From Kummersdorf

ff

faber and faber

First published in 2003
by Faber and Faber Limited
3 Queen Square London WC1N 3AU

Typeset by Faber and Faber
Printed in England by Mackays of Chatham plc, Chatham, Kent

A CIP record for this book
is available from the British Library

ISBN 0-571-21912-8

2 4 6 8 10 9 7 5 3 1

For Jo, with love

Chapter One

It was the rain that stopped the boy running. It made the night too dark to see anything much. He thought: I'm thirsty.

There should be some water left in his bottle. His hand went to his belt. The bottle wasn't there. He'd left it behind.

His hand went on past his belt, feeling the old knitted cardigan that was there instead of his scratchy uniform. The raindrops were coming right through to his skin. The trousers he had on were too short for him and his hair was getting soaked.

He wanted to be at home. With Wolfgang and Heide, and Mother. He didn't want to be standing shivering like this in the rain, in the middle of nowhere.

He could just see that there was a broken tree where he was standing, maybe it had once been a lilac. He put his hand out and felt the smoothness of burned wood. The Russians had already been here, or maybe some bomber had dumped an incendiary as it flew away from Berlin. I'm hungry, he thought to himself, and remembered that he'd had a pack with one square of chocolate left in it, a bit of porridge, a mouthful or so of ersatz coffee, a bit of bread. Only he'd left his pack behind, as well as his water-bottle. He was all alone with nothing to eat and drink, and he'd stolen the clothes he was wearing. From a dead man, a granddad who was too old even for the Home Guard.

You didn't have time to think when you were in action, but now it was as if somebody else – like a teacher – was making him remember. Wake up, boy! Do you even know your name? Or what the date is?

He thought, My name is Hanno Frisch and I really don't know what date it is but it's the end of April, maybe the twentieth, and it's 1945. I'm in the army – no, I used to be in the army.

He'd spent years looking forward to the army, hadn't he? When he was younger, Wolfgang and he used to lie in bed at night and imagine themselves in a doorway, gun in hand, holding a position single-handed against a whole squad of the enemy. Maybe Wolfgang would get winged by a bullet but Hanno would knot an improvised bandage round his arm and they'd keep on fighting. Sometimes their mate Emil was part of it, sometimes he'd been taken prisoner and they had to rescue him afterwards. They tried to make it different every time. Sometimes they'd start arguing about who'd killed more enemy soldiers and end up fighting each other, then Mother would come in to tell them off, or she'd just come in because she'd heard them talking. The best times were when they reached the bit where they were the only pair of twins ever to get the Iron Cross together and the Führer decorated them himself and they were on the newsreel.

Hanno wiped his eyes. The rain came down harder. If anyone saw him they'd think it was only the rain making his face wet, but he was still ashamed. He was almost fifteen – and a police captain's son – he shouldn't cry whatever happened.

He groped his way forward and came up against some kind of ruined wall beyond the tree. He leaned his head on it. The wanting to be at home came over him again. He couldn't stop it.

He wanted this to be an April shower after school last year, he wanted Wolfgang to be running for the house door with him. He wanted Mother to come home at the same moment. They'd climb the two flights of stairs to their flat together and she'd be complaining: 'Two hours I had to queue at the baker's and the greengrocer's and it kept pouring down, and where's that Heide, she's so scatterbrained, almost seventeen, you'd think she'd have some sense . . .' but Wolfgang would make a face and Hanno would give her a kiss and she'd laugh after all and say: 'I got the bread, though, I kept it dry in here, and look, potatoes *and* carrots, the rain doesn't do the vegetables any harm – and did you smell that lilac downstairs, there's nothing like the scent of wet lilac!' Her face would light up when she talked about the lilac. Father wouldn't be there, of course – he'd be at the war – but they were used to that.

It felt as if there'd always been a war – oh, he knew it had started when Wolfgang and he had been nine. He was too young to remember much what peace was like. They'd grown up with the war. At first the Germans had beaten everyone else – the French, the Poles, the Danes, the Norwegians. When they'd had to declare war on Russia they'd gone forging ahead there, too. It had been the usual thing of victory after victory coming over on the radio news. And then it all started to go wrong. There'd been sad music on the radio instead of fanfares of trumpets, because a whole German army had been wiped out at a place called Stalingrad. The Amis and the Tommies had landed in Normandy. Emil's father was taken prisoner then. Bit by bit, the enemy had forced the

German armies backwards, into their own country.

One day this February he'd found his mother at the kitchen table with her head down among the potato peelings and the knife lying on the floor at her feet.

'Mother?' he said. 'Mother?'

He might as well not have been there; she cried and cried, there was dirt on her wet face from the potato peelings so he tried to clear them away, but she just shrieked, 'Leave me alone!'

'Mother?' he said again, and then he saw the telegram. It said his father had been killed fighting for the Fatherland.

He stood still, he didn't know how the world would go on if Father wasn't in it. In spite of everything, he'd felt safer for knowing he had his father.

Then Wolfgang turned up and Hanno showed him the telegram. Wolfgang put his arms round Mother and kissed her face, dirt and all. Now Hanno put his arms round both of them, and Heide came in and saw the telegram and they were all crying together. After that the other police wives started arriving, Frau Schroeder and Frau Knop came in first from upstairs – of course the word was going round the house: 'Frau Frisch has had a telegram, let's go and see what's happened,' and it was: 'Ah, dear God, how can it be? When the Captain was only home at Christmas time?' Hanno caught Wolfgang's eye. Wolfgang knew what he meant. They went downstairs into the yard and started chopping wood for the stove. They didn't talk. But they hacked at the wood, making the chips fly, and then Wolfgang dropped his hatchet and grabbed Hanno. They fought, rolling on the ground. As if they were fighting off Father's death.

Two days after the telegram both of them were drafted

into the Home Guard. Mother went white when Becker came round to tell them.

'They're too young,' she said.

'We're not,' said Hanno.

'You are,' she said. 'You're only fourteen.'

'Almost fifteen,' said Wolfgang.

She said, 'Oh, God, yes, almost fifteen! What have we come to? Herr Becker, they're supposed to be sixteen for the Home Guard, you know that.'

Becker gave her a teacher's threatening stare through his steel-rimmed glasses. He said: 'We don't have enough sixteen-year-olds in Sternberg. Too many brave lads are already in the Regulars. I've got permission to draft boys born in 1931 and earlier. You're not trying to undermine the war effort, are you, Frau Frisch?'

Undermining the war effort was treason, you could be sent to prison or worse. Mother knew that, the boys knew that.

Unpleasantly, Becker added: 'You needn't think, Frau Frisch, that you can move mountains this time.'

Mother didn't answer. After Becker had gone, the boys asked her what he'd meant. She didn't answer them, either.

The uniforms were faded grey and patched because they'd been cut off wounded soldiers in the dressing stations. There were twenty old men and thirty lads from school. Old Becker lined them up and went on about how lucky they were to have uniforms; they could thank him for that, he said, he had connections. Then he said: 'This is the proudest day of all your life.' And started off about the last war, when he'd got the Iron Cross for knocking out an English trench single-handed, and old Rettig the baker wheezed and muttered, 'The Tommies were all dead before he got there.' That made everyone snigger because Rettig knew, he'd been in the same regiment, and Becker shouted: 'What was that? The next man to show disrespect will be shot!' That shut them up, but it didn't make anyone respect Becker. He was their Latin teacher as well as their Home Guard captain, they'd always known he was a self-important brute.

Rettig had terrible asthma: it was the flour, he always said, on top of the gas from the last war. He kept wheezing while Becker reminded them what the Ivans were like – 'You all know what happened at Nemmersdorf,' Becker ended.

They'd seen the newsreel pictures. The Russians were even worse swine than Becker, they'd killed everyone, but the worst thing was what they'd done to the women and girls before they killed them. Only Rettig muttered something like 'What do you expect? We all know –' and then he shut up because Becker was looking at him. Becker barked out, trying to sound like the Führer: 'We can stop the Russians. Never mind how old or young we are. The Führer has said we can. We must have faith. The German people will be telling our story for hundreds of years. How we made this last stand and saved the German people from the Asiatic hordes.'

It was because of the Russians that Mother and Heide had gone away in March – the police wives all managed to get train tickets to the west, where the British and the Americans were coming. Mother and Heide were going to Aunt Lisi in Frankfurt. Mother had thought she'd be able to take Hanno and Wolfgang with her: they could go to the Home Guard in Frankfurt, she said to Becker, but he wouldn't let them go, he didn't want his Home Guard under strength. Hanno couldn't forget her leaning out of the train, crying and kissing them each one more time: 'I wouldn't go if it wasn't for Heide. But you'll come to me in Frankfurt, when the war ends. Both of you. Do you hear?'

Old Frau Hamm came in to stay in the flat with them and cook. But the first night Mother left them a meal. Frau Hamm didn't care what they did, she just fell asleep in a chair after dinner. They talked about how they'd fix the Russians, then they fought each other, just fooling around. Frau Hamm stirred enough to say: 'Boys, don't fight,' then she nodded off again. She was tired because there'd been four air-raids in the last week. That was bad for Sternberg; it wasn't like Berlin where the planes came day and night. Tonight they were glad when the sirens went off and they had to go and fire-watch in town. It felt better to have something to do. It was better four days later too, when Mother's telegram came to say they'd arrived in Frankfurt. Then there'd been a time when they'd fallen into a spooky kind of normality. They'd gone to school, and Becker had lectured them, they'd fire-watched, they'd dug tank traps and fortifications and Becker had lectured them again. It had been strange when they heard that the Americans were in Frankfurt. They hadn't known what to feel, but Frau Hamm said, 'Better than the Russians.'

'Becker reckons we'll drive them all back,' Wolfgang said.

'The Home Guard?' said Frau Hamm. She bit her lip.

It was almost a relief when the orders came for them to go to the Front. There'd been that mess-up with Becker and the map and the compass; that had been funny – but three days later they were still wandering around the woods and getting on each other's nerves. Rettig kept saying they ought to go home. Till they'd met the SS unit and there was no more chance of going home. They'd fought the Russians.

Rettig had died first. Then Becker. It had been grim. All the old men and most of the boys had copped it. The next morning, the SS officer had put the last nine of them down in a ruined village with a Panzerfaust anti-tank weapon and a new lot of ammo for their guns. Wilke was in charge. He was sixteen. The Russians didn't come till the afternoon. Hanno and Wolfgang were together in a doorway, almost like their fantasy. They emptied their guns at the Ivans, and Wilke and Schroeder knocked out a tank with the Panzerfaust before the Ivans blew them up. Hanno and Wolfgang tried to reload but the new ammo didn't fit the guns. Then Wolfgang fell down.

Hanno shook him. 'Get up,' he shouted. 'Get up!' The Ivans fired again, but Hanno didn't get hurt. This is the bit where I put the bandage on him, thought Hanno. Only Wolfgang had no pulse and his chest had been ripped open. But how could he be dead? They'd always been together.

Wolfgang's dirty face was grinning, as if he was trying to reassure Hanno. Hanno thought: If I take him somewhere safe, maybe he'll wake up after all. Somehow he managed to pick his brother up and lift him over the remains of the house wall. When he put Wolfgang down he saw the old man lying there too; he hadn't been dead for long, by the look of him. Maybe half a day. The Ivans were firing shells and bullets and their tanks were grinding on, but behind the wall Hanno knelt next to Wolfgang. 'Wake up!' he said. 'Wake up!'

The Ivans went away and everything was quiet. Then something went cold inside Hanno because he knew Wolfgang was really dead. He laid him out carefully on the ground, arms by his side, he even went back over the wall and found the gun to lay beside him. He walked round the ruins of the village. He found five dead boys. Richter,

Langer, Mai, Kolbe, Thoma. That was everyone then. There was nothing left of Wilke and Schroeder. He went back to Wolfgang and looked at his still-grinning face. It was very like Hanno's, though they weren't identical. Wolfgang's hair was a bit darker blond, and wavy where Hanno's was straight. Hanno was a bit taller. Had been a bit taller.

He stayed there till dusk, sitting on the ground beside Wolfgang, but Wolfgang's face was getting less and less like him, somehow. There was a sound of more tanks in the distance, German or Russian, Hanno had no idea. Anyway, they were coming closer. Now he seemed to hear his brother's voice: 'There's nothing to stay for. Get out of here!' And Hanno knew what he had to do: he took his uniform off and took the granddad's clothes off him, but he left the long underpants and the long-sleeved vest. There were no wounds on the old man's body. Maybe he'd died of heart failure. It didn't seem right to leave the old granddad in his underwear; Hanno put his own uniform on him. There was blood on the uniform: it looked as if the granddad had died a glorious death fighting for the Fatherland like Rettig and Becker. And Father and Wolfgang. Wolfgang. Wolfgang. Then he heard how close the tanks were getting, and he ran for it.

He didn't know how far he'd run. He couldn't go any further tonight, that was all. He leaned on the wall and put a hand into his pocket – the old man's pocket, he thought, my pocket, it's all the same. There was a thin, hand-rolled fag. There was even a single match. The granddad had died before he could have his last fag, now Hanno would have the smoke for him. In his memory. Not Wolfgang's yet. He'd thought about Wolfgang as much as he could bear now.

Hanno sat down on the ground. He took the match and struck it on the wall, shielding it with his hand so that no one would see it and the rain wouldn't put it out. It flared: he lit up and took a drag. It was good tobacco, not civilian tobacco; the old man must have got it on the black market. You weren't supposed to smoke under eighteen. In the army, you got a sweet ration instead of fags, but Rettig the baker gave them his. 'If you're old enough to fight, lads, you're old enough to smoke.' He used to like grumbling, Rettig: 'Look at these potato-flour cakes, will you? Stiff as dried glue, and when the Ivans arrive we won't even have that muck.' You'd think the Red Army had come all the way from Moscow just to eat Rettig's dinner. But he handed out the fags. 'Don't thank me,' he said. 'You've none of you anything to thank anyone for.'

The clouds parted in the sky above him and the moon was there. Hanno forced himself up to look about him; the clouds would be over the moon again in a moment and he needed to find some shelter to sleep under, out of the rain. He was in the middle of a ruined farm: a bomb or a shell had hit one of the barns and knocked the other buildings down. No smell of dead bodies, probably the family had run away already. There was a stable or cow-shed or something that seemed to have kept its roof.

He picked his way across to the building, still shielding the warm cigarette with his palm. The farmyard had been paved with cobbles, and the blast had ploughed up half of it and left the rest untouched: those cobbles gleamed silkily in the moonlight and the wet. A bat flittered round his face; he shuddered, and it was gone. There *was* a roof on the building, a door even. He pushed it open, careless with relief, and saw a movement. Then someone grabbed his arm.

Chapter Two

All you have to do, Effi told herself, is grab whoever it is from behind, put the knife in the right place and stab or cut. You mustn't think it's a person, just think it's meat – it's a kitchen knife after all. Listen, out there they're killing God knows how many people every second, surely you can manage it once, Effi? And if it's an Ivan you can get his gun and work out how to use it.

Only it wasn't an Ivan. It was a boy with fair hair and long thin wrists poking out of a cardigan sleeve. A boy who was shivering. Oh, yes, she thought, we've both got something to shiver about. She could see him quite clearly in the moonlight. He was quite nice-looking, but moonlight was flattering, wasn't it? And he had a lit fag in his hand. The clouds went over the moon and shut the light off. Now all she could see of him was the glow from the fag shining red through his fingers.

She took hold of his arm and he jumped. She laughed at him. 'Have you got any more fags?' she asked.

He pulled himself together; he mustn't let himself down in front of a girl, must he? 'You can have this one,' he said, and held it out to her. When she took it his hand vanished, all she could see was her own in the glimmer of heat in front of her face. She drew in smoke. That was good. The door was still open.

He said: 'I wanted to go to sleep. I'm tired.' As if he had

a right to a bed for the night.

'I've got a gun as well as this knife,' she said, lying, 'and I can see you in the dark. I've got night eyes like a cat's. You'll sleep here if I let you.'

She had to show him she was boss. Oughtn't she to send him away? Supposing he was a deserter, and the military police came along? They'd both be strung up. There was a beam in the stable just the right height for the job. If the Ivans came – she had to stop thinking bad stuff. If the Ivans came she'd get away.

The cigarette was burning her finger, there hadn't been much tobacco in it. She stubbed it out on the wall and put the end in her pocket.

'OK,' she said in the end. 'You can sleep here tonight. You go when I tell you to.'

She could see he was relieved, too tired to think about anything except getting his head down. He had army boots on his feet, giving him away.

She gave him a push.

'This way, this stall.'

'What?'

'There's some hay here. And if you light a lamp, it can't be seen from the yard. I've been out to make sure.'

She lit her tiny lamp. His eyes were drooping half-shut, and yes, he was good-looking, if you liked that type. Blood on his civvy clothes.

'Is that yours?' she asked, pointing to it.

He shuddered. 'No.'

He lay down on the hay, his eyes fell shut and he was asleep. Then there was the sound of engines in the sky. Bombers going to Berlin. She sat still, as if that would make her safer. Her heartbeat grew huge and loud, filling her chest, she felt her hands and feet grow small and cold.

There was nothing new about that. Now she had to think about America. The lights on the stage and the music. It was all right. It was going to keep on being all right.

When the planes had passed she poked a piece of hay at the boy's hand, and listened to his breathing as carefully as if she was a doctor. He was flat out. She took the lamp and went into the other stall. Moving softly and still listening, she cleared away the straw in the corner – it was mucky on the floor, the hay next door had been up in the rack before she brought it down to sleep on. She laid bare the loose half-brick in the wall. She pulled it out and reached inside, then she noticed that her hands were dirty. She'd better wipe them on her clothes. She got them clean and felt for the bag. It was still there, it was all right. She set the bag on the straw and made to open it, but she mustn't, not yet. She picked up the lamp again and went softly back to the stall where he was lying, his mouth open, his face turning gold with the faint light on it. He really was asleep.

She got a handful of clean hay, took it back with her and spread it out on the straw next to the bag. Here were the cotton reels. She counted them as she turned them onto the crinkly hay, fingering their angled wooden shoulders. Twelve. All she'd been able to salvage from the hoard Aunt Annelie had made, that she'd said would be so useful when the war was over.

Effi swallowed hard. Making it through, she told herself, that was still what mattered. And she had the cigarettes, ten packs of these, good cigarettes, Schulz's Nazi fat cats' cigarettes that had flown out of the car along with her when it crashed. Everything else had gone up in flames. They were good fags, but not for her to burn, they were what people were going to use when money was worthless – and it would be soon. Nice smart packages, shiny paper: the high-ups in Berlin were still doing themselves proud, they had plenty of good stuff to take with them when they got in their shiny cars fuelled with the petrol ordinary people couldn't get hold of, and high-tailed it out of Berlin before the Russians came. Schulz had meant to go to Argentina. Well, she'd been glad enough to get a lift with him when she needed it.

She had to put the stuff back in the bag. Then the bag went into the hole, she slid the half-brick back in place, dirty straw against the half-brick. It was a work of art to put the straw back as if it hadn't been disturbed, ruffle it up a bit. That looked OK. Then she gathered up every last piece of hay and took it back to the other stall. She put the lamp out and sat in the dark for a few minutes before she wrapped herself in the blanket and lay down on her side, cradling her front with her arms, curling her legs up to her chest. The Russian planes came over twice more in the night, and each time she woke up and felt her swollen heart thumping, and each time she went back to sleep again.

Hanno woke up, and looked for Wolfgang. He wasn't in the stable. So where was he? Then he remembered. But it can't be true, he thought. And how could he be alive when Wolfgang was dead?

The girl was there.

'You're awake, are you?' she asked, sitting down beside him.

She didn't seem quite real, though he could see her clearly enough, thin body inside a grey skirt and a grey cloth jacket over a shirt that used to be white. Huge hungry black eyes above high cheekbones, a snub nose and curly black hair down to her shoulders. And solid boots on her feet.

She asked: 'I suppose you want food?' She had a Berlin accent.

'You've got food?'

'Would I promise it if I didn't? It isn't much. Just porridge.'

She looked at him, narrowing her eyes and whistling for a few minutes, like a boy. Then she said: 'Cold porridge. I don't light the fire twice in a morning, once is dangerous enough.' She pointed to the other side of the stall. 'Look, it's there, in the pot. You can borrow my spoon. Get up and help yourself – I'm not going to bring it to you.'

He fetched the pot; it was black and encrusted on the outside but the inside was clean, and his nose caught the smell of food. He picked up the spoon.

'I've had my share,' she said, then: 'There's some water in my mug. It's clean water, the pump's still working in the yard.'

He ate it quickly, licking the last little blob off his fingers, but he didn't enjoy it. It stilled his hunger, that was all. There was a noise overhead. It was louder than the guns. The sky beyond the door was dirty with planes.

'Ivans,' yelled the girl against the racket.

Hanno yelled back: 'They'll be Tupolev bombers. Or ground-attack planes, tank-busters.'

'Expert, are you?' she jeered.

She doesn't like me, he thought.

The quiet was shocking after the planes had gone. He stood up.

'Where are you off to?' the girl wanted to know.

'I don't know.'

She looked him over, biting her lip for a moment. 'I'm going to the lake, to wash the pot and the spoon. There are fish in it. Mind, we can't cook again till after dark, the smoke doesn't show then.'

'The lake?'

'Just beyond the farm. It's pretty.' She laughed. 'Do you think you could catch a fish in a flour bag? I forgot to go to the angling shop for a net.'

He said: 'I've got to piss.'

Her lips puckered upwards at the corners of her mouth. 'Is that where you were going? You could piss behind a tree on the way to the lake.'

'All right,' he said. 'I'll come to the lake with you.' He thought he might as well do that as anything else.

She whistled again, a bit of a tune he thought he knew, but he wasn't going to ask her. 'Your choice, kid. If you want to crap, the earth closet's behind the old cowshed. It smells. Don't fall in.'

'I don't need to crap.'

'Good for you.'

The lake was pretty if you looked to the left. To the right, there was a big messy crater flooded with water. There were white birch trunks floating in it like belly-up fish. Some of the stems had even burst out in little glossy leaves and gold catkins.

'Look,' he said, half to himself, 'they don't know they're finished.'

The girl ran to the tree-fringed beach on the other side, sat down and took her boots off. 'You have to wade in to find the fish. They taste good, what there is of them.'

She took her jacket off and rolled her skirt up so that he could see almost all of her legs. He looked away.

'Come on,' she said. 'If I catch a fish, I shan't share it with you.'

He asked her, 'What's your name?'

'No time,' she said, going into the water.

He followed her. The lake was cold; it was a fiddly hunt for fish that were small, as she said, and nimbler than his fingers with the clumsy flour bag. But he caught two. She didn't catch any.

'I don't like to stay too long in the open,' she said. 'Might get spotted and bombed. You can take your fish and go if you like.' She stared at him.

No, he thought, I can't yet. He said, 'I'll stay till tomorrow.'

She didn't answer, but turned round and started walking back through the wood. The birds were singing as if it was an ordinary spring. They reached the stable and another lot of planes came over. He laid the fish on the floor, but she shook her head at him.

'No,' she shouted against the racket, 'safer up there,' pointing to the hayrack. 'Though the rats'll come for it anywhere.'

When the planes had gone, she said, 'Nothing to stop them. No Luftwaffe heroes.'

'They said there was a secret weapon.'

'Oh yes, I forgot about that. It's going to go up into space and come back and set New York alight, isn't it? Pull the other one.'

'My name's Hanno,' he said. 'You can have one of my fish.'

She narrowed her black eyes and stared at him.

'I'm Effi,' she said at last. 'Do you mean it about sharing the fish?'

'Yes.'

'More fool you.'

He heard the guns in the distance. 'Tomorrow,' he said suddenly, 'I'll go back and fight again.'

'What'll you tell the military police?'

She thumbed at the beam: in a flash he saw himself hanging there. He felt as if someone had kicked him, hard, in the stomach, and now he knew what he was: a deserter.

'Cheer up,' she said, 'do you think you're the only one to run away?'

A squad of bombers flew in, not far away, but not directly overhead either. Suddenly he knew he was listening, all the time, for sounds outside, for footsteps or approaching engines. The girl – Effi – must have listened like that, last night. The rain came down on the roof.

There was an explosion somewhere. He said, 'My mother went to my aunt's in Frankfurt. The Amis are coming there.'

There was a second explosion, further away, and a plane flew right overhead. It was gone before he could be afraid of it. Now the girl made a comic face. That made him laugh, whereupon she stared at him with an expression of ludicrous, teacherish outrage. He kept laughing, though it felt wrong to laugh when Wolfgang was dead.

She said, 'Let's cook that fish. The rain hides the smoke, and I'm hungry.'

'I thought you said not till dark?'

'Oh, I don't care,' she said. 'If a bomb's got our names on it –'

Chapter Three

There was something wrong with the boy. His eyes were too wide open, and when he laughed he was out of control. Oh, well, thought Effi, a lot of things are war-damaged nowadays. She took him through the rain into the wreckage of the farm kitchen. The huge chimney was still standing, and a bit of roof round it, though they had to duck under a fallen beam to get there. The big range was battered and pitted, several of the doors hung open at crazy, useless angles.

'I stayed here because of the chimney,' she told him. 'And the stable.' (And the sack of swedes she'd found in the wreck of the cowshed.) 'Good if you can cook.'

They'd done a brisk trade with electric hotplates in Berlin after all the gas mains were broken. Aunt Annelie had got one and cooked black-market stew on it; there'd been enough for them and six of the U-boats. Effi shook herself: there she went again, thinking about things that would trip her up. And why had she decided to make the smoke? Well, now she'd got going, she wasn't going to stop. She was really hungry.

The boy said, 'We used to have carp on Christmas Eve. And poppy-seed dumplings. My mother used to let the carp swim in the bath. My sister always wanted to let it go.' He smiled but looked worried at the same time.

Effi had a little heap of firewood on the other side of

the range. She broke it into small pieces, calculating how much heat it'd take to cook the fish. Then she reached into her pocket and got a match. She had two boxes of matches. What was his family life to her?

'Can't we cook those nettles?' he asked. 'There, behind the ruined wall.'

'Go on then,' she said. 'Pick them.' He walked over and set to, using his finger and thumb. Fish, she thought, nettles – he's quite useful.

She lit the fire. She'd been baking the fish in the embers: the skin got black but that didn't matter.

'How old are you?'

'Sixteen.'

He was lying, of course. 'So am I,' she said at once. She thought he was fourteen, like her. Maybe fifteen. 'Where do you come from?'

'Sternberg.'

'Where's that?'

'About forty kilometres south-east of Berlin. It's only a small place. There's a big wireworks there, though.'

'You've come quite a trek, haven't you?'

She wasn't quite sure where they were now, but Schulz had meant to drive south-west, towards Wittenberg, and had been forced to take the Zossen road south-east instead when he'd found the road blocked by Home Guard tank traps. He'd sworn a lot. About an hour later, the Ivan plane had opened fire on the car. She guessed they were somewhere round Zossen. That could be bad, because the army headquarters was at Zossen, or maybe good, because the Ivans might home in on Zossen and leave the countryside alone. She thought it was probably best to wait here till the shooting stopped. Probably.

The boy said: 'We went to fight the Russians but our

captain – Becker – he was old and he lost his reading glasses so he couldn't read the map. We were going round in circles.' For a moment he almost grinned. 'We tried to tell him, but he kept shouting that he'd been in the Great War, he had the Iron Cross, how dared we? Then we met an SS unit and the officer made Becker own up. He slapped his face. They found us somewhere to fight.'

'Pity you met them, isn't it? Or you could have carried on being lost till it was all over. Did Becker get killed?'

His face went quite blank. She didn't like to see that.

'Put those nettles down,' she said. 'Go to the pump, get me some water to cook them with. It's round the corner there, by the door hole.' She passed him the pot.

He said, 'The first lot of ammunition was all right, but the second lot didn't fit the guns.'

'Of course,' she said, wanting to shut him up. 'Germany's finished. When you're finished, you make a mess of things. So they gave you the wrong ammo, so what? Look, boy. What you've got to realize is that you're lucky. You're still alive.'

Hanno went away to the pump. He walked out through the gap in the wall and stood in the rain outside the shaky wall working the iron handle till a spurt of water came out. He hated himself for telling the girl things. He wasn't going to tell her about Wolfgang.

When he came back, the girl picked the nettles up and swore. However carefully you took hold of a nettle it'd whip round and sting you somewhere, Hanno had three throbbing spots on his fingers. He was glad she'd got stung. She was a bad girl, anyway. Heide didn't even know that word. She put the pot on the stove and threw the greens in to boil. She didn't look at him.

*

Eating the fish was a performance. You needed all your wits about you to separate the scraps of sweet flesh from the bone and keep from choking. Effi took her time over it. The nettle leaves were slimy and strong to taste. Aunt Annelie used to say they cleaned the blood.

Suddenly the sun came out and the wet on the black fallen beams glittered like snail-tracks. Effi jumped up with the fish still on her tongue, and put the fire out with sandy soil she had ready beside the wood; she'd been too careless already, and now she felt a wildness howling inside her, she wanted to let go, she wanted to be careless.

Pierre must have felt like that in the end, tired of hiding and taking precautions, so they caught him.

There were planes coming, swarms of little planes like insects going to a dead horse. The sun warmed her side as she and the boy crouched in the shelter of the chimney. She put her hands across her belly, comforting it. Potatoes or bread would be better comfort. Pierre used to go on about French bread, long white sticks, crisp on the outside, soft as butter on the inside. It only kept a few hours, he said. She'd asked him what the point of that was. She'd have liked to taste it now, all the same. It wouldn't need to last: she'd eat the lot. When all she had to look forward to was tonight's turnips and some nettles, and porridge again tomorrow morning. Fish if she was lucky.

She was thinking about Pierre now, and Aunt Annelie. She could see them both in her mind, as if they were looking at her. Pierre pushing his floppy brown hair out of his eyes, and needing a shave – there were more important things to buy on the black market than razors. Aunt Annelie with her blonde hair tied back with a blue ribbon; she'd always liked little bows. But she'd kept a big red flag in the cellar for when the Russians came.

When it was safe, Pierre liked to talk German with a French accent, though he didn't have any problem passing for a German, because he came from Alsace and talked Rhineland. He'd been in Paris, playing jazz piano and harmonica in a bar, when the Germans picked him up and brought him to work in the munitions factory in Berlin. 'Volunteers,' they called them. There were Dutchmen and Belgians, too. Pierre had worked night-shifts underground; he was used to that, he said, but he didn't like putting shells together in a factory as much as he liked playing jazz in a cellar. He said the conditions were worse for the slave labourers from the East; he hadn't suffered much. Still, when the camp was bombed he got out smartly enough. And was clever enough to find his way to Aunt Annelie's bar, and Effi, and the German Resistance. Such as it was.

Aunt Annelie got Pierre a set of false papers and a ration book, Peter Sachs he was supposed to be called, her cousin from Bonn. Pierre was supposed to be a nickname. And he pretended to have a bad leg that had kept him out of the army – he got so used to limping he said he couldn't walk properly any more. He helped her run the bar, which was on the ground floor of a big workers' tenement in Prenzlauer Berg. Underneath it was a cellar, it was the air-raid shelter for the whole block, but once Pierre was there it became a jazz club too; they even managed to get a piano for it. There was Jochen Roth on violin – he was out of the fighting since he'd been burned and blinded in North Africa – and anyone else who was on leave with any instrument they happened to be able to play jazz on. Effi used to go, though she wasn't supposed to, but kids weren't supposed to be in Berlin at all; half of them had been evacuated. She used to keep quiet in a corner. It was a good place to exchange information when the music got loud and if any Nazis turned up, Pierre would change to sloshy square stuff like 'I Know There'll be a Miracle Some Day'. In the daytime, Pierre gave Effi music lessons there. She didn't go to school any more. He even taught her the harmonica, though he said it wasn't a girl's instrument.

Whenever the bombs came down the music had to stop. Pierre was an air-raid warden and Effi was a fire-watcher. If food was short for the U-boats, they'd skip over to the posh areas and do a bit of looting while the fun was going on. Once they got caviar. Aunt Annelie said it was very nutritious. Aunt Annelie had a false wall at the back of their living room and a little, secret space behind a cupboard. Once, before an action, she'd kept leaflets there, and sometimes U-boats – Jews and Communists – went to ground there, if they were on their way out of Berlin, or if the place they'd been staying had been wrecked, or people had got suspicious. Berlin was supposed to be empty of Jews but there were still a few hiding out. Also, Aunt Annelie kept food and useful things in there. She'd started to put those away after 20 July 1944, when the plot to kill Hitler failed. They'd had some bad days then, always expecting the Gestapo, but somehow they didn't get arrested.

Aunt Annelie had always said Hitler would make Germany fight till the end, so they'd need to last out a battle. She'd been right about the battle.

The plan had been that Pierre, Aunt Annelie and Effi would stick it out till the Ivans came, then Pierre would show them his French papers, which he'd kept, and claim Effi and Aunt Annelie were French too. So the Ivans wouldn't do anything bad to them and they could go west with Pierre. He wanted Aunt Annelie to go to Paris with him. They'd get married there and live happily ever after.

Only then came the night of 18 April. When Hitler had called on the people of Berlin to die for him, and the left wanted to show him how many Germans didn't agree. Everyone was to go out and paint NO on the walls. Aunt Annelie said there weren't many walls left to paint and Pierre said, 'We'll find some.' Aunt Annelie didn't go, she wasn't feeling well. Effi went with Pierre. And somehow Pierre went crazy, he wouldn't let Effi check the streets first; he said it was blackout, no one would see him. It was as if he thought liberation had already come. But the police came round the corner and they got him.

He shouted at Effi: 'Run for it!' The swine got their noose out straightaway. There was a lamppost nearby, they didn't waste energy taking him anywhere else. She watched, it made her feel sick to remember it, she forced herself, she hoped they might go off at once and she could cut him down, but the swine made sure he was dead before they left. Effi ran back to Aunt Annelie's and inside her the voice was wailing, No, not Pierre, he can't have copped it. Only when she got there an incendiary had come down on the bar, the whole block was in flames and Aunt Annelie was inside there. Some arsy Hitler Youth – like that boy – was acting as air-raid warden and he wouldn't let Effi go in to get Aunt Annelie. Afterwards they found her body, and later Effi found the cotton reels among the ruins. She'd been looking for Pierre's harmonica but everything else was burned up.

The next morning there were plenty of NOs painted on the few walls the bombers had left standing. It hadn't been worth Pierre losing his life for. Then Schulz had turned up like the fairy godfather. Or something. 'My God,' he said – as he did every time he saw her, 'you're so much like your mother. I'm leaving Berlin. I want you to come with me.' She'd said, 'Nothing worth staying for, Herr Schulz.'

She made herself think about her father. He was coming back to Germany. He'd sent word, he was a US citizen now and he'd joined the army. When the war was over she'd go to the Amis and ask for him. Bruno Mann. 'You know,' she'd say, 'he wrote that hit song: "Raindrops Shining in Your Hair". They even play it in Germany, only with a different name.'

She'd know him when she saw him. Aunt Annelie had a photograph and she'd learned it by heart.

The planes had gone. She glanced at the boy.

'What are you staring at?'

He hesitated. Then: 'There are some buttercups there.'

'You can't eat buttercups.'

He said, 'They're so yellow.' As if it was amazing to see yellow buttercups. And she looked at them, trying to see what he saw.

'They look sticky. Like wet paint.'

He gave her a sudden grin that surprised her. It was the kind that made you grin back, you couldn't help it.

'My mother used to put them under my chin,' she said. 'I thought the yellow really came off on me.'

He asked, rather hesitantly: 'Is she alive, your mother?'

'No.'

'I'm sorry,' he said. As if he meant it. Then: 'If we went down to the lake again we could catch more fish.'

'Too dangerous. If you're always trotting around the place, someone might notice. We'll go back to the stable.'

His friendliness faded. He looked out at the world as if he hated it.

'I'm going to fight tomorrow,' he said, as if he thought she'd be sorry.

She shrugged her shoulders. 'I've been wanting a bit of time to myself.'

In the stable she took her boots off, stretching her bare feet and long toes, slipping her fingers between her toes to flick the dirt out. She told him: 'You should take yours off. Or your feet'll rot.'

'I know,' he said, but he kept his boots on.

Suddenly she wanted to make him laugh again, so she pulled the comic schoolmistress face. Pierre used to love that.

He was trying not to laugh, but he couldn't stop himself. Then he stood up.

'OK, watch,' he said. 'Who am I?' He walked about doing the goose-step, it was good; he doubled his chin and made his stomach poke, he looked so fat and yet mean at the same time. Now it was her turn to laugh.

'You're fat Reich Air Marshal Göring,' she said. She liked him for making fun of the stinking Nazi.

He dropped down beside her again, and they went on laughing, leaning back against the splintery wooden wall. But they were making much too much noise.

'We shouldn't,' she said. 'You don't know who's listening outside.'

He fell silent at once, and started undoing his bootlaces.

She thought she'd get some information out of him. 'So your mother's in Frankfurt. What about your father?'

'He was killed in February.'

'Do you miss him?'

'Yes.'

'What did he do before he was in the army?'

'He was a policeman.'

The boy was a policeman's brat?

Sharply, she said, 'What kind? Detective? Or –'

'Not a detective. Not Gestapo, either.'

'Military police then? Or just on the beat?'

'He was in a police regiment. In the Ukraine, and then he had to retreat with the rest. He was a police captain.'

Effi interrupted. 'Shut up. I heard something.' She hadn't, but it gave her the chance to calm down.

Pierre used to say: 'Look, kid, don't get angry. Angry makes you careless.' Now she wouldn't think about Pierre's own carelessness. She'd think about keeping safe, that was what he'd wanted. She whistled under her breath, 'Body and Soul', nice and slow. It did calm her.

She'd have to get rid of the boy. Police had killed Pierre, and she knew what the police regiments had done out in Russia. Killings. Just as bad killings as the SS. Probably he was proud of what his father had done. Imitating Göring didn't mean anything, people were always making jokes about the Nazis, even about Hitler. It was just like kids poking fun at the schoolteacher. It didn't mean they'd rebel against them. Anyway, it was all right, he wanted to go off and fight again, get killed with the rest, good riddance. She'd encourage him.

'I'm going to get some kip,' she said. 'Got to do something to pass the time.'

Mother had darned Hanno's socks with yellow and pink wool from a couple of her old jumpers. Hanno had said, 'I'm meant to fight the Russians with pink and yellow socks?'

'The Russians won't look inside your boots,' said

Wolfgang.

'It's all very well for you,' Hanno had said crossly. 'She used up all the grey wool on yours.'

'OK,' said Wolfgang. 'Dye them.'

'What am I meant to dye them with?'

Wolfgang had gone to Father's desk and come back with a bottle of black ink. He'd dribbled it over the socks. 'You see,' he'd said. 'I'm saving our soldiers' honour, making sure you have decent socks.' Then he'd put them on the stove to dry and the ink had run down and Mother had come in from queuing for bread and she'd been angry. Heide thought it was funny.

He couldn't understand why he'd done that imitation for the girl. Maybe just because he was so used to being one of a pair, having someone to laugh and clown with. Wolfgang was the funniest, though. Once he'd made Hanno and Heide spit water all over the table at Sunday dinner. Then they all got into trouble. 'You shouldn't encourage them,' Mother said to Heide. 'You're two years older – you should set a good example.'

Wolfgang could even get out of a fight by making faces at the other boy. Pity the Russians hadn't been able to see his face.

He was tired, but he couldn't sleep. He had an odd feeling of lightness and pain, as if a limb had been hacked off him. His chest ached; he told himself he didn't know why – he didn't want to admit it was the tears he needed to shed. He wasn't going to cry.

One of the girl's bare feet was poking out from the blanket: she had nice feet. He stared at the lines of her foot as if he had a pencil and was working out how to draw it. But really, he thought, it ought to be a carving in wood. Wolfgang wasn't interested in carving, he liked making model aircraft, but Hanno had used to whittle wood, he'd done animals and birds and faces. Mother said once it was as good as the carvings at Oberammergau but that was the kind of thing mothers always said about their kids' stuff. Hanno was never really pleased with what he did, he thought he'd need a lot more time, and time to think, too. Anyway, in the last while they'd needed every little bit of wood for the heating stove.

In the evening, the girl brought out swedes from somewhere. They ate them with more nettles, taking turns at the spoon and the pot. She said they had to put the lamp out as soon as they'd eaten, to save the oil.

'When did you last eat a potato?' she asked him.

'In the army.'

'The good breakfast before you're hanged, hey? Crazy, really. When a pig's to be killed, they starve it. Only nowadays,' she went on in a singsong comedian's voice, 'they just string people up, no food. Can't have people fiddling themselves extra rations that way. Still, the number of people there are hanging around in Berlin, you'd think no one had spread the word.' Her face twisted up for a moment, but she passed her hands over it and came out the other side grinning. 'Your turn to eat, Hitler Youth.'

'Is that where you come from, Berlin? Don't call me Hitler Youth.'

She glanced at him, whistled again, and said, 'Yes. I was with my two aunts. We were trying to get to Leipzig, where my grandfather lives, and I lost them.'

'And your father?'

'He died,' she said. 'At Stalingrad.'

Now there were tears in her eyes, and he didn't know

what to say.

'Are you going back to the war?' she asked.

He told himself that he ought to revenge Wolfgang's death.

'They told us things we could do. Werewolf actions. Sabotage behind the enemy lines. They showed us how to unscrew a tank's petrol cap and pour sand in.'

'Well,' said the girl, 'the soil's all sand round here so that's easy – now all you have to do is find an Ivan tank; plenty of those round here, too.'

Suddenly he saw how stupid the whole idea was. 'An Ivan tank on its own with no soldiers guarding it?'

She shrugged her shoulders. 'I'm not the werewolf. You are.'

Hanno woke up and again he turned round to look for Wolfgang. Only Wolfgang was dead. He kept having to realize that. It hurt so badly.

There was a bright thin wedge of yellow light lying on the stable floor beyond the grey wood of the stall. He lay still, watching the dust dance in the air. Somewhere there were big guns pounding outside, but there was a bird singing too, really close. He shut his eyes again.

It seemed wrong that he could just lie there. Every morning, for as long as he could remember, there'd been work waiting for him and Wolfgang as soon as they woke up. Wood to chop, wild mushrooms to pick, jobs for Mother, scrap metal and rags to collect for recycling, labouring jobs, school. Fire-watching at night. Sometimes you couldn't keep awake in school. Some of the teachers would let you sleep in class if you'd been up all night. Becker wouldn't. Once he'd crept up on Emil and woken him up with a massive clout round the ear hole, then he'd started yelling about superhuman efforts.

The sun was really warm, and his clothes were steaming. Hanno remembered that there was a job waiting for him. Becker used to say to the lads: 'You were born to die for Germany.' Wolfgang wasn't there because he'd done that job already.

His eyes wandered aimlessly round the stable and he

saw that the girl had left the porridge for him in the hay. It was still warm, and he was hungry. For a few minutes it tasted really good. Then he started to think again, and the taste went away. He ate it all, though, and licked the pot out. His belly wanted it.

Mother had said both of the boys must come to Frankfurt. He imagined himself coming through the door. She'd say, 'Where's Wolfgang?' There could only be one thing worse than knowing Wolfgang was dead – having to tell Mother about it. And Father had done his duty for his country. Who was Hanno to shirk it? He thought, but it's finished. Frau Hamm knew that. Then: Frau Hamm was only an old woman. What did she know?

A cat came in through the open door, a scrawny miaowing tortoiseshell. He put his hand out to her. She purred, then clawed at him. He pulled his hand away and licked the blood off. The cat started to rub her cheek against him. He scratched her behind the ears. She loved it, twisted her chin round for him to scratch underneath it, rubbed and caressed him. Suddenly she bit him and shot up to the hayrack, where she sniffed and miaowed again. She must be able to smell that there'd been fish there. She kept miaowing now, a loud, demanding call.

'I don't have anything,' he told her.

The cat shot him a disgusted look and started to wash. Hanno didn't want to stay still any longer. He got his boots on and went out to ferret around the buildings, looking for Effi. She wasn't anywhere, so he thought he'd try the lake. He went back to the stable to get the pot and spoon to wash. The cat had gone away.

He went through the wood. The smell there was clean and sweet, quite different from the musty smell of old animal mess and broken buildings at the farm. Every now and then his face brushed the yellow, tasselly birch flowers. It was as if these things were shouting for his attention, like the cat, like the loud yellow buttercups yesterday and the birds singing their heads off. Half of him said, I don't want to – but he started to run to the lake.

Effi was standing by the shallow water. She was pulling her jacket on and her hair was wet. She heard him come, stared at him with her black eyes wide.

'Have a swim, Hitler Youth,' she said. 'I won't look when you get to the interesting bits.'

He found himself answering in the same teasing voice. 'So you think I'm interesting? That's nice.'

'Here.' She threw him a thin, damp greyish towel. 'Actually,' she said, 'I won't look at all. Don't want to see how dirty the war has made you.'

He took the old man's cardigan off, and the shirt, and washed his face and neck. Then he made sure Effi really wasn't looking, stripped his trousers off and went into the lake. The water shouldn't feel colder than it had done yesterday, when he had his clothes on, but it did. He remembered how the Hitler Youth group had had to swim in the frozen lake at home to harden themselves.

A duck splashed down into the water. The drake came next, with his blue-green head, and they looked round them smugly, taking possession of the lake. About five more pairs followed them, ha-ha-ing at each other.

Effi shouted: 'Why did you throw away your gun? Oh, I forgot, there wasn't any ammo. Couldn't we make catapults? There are enough stones back in that farmyard. Duck. Duck! Gourmet stuff.' She accented the gourmet, and drew it out, long and husky. 'Oh, sorry, Hitler Youth.

I didn't look at you, only at the ducks. I'll look away now.'

He made sure she really was looking away before he came out of the water. He thought she'd seen something, anyway, but not the important part, only his bum. He rubbed himself down with the towel and got his trousers on quickly. When she took the towel off him, he startled himself because he wanted to kiss her. Only he didn't know how to start. He had kissed a girl before, but that was only Trude Streicher – it was easy with her, you just went up to her and took hold of her; she'd kiss anyone back. Wolfgang and Hanno had both done it. And there were stories that she'd go all the way if you tried it, but neither of them had.

They went among the trees and found forked pieces of wood. He remembered that they'd need elastic if they wanted to make catapults.

'We can use the stuff in my knickers,' she said.

He found himself laughing again.

'I'll take them off and put the elastic back afterwards.' She made the schoolmistress face. 'So no bad thoughts, young man.'

She couldn't say anything else, because the planes came over, flying lower than they had done before. Hanno dropped flat on his face and lay on the ground without moving, but some kind of little animal – a vole or a shrew – ran over his hand: lucky thing, he thought, on its way to its own private bunker. He could see each separate blade of grass and the pale sandy soil underneath. Then he felt Effi's hand in his, felt her fingers lock round his: her palms were sweating.

After the planes had gone, he said, 'The birds have stopped singing.'

'Maybe they've all gone away,' she said. 'Maybe the ducks have gone too.' Her voice was quiet and shaken. Then it perked up. 'Well, never mind, life goes on.' She rolled over onto her back and stood up all in one movement. Hanno did the same, and not just to show her. He wanted to. She gave herself a shake, then turned a cartwheel without warning, bowling herself unerringly between two tree trunks. Then she bowed, smiling round her like a movie star; he could almost hear clapping.

Who is she, he thought, where does she come from? A moment later the first bird began to sing.

They came back into the farmyard: Hanno saw Effi stiffen and stop. There was a man standing there – waiting for us, Hanno thought, and his throat closed up. That'll teach you to be happy, a nasty voice said inside him.

The man was dressed in a come-down suit of clothes, but Effi saw the strength of his back even while he tried to slouch. He took his hat off. He had army-cropped hair. Or police-cropped. It was a squashy civvy hat and he looked at it as if he didn't recognize it. He waved to them and came over, stumbling round the heaps of wreckage. He was drunk.

'So,' he said, 'there is life here, after all.'

Oh, that Nazi sarcasm, heavy as a bomb, any moment now he'd drop it on his toes and swear. And she hadn't got rid of the boy yet. She didn't want to think how she'd held his hand when the planes came over; it had been a moment's weakness, she'd get over it.

She thought about the knife in her pocket, but this fellow probably had a gun. Of course the boy knew how to shoot. If the man had a gun and if she could get it off him the boy could shoot him and then use it to bag a duck. If only.

'I've got a car,' said the man. 'It's on the main road, about a kilometre from here, but the petrol's given out. There must have been a leak in the tank when I bought it. Any petrol here?' He smelt of enough booze to tank his car up.

'Mister,' said Effi, 'where do you expect us to get petrol from?'

Then she noticed how the boy Hanno was staring at him.

'Police Major Otto,' he said.

The man's shoulders went up round his neck and his trigger-finger twitched, probably he'd come straight from torturing people and killing them, but now he was scared and angry, a beast on the run, more dangerous because he was drunk – and the boy was staring at him as if he hated him. Effi's heart raced. Keep calm, she thought. She did the whistling under her breath again, 'Smoke Gets In Your Eyes'.

'My name's Braun,' the man said, giving the boy an evil look. 'I had a business in Berlin, but an incendiary got it. I've lost everything now the car's gone.'

Lies, thought Effi, you've probably got a dozen numbered bank accounts in Switzerland. Like Schulz.

'I'm a diabetic,' the man said roughly. 'I never got called up. I suppose you're a deserter, boy.' He pulled a flask out of his pocket and swigged. Effi smelt cognac, worth any amount of food, and he was wasting it getting drunk. But he was used to not worrying about food, he smelt of meat as well as drink – real meat, not blue-stripe sausages made of cereal.

'You used to be in the police in Sternberg,' said Hanno.

The man said: 'What do you know about the police in Sternberg?'

'I'm Johannes Frisch,' said the boy. What was going on between them? 'Captain Frisch's son.'

'Never heard of you,' the man said, but he gave the boy a really wicked look now and the boy returned it; they stood there eyeing each other as if they were going to fight.

There was a sound of planes again. No time to get to the stable so she ran for the cook-place. The boy came after her, then Braun-Otto was there beside them, all three of them skulking against the wall. The planes flew right over the yard and went away. They'd be back. There you are, thought Effi, while a small shiver ran all the way up her spine – a girl never has to feel lonely, people always turn up. Armies of them, even.

What was Otto doing? He was reaching into his pocket – so he did have a gun, what was he going to do with it? He was holding it in front of him and playing with the trigger. Her heart drummed a scary solo. But she must act brainless, that's what Aunt Annelie always said you had to do if it got sticky. 'They think women have nothing between their ears, play up to it.' Aunt Annelie had spent the last twelve years acting the good-hearted dumb blonde barmaid and in the end only the comrades knew how smart she was.

'Herr Braun,' Effi said. She'd better think of him as Braun, then she'd be less likely to slip up when she talked. 'Please be nice to me, don't fire that thing off.' And rolled her eyes at him like stupid fat Zarah Leander in that Nazi feel-good film, *The Great Love*.

Braun's face turned cheese-white. Suddenly he ran out into the yard and threw up. The wastefulness of it, how could he spare the food? Only –

'Come on,' she whispered to the boy. 'Run. Now.'

He didn't even hear her. He was waiting for Braun with that furious look on his face. It was too late now anyway, Braun was wiping his mouth and coming back. He was holding his gun properly now.

He ignored the boy and started interrogating Effi.

'Who are you, girl, what are you doing here? You're from Berlin, aren't you?'

'Prenzlauer Berg. My aunt had a bar there. But it was bombed out and we went to stay with my other aunt out in Grunau but then we had to run away from the Russians. We were trying to go to my grandfather in Leipzig and I lost my aunt and – and my father died at Stalingrad, Herr Braun.'

'Otto,' said Hanno. 'His name's Otto. He was a veteran Nazi, he joined before the Führer came to power in 1933, he used to make a really big thing out of that. Now he's running away.'

Braun's finger twitched against the trigger.

'Stop yapping, boy.'

'No,' said Hanno.

'Do as you're told!' Braun threatened him with the gun. At last the boy got the message and he shut up.

'Prenzlauer Berg's a bad area,' said Braun to Effi. 'Too many Communists there. Traitors.'

'Oh, I love the Führer, Herr Braun, so do my aunts. I hate the Communists, they're in league with the Ivans.'

He didn't believe her, she could tell. He said: 'How do you and the boy come to be together?'

'He just turned up here today,' she said. 'His friends were all killed, but he's not giving up. He's going off to do werewolf actions. Sabotaging the enemy.'

'Where had you been together when I met you?'

'There's a pretty lake, with fish in it. And ducks. We

were thinking about eating duck – you could shoot us one, Herr Braun, we could all eat it together.'

'A duck?' Braun laughed. It was a bad laugh. 'Why not? I might even let you have a bone or two to chew. But I don't want to waste a bullet. You can catch us a duck, boy. You'd better. Or –' and he pushed the gun muzzle towards Effi.

At least now Hanno knew what a fool he'd been.

'I don't know how,' he said.

'Not so cocksure now, are you? You'd better have an idea. Quickly.'

Effi said: 'We were thinking about a catapult . . . Herr Braun, I've got to pee.'

'Go round the back there. If you run for it I'll know. I'll shoot you.'

She went behind the chimney and got the elastic out of her knickers. It wasn't easy because her hands were trembling. How had she come to be the hostage in some kind of police feud? At least Braun wouldn't know where the elastic came from. She stuffed her knickers in one pocket, kept the elastic out.

'I've got this,' she said. She took it to Hanno. 'That'd do for the catapult, wouldn't it?'

Hanno's eyes opened wide for a moment. He knew.

There was the distant sound of planes again. Braun shut his eyes and muttered. There was something nearer. The sound of an explosion on the ground. Braun didn't seem to hear, but it must be his car. And there was a rattle of bullets. Fighting on the main road.

'We can't stay out here,' said Braun. 'You, boy –' he grinned, jeering at Hanno – 'go for the duck and the girl can come in that stable with me. If you're not back in forty-five minutes, I'll shoot her.'

Hanno went. Please, boy, she thought, don't run out on me and leave me to die without my knickers on.

When they got into the stable she couldn't see anything because the sunlight had made a blue fog in her eyes. She sat down by feel. Slowly her vision cleared. She couldn't hear the fighting any more, only the planes. It was dreadful not to know. She strained her ears in case people were running into the farmyard. Oh, why had Braun come? And the boy?

Keep your head, Effi, she told herself. And make yourself look as if you had nothing but fluff inside it.

chapter five

The wood was full of frightened animals. Deer jumped away from Hanno, rusty squirrel tails shot up the trees and two foxes slid into the undergrowth. Somewhere quite close by there was more firing. Now even the trees stood still, fearful, listening. They could be killed, too.

He had three-quarters of an hour to catch a duck, and no watch to time himself with. He'd been such a fool. When he'd seen Otto he'd got angrier than he could ever remember in his life because Otto was running away from the fighting when Father and Wolfgang were dead. He'd felt he could do anything. Even when he'd seen Otto's gun it hadn't made him careful. And now he'd put Effi's life in danger. He should have done like her, sweet-talked Otto, pretended not to know him. He thought – he'd no idea why – that he ought to have known how vicious Otto was.

He was almost at the lake. He had a pocket full of stones from the farmyard; now he had to find a piece of forked wood for his catapult. He thought he'd get it off one of the broken trees that were lying in the water. He ran, and all the time he saw Otto's face, the fleshy jaw thrusting forward at him when he'd said whose son he was. He'd looked as if everything that had gone wrong for him was Hanno's fault.

He waded into the water and looked up and down one

of the fallen trees for his catapult, but all of a sudden he couldn't make himself concentrate. He wanted Wolfgang. It felt as if he couldn't make the catapult properly without his twin to help him. He shook himself. It was worse than useless, mooning around like this.

The firing moved away. How much time had he got left? But there was a thin forked branch and after all it was easy to break it into the right shape. He fetched out the elastic – Effi's knicker elastic. His throat felt tight again.

The ducks were still there, puttering around and quacking, their faces smug as ever, they looked like park ducks, ducks from a past he could still remember, when people used to stroll around in nice clothes on a Sunday and push sun-bonneted babies in prams and had bits of bread to spare for birds. They were just too far away, maybe they'd come if he pretended to throw food to them.

He pulled some crumbly bark from a willow tree and scattered it on the surface, putting the elastic round the catapult's fork and pulling it back. The ducks were too clever. They glanced at the bait and left it alone. Then he thought he'd wade into the water and see if he could get closer to them, but however gently he went, they swam away. One of them even took off and landed clumsily in a tree, but the rest only paddled out of range, squiggling the water behind them. Suddenly the thought of Wolfgang twisted in his stomach like a bayonet and he didn't want to kill anything. He remembered how he'd aimed at a Russian and shot. The man had put his arms out and fallen down. Dead. I killed a man, he thought, maybe more than one. So why don't I want to kill a duck?

Anyway, he had to.

There was a thrashing of leaves. There were deer running towards the lake. They splashed off the further bank and sprang through the shallows. The ducks took off and flew towards Hanno, landing like seaplanes, braking with their feet. They were only a metre or so away from him. He put a stone in the elastic, pulled back, and let go. He wasn't sure if he'd hit anything, then he saw a duck lying dazed in the water: the rest were up in the air and making for the trees. He reached for the duck and there was a commotion beneath it. Something had hold of the feet. Quickly, he grasped the neck and put his hand under the belly. There was a pike there, it wanted to eat the duck too. He thought they might pull the duck in half between them, and again he didn't want to kill the duck, but he knew he had to. Angrily, he kicked towards the brute, then remembered Father saying pike sometimes attacked people. It didn't matter. He wasn't going to lose this fight.

The pike let go. Hanno waded out of the water. Then he remembered the catapult, with Effi's elastic. He'd dropped it and it was bobbing up and down out there. He waded out to it. The duck was moving feebly under his arm. He was going to have to wring its neck.

He didn't know how to do it and it took far too long. He felt sick before he'd finished. Then he ran back to the farm, terrified he'd hear a shot, but when he got back to the stable Effi was sitting there chattering to Otto about how much she loved the Führer. Then she had to pretend to go and pee again. Luckily, Otto let her go.

'Right,' said Otto when Effi came back. 'Get that thing plucked.'

'I've never plucked a duck before,' she said, giving a silly giggle. 'I've plucked a chicken, is it the same?'

She took the duck from Hanno, sat down cross-legged and started tugging at the feathers.

'You start plucking a duck from the tail,' said Otto, and he got his flask out again and drank. It was a silver flask with engraving on it. 'You won't find it easy.'

'Oh,' said Effi, 'do you know how to do it, Herr Braun?'

'I've watched it done,' said Otto. 'It's women's work.'

'Of course,' said Effi, and giggled again. Then she started to attack the tail feathers. Fluffy bits of down flew up and settled in her hair, landed on her face, and drifted through the air. There were filaments of duck-down on Hanno's dirty trousers.

Otto stared at Hanno. His eyes were bright blue, but not soft, like forget-me-nots or the sky. They were like blue glass, a hard clear colour without a trace of grey in them.

'All right, boy,' he said, pouring more cognac down his throat. 'I know who you are. Bernhard Frisch's son. And stupid as your father, I see. But I'm not Otto, I'm Braun. Have you got enough wits to understand that now?'

Effi gave Hanno a look. He nodded, and kept his mouth shut.

The plucking didn't look easy. The duck-down went everywhere, coming out with the big feathers. Effi sneezed. Hanno felt something hairlike at the back of his throat. He shoved his finger down to try and get it out, but it stayed there. It was disgusting. He coughed.

'Stop that noise!' said Otto. 'Both of you.'

'If he went to the pump,' said Effi, 'he could get a drink of water, Herr Braun.'

Otto thought. 'Go and come back quickly. Or else –'

Hanno went, and drank. Now at least his throat felt better.

When he came in Otto was sprawled in the corner, shaking his flask. 'It's all gone,' he said.

'Oh, dear,' said Effi in a prim, mousy voice.

'I should have had more,' Otto said. 'It stinks. And here I am with Frisch's boy, and that really stinks. Where is the fellow, anyway? Has he deserted too?'

'He's dead,' said Hanno. 'He died fighting the Russians.'

'You expect me to believe that? Rats don't die easily, they know how to get themselves out of trouble.' Otto laughed. 'He knew how to make friends for himself, I'll grant him that. And how to watch his back.'

Hanno felt the rage flare up in him again. He pushed his lips together.

Effi stifled a cough. 'This stuff is horrible, it gets down your throat.'

Otto pulled a handkerchief out of his pocket and tossed it to her. 'Put this over your face and stop complaining.'

'Oh, thank you,' said Effi. 'Herr Braun, you're a real gent.'

Otto said to Hanno: 'Your father was a criminal. A bad element. A disgrace to the police force. But a rat. A clever rat.'

Hanno remembered Mother crying into the potato peelings. It was hard to control himself.

Effi made a triangle out of the handkerchief and tied it round her face.

'Now I'm an outlaw in a Wild West film,' she said, giggling. And whispered to Hanno: 'No. Don't get angry.'

A plane came over and there was a series of explosions not far away. The stable wall shook and the farm cat came down out of the hayrack.

'A pussy cat,' said Effi quickly. 'Puss, puss!'

The cat walked round Effi, wanting a taste of the meat.

Otto had his gun out. 'Animal gets on my nerves.'

Hanno thought he was going to shoot the cat, then: 'Out,' he snapped, suddenly. 'Out into the yard, you two.' The cat kept on miaowing, it didn't know about guns. Otto pointed the gun at Effi. 'Get a move on, girl.'

Effi stood up. She was white as chalk, but she kept hold of the half-plucked duck.

'You too, boy,' said Otto.

'The Russians might come,' said Effi.

'If the Russians come,' said Otto, 'd'you think they won't find you in here and make you wish you were dead? Out!'

He gave Hanno a shove with the gun. They stumbled out into the yard. The sun was shining out there. There were no planes, but they could hear the sound of fighting coming closer.

The cat had come out with them. 'Miaow,' she said, gooseberry-green eyes fixed on the duck. 'Miaow!'

Otto herded Effi and Hanno into the cook-place. The cat came too. Effi was still holding the duck.

'Turn round,' Otto said. 'Face the wall.'

He was going to shoot them. No, thought Hanno. No.

'Bernhard Frisch's son,' said Otto like a judge passing sentence, 'and a little tart from Prenzlauer Berg. Scum, both of you. You can tell as many lies as you like, trying to save your skins, but you don't fool me. Now which of you shall I shoot first? No – why should I make it so easy for you both? Come here, girl. You, boy, stay where you are.'

Effi went from beside him. He thought Otto grabbed hold of her.

'Herr Braun,' Hanno heard her pleading, 'we're Germans, your own people –' then she cried out, gasped, and shrieked.

'What are you doing to her?'

Otto laughed. It was a bad laugh. 'I'm twisting her arm, boy. I've even made her drop the duck. You can turn round now, I want you to see her arm go out of its socket.'

Hanno turned round and saw the cat dart forward to get the duck. It ran right between Otto's legs.

'What?' Otto shouted.

All at once Effi was free. She'd yanked herself out of Otto's grip and nipped round the corner out of sight. Otto went after her but Hanno jumped forward and stuck his foot in Otto's way. Otto stumbled. His gun went off and the bullet hit the ground. There was a spray of earth. Now suddenly the fighting was much closer, there were soldiers coming and shooting. Otto was running away, right out of the farmyard, and the cat was running too with its tail hooked in fright. Hanno was round the corner before he thought about it, but he couldn't see Effi. There was just the chimney poking into the sky and the broken beams all around it, and the rubble.

'Hanno!' It was Effi's voice. 'Down here.'

There was a hole in the ground; you couldn't see it very easily because a beam had fallen half-across it. There were wooden steps going down into the old cellar. Hanno felt carefully with his feet as he went down them, but only one was missing. It was very dark.

'Effi? Where are you?'

Her hand touched his shoulder. 'Here.' She moved up to him. They stood still, close to each other, hearing guns and then something came driving through: an armoured car, maybe, he didn't think it was big enough for a tank but it made the roof shake and debris came down on their heads. After that everything went quiet.

'I've got the duck,' said Effi. 'I never noticed I'd picked

it up till I wondered what I was holding.'

'It's my fault,' said Hanno. 'I was a fool. How's your arm?'

'Don't do it again, kid, that's all. I'm OK; I started making a noise before he hurt me. I got away from him nicely, didn't I? He thought I was too silly to know the trick. P – my uncle taught me. My aunt's husband. I just untwisted myself, there he was holding the air.'

'You're shaking.'

'No, I'm not. I'm OK. Where did the swine go?'

'He ran when the soldiers came. Right away. I don't know if he'll come back.'

'Maybe they killed him. I hope they killed him.'

'So do I.'

'Why does he hate your father so much? And you, now.'

'I don't know. He used to be in Sternberg, but the police regiment went to Czechoslovakia in 'thirty-nine and he was moved to a different unit. He came back visiting the year before last, when Father was on leave. We'd gone to the bakery and we met him on the street.'

Wolfgang had been there, but he couldn't mention Wolfgang.

'They talked about the war, they were both fighting partisans, Otto was in Yugoslavia, Father was in the Ukraine. There was something – I thought Father was wary of him. And when we came home he didn't tell Mother we'd met him.'

'Did you tell her?'

'No.'

'Why not?'

'It felt as if I mustn't. He was lying about my father, you know. Father never did anything wrong.'

She didn't answer. Then she said: 'I can get the feathers

out of this thing by feel. Better to stay down here till I've plucked it, what do you think? Then we can cook it.'

'Don't you want to go, in case he comes back?'

She hesitated. 'Maybe. Only – I'm so hungry. Aren't you?'

'Yes. More than I'd have thought.'

'And there's a good place to cook it here. We'll eat some, then we'll go.'

She'd said 'we'll go' as if she wanted them to be together.

'Do you want to go to your grandfather in Leipzig?'

She said: 'What do you want to do?'

'I don't know. But I can start off with you. If you want me.'

She didn't say anything. Maybe she didn't want him after all? Then she said: 'We'd better go together and share the rest of the duck.'

There were two dead German soldiers in the yard when they came up. Effi didn't say anything about them, neither did Hanno, but they walked round the farm to see if Otto was there. There was no sign of him, dead or alive. Effi put the duck in the pot and cut up chunks of swede to roast with it.

The cat was sitting about a metre away, still miaowing.

'Puss,' said Effi, 'you almost got both of us killed back there.'

There was one thing, though, the time she'd spent practising her fairytales had paid off, she'd got them out pat – it was a mistake to admit to Prenzlauer Berg, though. Another time she could say Aunt Annelie kept a teashop in Wannsee. That didn't sound so subversive.

The cat kept her eyes fixed on the pot.

'Miaow!' said Effi to her. 'Miaow!'

But she was listening all the time, taut and frightened in case Otto came back. Maybe it was stupid to roast the duck, but she'd started now. Had she been right to tell the boy he could come with her?

He'd come back from the lake with the duck, he hadn't needed to do that. And he'd said he was sorry. So what if he was a policeman's kid? You judged people by what they did – Pierre and Aunt Annelie always said that was what it was all about. Suddenly she was really happy he was there, but: Effi, she said to herself, just remember to mind your tongue with him.

She said: 'Aunt Annelie used to like duck.'

'One of the ones you lost?'

'Yes.' She'd kept a lot of the truth in her story, it came out naturally then. 'Come on, we'd better pack up while the duck cooks.'

'There's nothing to pack, is there?'

She hesitated, then said, 'I've got some stuff.'

'What kind of stuff?'

She shook her head. 'It's in the stables. You can get some swedes, only a few, we can't carry them all. The porridge is finished.'

The sun was sinking. She went into the stable, got the bag from its hiding place, hung it on her front and buttoned her jacket over it. Lucky that the jacket had always been too big for her, it had been Uncle Max's before the Nazi storm troopers killed him in 1933. Aunt Annelie had cut it down for Effi. The buttons strained a bit, but this wasn't a fashion parade.

Hanno came out of the ruined cowshed with the swedes. He stopped and stared at a heap of soil beside one of the dead soldiers. What was he staring at, Otto couldn't be in there, surely, waiting to jump out?

'There's a milk can,' he said.

You could just see its shoulder shining faintly in the red evening light. Hanno got down on his hunkers and dug the can out with his hands and nails. He moved quickly and cleverly, the strangeness that there'd been about his movements before had gone, but when something exploded a kilometre or so away he jumped. Then they both laughed. It was jittery laughter.

The can wasn't very big, probably held about a litre and it was battered and dented but there was even a lid.

Hanno said: 'We can fill it up with water before we go.'

'Smart,' she said. He went off to the pump.

When he came back, he said: 'I used to get so excited when we went away, when I was a kid. I could never sleep the night before.'

'Where did you used to go?'

'To the Baltic.'

'I used to go to the Wannsee Lake.'

'With your aunts?'

'With my mother. She died of tuberculosis and then I went to live with Aunt Annelie'

'Was your father in the army then?'

'Yes.' Effi, she thought, you're a smart liar.

The duck's skin was crisp and brown round a thin layer of fat. A curl of fat sneaked out when Effi put the knife in. They gobbled it up, oh, God, the taste of it, something you could lay your tongue round and get your teeth into! The swedes were soaked in gravy and more fat. Only potatoes with it would have been better still.

They ate a breast each and didn't give anything to the cat. They'd agreed to save the legs and wings and the carcass. They knew they'd both be glad of food later on.

As soon as they'd finished they went away from the farm together. They walked all the way through the wood. It was dark by the time they came out the other side, but the moon was up. There was a field of sandy soil that they had to cross.

'It's like the beach,' she said. 'Your feet sink in. I hope that swine Otto doesn't turn up, it'd be hard to run here.'

Hanno didn't answer. They kept walking. It was scary, out in the open, with their long moon-shadows floundering across the field ahead of them. Cheer up, Effi, she thought. You're on your way to the Americans and Papa.

Chapter Six

Effi spoke English well enough to talk to the Americans when she found them, maybe she didn't speak it as well as she used to when she was at school in London – after all, she'd only been eight when she'd left. But Mama and she had used to speak to each other in English and she'd practised it with Pierre.

Pierre would say in English: 'You lived in Paris when you left Germany first, and you say you don't know French bread – don't you remember anything about Paris?'

'Pierre,' she'd say, 'I was only two and a half when we went away from there to Amsterdam.'

He'd shake his head and say: 'One day, kid, you'll really experience Paris.'

'I can't wait,' she'd say.

'So Amsterdam – can you remember Amsterdam?'

'Only some tall brick buildings and canals. But I can remember London.'

'OK, kid, tell me about London.'

'We had a flat in Chelsea; it was really small but it was cool because I could get out of bed in the morning and look at the river. I can remember my school, too. It was called an 'advanced school'.

'What's this – "advanced school"?'

'Nobody was ever hit and you could choose what you studied.'

'So what did you study? And were the other children nice, or were they horrible because no one ever disciplined them?'

'I studied music, of course. The teachers were really good at music. And art. That's why my parents sent me there. But I did the other things, too: arithmetic and reading and writing. The kids were nice. There was another kid from Germany, she was called Nini Engelmann. Her family were Jewish – that was why they'd come away – and her father was an architect, but he couldn't get enough work in England and they went on to America. The other kids thought I must be Jewish too, quite a few of them were. I had to explain to them how Papa was a Communist and Hitler wanted to kill him, and some of them didn't know who Hitler was, and I told them he was the Government in Germany and he was a bad man. They used to giggle if Nini and I talked German together. Not nastily. They really were nice kids, and a lot of their parents were artists too, like mine.'

'And your father was a composer even though his father kept a bar. He rose from the working class. And your mother?'

'You know she was a film star and a singer.'

'I'm making you practise your English.'

'You should have been a schoolteacher. Anyway, my accent's better than yours.'

'And can you speak French as well as I speak English, kid?'

'No. OK.'

'Your mother came from a rich family, didn't she? Did she work when you were in England?'

'Not very much, she had to look after me. She gave singing lessons, and sometimes she sang at concerts.'

'And your father was a composer but he ended up writing popular songs? Not that I have anything against popular songs, kid, I'd rather listen to them than to symphonies myself, though good music is good music.'

'It was hard for him to get work, there were so many artists who'd had to leave Germany. I can remember him always writing letters to people in concert halls and opera houses and then getting angry and saying he'd been ruined when he left Germany, he'd had a reputation for classical music once and now he could only write schlock for Tin Pan Alley. But he was good at popular music. Everybody liked it.'

'So did he never get his classical work performed?'

'Sometimes. Not enough to make money. The popular music kept us fed.'

'So you can remember your father?'

'He had fair hair and blue eyes, and he was quite tall.'

'You got that from that photograph your aunt has – you look at it all the time.'

'I do remember him.' And now she started to talk in German after all. English was too slow. 'He used to take me to the piano and put me on his lap, and he'd make me play music, well, really it was my fingers on top of his, but there I was suddenly playing something really good and difficult. He was a wonderful pianist, my Papa. And when I was playing my little kid pieces he used to come and listen and then he'd tell me things, the way you do, and I always played better after that. And he'd play the piano and we'd all sing. And I can remember one Sunday afternoon we were out for a walk on the river bank. Mama was wearing red sandals and she had a red hat and a white dress with short sleeves and a big skirt, and I had a white dress and black patent leather shoes with ankle-straps and I had a red hat too, I always wanted to dress like Mama, she was the elegantest lady in the world. And Papa was wearing a summer jacket; it was a lovely day, the river was dancing and all shiny, there was an old dirty dredger tied up at the bank and even that looked like an oil painting and then Mama and I started skipping along the pavement, singing: "London Bridge is falling down, falling down, falling down, London Bridge is falling down, my fair lady." There were people staring at us – English people don't sing in the street, you know, and usually we were careful to try and behave properly, because of fitting in, but that day we just didn't care and Papa stood there and clapped and there was an old man walking up the street and he stopped, and said: "Lovely! Lovely!"'

Pierre said: 'You've never told me that before.'

'I never will again. It's a special memory, I don't even remember it a lot to myself, I'm scared it might get spoilt if I bring it out too often.'

There were other things she remembered that she didn't want to talk to Pierre about. Like when letters used to come from Germany, letters with thin skins, she used to call them in her little-kid way, they didn't weigh much but what was inside them was pretty heavy. There was Grandmama in Germany, she had tuberculosis, and she was getting worse. And there were whisperings; Effi hadn't understood them at the time.

Papa whispering to Mama, 'Hansen has got rid of his wife.'

Mama saying: 'Hitler is the devil. Destroying people's lives. Oh my God, the Sachers are dead.'

'What happened to them?'

Mama, pushing the letter over to Papa. 'Read.' And then, not waiting for Papa to read, whispering: 'They gassed themselves, and the child, too.'

She knew what it was about now. The Nazis had told actors and artists who had Jewish husbands or wives that there'd be no more work for them unless they divorced. The Sachers had killed themselves so that they wouldn't have to part. But she'd felt safe at the time with Mama and Papa, she'd never have imagined Hitler could drive them apart.

A letter came from Grandmama. Mama said, 'She's not got long to live. Six months maybe, the doctors say.'

There were arguments. Mama was desperate to go, Papa didn't want her to. Mama was miserable. Effi remembered her crying beside the monkey cage at the zoo, the two of them had gone there to be cheered up. A little monkey with a wrinkled face came and made faces at Mama but he couldn't make her laugh. Effi kissed her and she wiped her eyes, gave a kind of smile. She sent Effi off on an elephant ride. 'Have a nice time,' she said. Effi came back and waved to Mama and shouted to show her what a good time she was having on the elephant. Mama looked up at her as if it hurt to see Effi smiling, and her face was all wet again.

The next thing Effi could remember was all of them standing by a taxi in the rain, waiting to get in and catch the boat train from Victoria Station. Papa wasn't coming. Papa and Mama were angry with each other. That was when Effi heard about Schulz for the first time, though she didn't know why they were standing shouting about this man called Schulz when the taxi driver had got his meter going and it was ticking away, making the ride to Victoria more and more expensive by the minute. Papa didn't want Effi to go to Germany, he wanted her to stay behind if Mama was set on going, but Effi wanted to stay in London with both of them.

Papa shouted: 'There's going to be a war. Any day now. And you're going off to Germany?' He kissed Effi goodbye, he said: 'Remember I love you.' He gave Mama a quick kiss on the cheek, it was a nasty kiss, as if he hated her, and went back into the house. She remembered the door banging and she felt as if it had slammed on her finger. That was how much it hurt.

She couldn't remember the crossing, just how they got off the boat at Ostende in Belgium and walked down the platform. The porter was wheeling their luggage up the platform to the train, their bags were all wet and shiny. And they had a sleeper compartment and Mama pretended to sleep, but when Effi got up and went into the corridor to look out of the window, Mama jumped off her bed and came out, she grabbed Effi's hand as if she was a kid herself, younger than Effi, and couldn't bear to be left alone in the compartment.

There was steam flying past the windows and it was dark outside, there were empty lit-up stations with weird names, they shone up out of the night and then were gone, and Effi was scared of Germany because Hitler was there, and one of the things she'd always known was how Hitler had killed Uncle Max in a camp and how he'd wanted to kill Papa too, that was why they'd cleared out of Germany, so why are we going back there? she asked herself, but she couldn't ask Mama because Mama was upset enough already.

When they got to the border they had to get out of the train and sit in front of a desk in a big shed and a man in uniform looked at Mama's passport and then stared at

Mama's face. Mama's hands clenched in her lap. Effi was such a kid still, she was scared that Hitler would come along himself and drag them off to a camp. But the man just stamped the passport and said: 'Welcome back to Germany. Heil Hitler!'

Grandmama lay coughing in her big bedroom in the villa in Wannsee, coughing and crying with joy to see Mama and Effi. And Schulz came round, he was a big man in a big suit who started on at Mama about working in Germany, but she said she had to go back to Papa.

'Why?' said Schulz. 'You could get rid of him so easily.'

'Get out,' said Mama. So he apologized, but it showed Effi why Papa hated Schulz and she hated him too. And she wanted to go back, they'd seen Grandmama, hadn't they? But Mama said Grandmama needed them to stay awhile.

She learned all about Schulz later on. How he'd been a film producer, though not a very important one, but Mama had worked with him once and he'd always had a thing for her. How he'd got his big chance when all the Jews and anti-Nazis had left in 1933, and now he worked in the film section of Dr Goebbels's Propaganda Department. Mama had been a really big name in the old days and it'd be a propaganda coup for the Nazis if Schulz managed to sign up Leni Valentin. There was more to it than that, though. He was in love with Mama.

Mama kept telling Schulz she was only in Berlin to visit her mother.

It was like a weird, gone-wrong summer holiday, beautiful weather, and the lake was just down the road from the villa, it had a sandier beach than the seaside in Brighton where they used to go for outings from London. Mama took Effi down there and they swam. But Effi couldn't enjoy herself properly, she was longing to go back to London. And then the war started, just as Papa had said it would, and they were trapped.

The story was that the Poles had attacked the Germans at a place in the East called Gleiwitz. Most people swallowed that, though they were bricking themselves because of the war. Nobody wanted a war, so they kidded themselves Hitler couldn't want one either. Maybe some of them guessed the truth, but they only ever whispered about it after they'd looked over their shoulder – that was 'the German glance', the quick once-over to make sure no one was listening who might shop them to the Gestapo. And Grandmama's maid Anna said to Mama: 'Why did the British declare war on us? Didn't they realize we had to defend ourselves?'

Mama just spread her hands; she was so miserable she didn't want to talk about it.

Letters came from Papa via the Red Cross. Things were bad for him, he'd been locked away in a camp. Mama said: 'If we'd stayed we'd have been locked up, too.'

People got killed in camps; they were a Nazi thing, so why were the British setting them up? It didn't make sense. The British were supposed to be OK. Mama said it was a different kind of camp, Papa had only been sent there because he was German and Britain was at war with Germany. That didn't make sense either.

'He's not an enemy,' Effi said. 'He hates Hitler!' She said it too loudly and Mama shushed her, even though she was speaking English. She understood, she'd learned quickly how careful they had to be. Everywhere. She was only a little kid, though, it was hard for her to remember all the time. Papa's letters all got read by the German censor, but Mama always destroyed them anyway after she'd read them, and she kept his photograph hidden under her mattress.

Papa had written 'Raindrops Shining in Your Hair' before they took him into the camp; he'd sent the sheet music to Mama, and Effi had to sing it under her breath, but when it became a big hit in America, the Nazis pretended they didn't know who'd written it and it was allowed to be sung in German cafés here, just with German words. So Effi could hum it – she wouldn't sing the German words, they were rubbish. The record made Papa's name, so that later, after the English let him out of the internment camp, he got an offer from Hollywood to come and write music for the movies. He accepted because Germany wasn't at war with America so if he went to Hollywood Effi and Mama could come and join him.

The song was about how much he missed Mama, and how sorry he was that he'd been angry with her on the day they left. That was why Effi hummed it so often, bit by bit it did away with the hurt from when he'd slammed the door on them.

She hated the school she had to go to in Wannsee. It was all girls, they were all called by their surnames and the teachers shouted at them and hit them for stupid reasons. They made you do a lot of games and gymnastics – that wasn't too bad, though the games teacher was a real bitch and she used to drive terrified girls right to the top of the climbing bars to toughen them up. Effi wasn't afraid of climbing and she was good at gymnastics, but there was too much cookery and sewing. She wouldn't sing at school because if it came out how good she was she'd have to sing in Nazi concerts. She pretended not to be able to sing in tune. Mama was teaching her music at home and she told Effi that what the teachers were getting the kids to do was rubbish, they had to sing too loudly, they'd wear their voices out. The songs were rubbish too, they were all about loving Hitler and invading Britain. People were pleased because France had fallen so quickly, they wanted London to be bombed so the British would surrender and then they thought the war would be over. A nice Europe that would have been, but anyway, Hitler had other ideas and he invaded Russia.

Claudia Anders was a girl Effi really got on with – clever and good at art. She had some Jewish blood, something like a great-grandfather, it wasn't enough to get her chucked out of the school, but some of the teachers were truly bad to her. They made her sweep the classroom and empty the bins, or clean out the kitchen after domestic science. It wasn't easy for her to do those jobs because she had one leg shorter than the other and had to wear a special shoe. Once Effi found her crying and she put her arms round her while all the other girls walked past. They weren't nasty exactly, just soggy. They didn't want to stick their necks out. That was the only time Claudia cried openly, anyway. She had guts, she didn't want the teachers to see they'd upset her. Then one day Schulz came round and told Effi she shouldn't be so pally with Claudia.

It turned out that Schulz was protecting Effi, or else – with Papa a 'filthy émigré' (that was what the Nazis called people like him) – she'd have been made to do all those jobs too. He stood there in his sharp suit with those huge padded shoulders and laid down the law to her and Mama about it. The next day the games teacher told Claudia she had to clean the toilets out. Just to show Schulz, Effi stayed behind and started to help Claudia. They were halfway through when Frau Bitch-face came along to check up on Claudia. When she saw Effi there she stood still and her mouth tried to smile; it said, That's what I like to see you doing, Mann. But then you could see her remember Schulz. She frowned and shook her head too fast – she looked like an idiot. Almost gabbling, she told them both to stop work, they'd done enough, she said, the caretaker could finish. That would have been a good memory – only a week later Claudia wasn't in school any more.

Somebody said she'd gone to hospital to have her tonsils out and she'd died of pneumonia. But a girl called Karin Koch told Effi: 'You know, if a child goes to hospital and they're, you know, undesirable, the wrong race, or from a delinquent family, or epileptic or deformed – well sometimes they give them something and then they die. Nobody ever worries about it.' Karin Koch's father was a doctor, so she knew. The girls never talked about Claudia again.

Grandmama died in September 1941. Papa wrote a kind letter to Mama; he said he was just leaving for America and once he was there he'd organize a visa for them. Only Germany declared war on America before Effi and Mama could leave. So they had to stay on at Wannsee. Grandmama had left them money to live on and the maid Anna did their housework. And Mama sat looking at the atlas, trying to work out routes she could take to get to America after all. They could go to Sweden, she said. Sweden was still neutral. Then get a boat from there to America.

The doorbell would ring: Schulz had come visiting again. Anna was always pleased to see Schulz – a Party bigwig with a huge Merc and a badge and a chauffeur, she thought he was a real classy number.

He was still on at Mama to go into the German movies. He said she could be bigger than Zarah Leander, and Mama, who was so slim, said, 'I'd have to eat a lot to manage that.'

Even Schulz had to laugh, because for all everyone in Germany was gooing over Zarah Leander and her schlocky films and songs, she was putting on so much weight all her costumes had to be specially designed to hide it and the publicity shots were airbrushed to hide the blubber.

'*No,*' Mama said then. 'Anyway, I'm always so tired.'

At school the teachers started to say: 'Children, if you hear your parents doubting that we will win, you must contradict them.' There were fewer girls in the classroom anyway, kids were being sent away to the country because there'd been a few air-raids on Berlin, which Fat Man Reich Air Marshal Göring had said would never happen. Nothing compared to what was going to hit Berlin later, of course. Mama didn't want to go away again, she'd even stopped looking at the atlas. All she wanted to do was rest, or go down to the beach and sit there while Effi swam. She was getting thinner, though she told Effi it was only the wartime rations. Then she started to cough. She had TB like Grandmama. And she died of it.

chapter seven

Effi remembered all that as they walked through the night, but it was bad, thinking how Mama had died. It'd make her cry if she didn't put it out of her mind, and this wasn't the time to cry. She said to herself: 'I'll cry when I'm with Papa. Not before.'

They'd been going maybe an hour or two when they came to the edge of a pinewood. It stretched as far as they could see in either direction, so they had to go in between the trees.

The moonlight didn't reach in there and they had to feel their way: the pine-bark scraped at their hands and the unfriendly sharp broken branches reached out to jab at them. The boy swore.

Effi laughed. 'That's the first bad word I've heard from you.'

'Did you think I didn't know any? It's going to be grim going through here in the dark.'

'We'll have to go on till we find cover. I'm not just going to lie down in the woods – supposing the Ivans came in the morning?'

'I *know*,' he said. 'I did scouting in the Hitler Youth, they taught us about cover.'

'Clever Hitler Youth.'

She was tired and scared; she thought he'd get annoyed now, she half-wanted him to, but he didn't.

'Come on,' he said, calming his voice down, 'don't let's row. I guess we'll find some cover, sooner or later.'

So on they went. At least the forest floor was easy to walk on, needly and bouncy, and the night air smelt of wild mushrooms, though you wouldn't get mushrooms in the spring. All at once they were walking into branches. A fallen tree maybe. Effi lit her lamp to see.

It looked as if a bomb blast had thrown two trees down and they'd fallen across each other, roofing each other's trunks. Effi crawled in and waited for Hanno to follow before she put the lamp out. She shuffled the bits of broken tree away, it'd be more comfortable to lie on the soft underlayer of decaying needles.

Hanno said: 'That was lucky.'

Effi laughed. 'Luck is my middle name, kid.'

They both lay down to sleep, but it was cold in there. The boy's teeth were chattering. He didn't have a blanket, did he?

'You're keeping me awake,' she said. 'Roll over here.'

They lay back to back and she put her blanket over both of them.

'Just mind your hands,' she whispered. 'Any cheeky stuff and you're out.'

'I'm too tired.' There was a laugh in his voice, though.

'Good. Stay tired.'

She started to hum Papa's song under her breath. Hanno fell asleep, making little movements against her. She heard an owl call, its wavery voice tracking across the wood, then another answered. The warmth was building up between her body and the boy's; it was good.

In the morning when she woke up, there was a lot of scuffling and chittering going on in the trees above them.

She felt Hanno wake beside her.

'What is it?' she whispered.

'A bird, or a squirrel maybe. I think it's a squirrel.' He yawned and stretched his arms in front of him. 'I dreamed about my best marble.'

She'd hardly been with other kids the last few years, she'd forgotten what they were like. The boys at school in England used to have marbles.

'What colour was it?'

'It was a cat's-eye, I found it in the garden when I was seven, it was sort of orangey-red and gold. Like two goldfish swimming together in a bowl. I always used to win with it. I dreamed I was back at my house, only it had been bombed and there was nothing but a heap of ash. I was digging through the ash trying to find the marble. Then I woke up and I remembered that it isn't in Sternberg any more. I gave it to my sister when she and my mother went away. She's got it in Frankfurt.'

'That's nice.'

His back felt hard, warm and alive. It shifted with his breathing. Her skin crawled pleasantly. She thought she'd like it if he turned round and put his arms round her.

All at once there was someone out there, walking in boots, talking loudly, she wished it was the Amis, but this wasn't even American English. This was Russian, she'd bet; strange, a language that was heavy and light at the same time. Papa once said every language had its own music, well, she thought, I couldn't expect these voices to be music in my ears.

They were laughing, one of them fired a gun off. She felt Hanno's heart pounding, even through his spine she could feel it, but he didn't move, neither did she. Further away there was more fighting going on than she'd heard yet, and it wasn't a nice day. Not ordinarily cloudy. The air felt dirty.

There was another shot, and another, and this time the bullet came right into the hideout, whacked into the layer of needles, making a puff of dust. This was worse than a raid, it felt more personal. And she wanted to sneeze. Carefully, noiselessly, Effi took her hand away from the pouch and squashed her nostrils with two fingers.

Don't sneeze, Hanno lad, do what I'm doing.

The Ivans weren't shooting at them, they were taking a break from the battle, pot-shotting at squirrels maybe. Another shot tore her jacket and scorched her arm.

Hanno knew Effi was hurt because he felt her wince. He had no idea how badly, but he had to lie quiet with his back to her. If he moved or spoke he'd betray them both. He thought, she's got to be OK. But he'd thought that about Wolfgang and Wolfgang was dead. He felt sick.

The Russians laughed again. He could hear a faint tremble in Effi's body, and the shots died off: he heard the boots and voices getting further away but he didn't dare move yet or even whisper to her. Now he couldn't decide which of them it was who was trembling, and he remembered the Jew in Sternberg, the old man in his shabby overcoat with the yellow star on it, shivering as the two of them were shivering now. It was a bad memory.

Effi rolled over slowly and sat up. 'They're gone,' she said.

He sat up too, there was just enough head-space.

'The swine winged my arm,' she said. She pulled it out of the torn grey sleeve and rolled her shirt-sleeve up. The wound was just below her shoulder. She hunched round and licked at the blood but it kept coming.

He said: 'Let me tie it up for you.'

'Have you got a bandage on you, kid?'

'Have you still got Otto's handkerchief?'

'The big First Aid expert, is that you?' She put her head on one side and made her eyes big and flirtatious.

'I do know how to do First Aid. We learned, in the Hitler Youth.'

'So I'm lucky, aren't I?'

'Look,' he said, though it was hard to concentrate, the way she was looking at him, 'you've got blood all the way down your arm, do you want me to help you?'

'It hurts,' she said. 'It's only a graze, though.'

'I know.'

'You know everything, don't you?' Her eyes narrowed.

A moment ago he'd thought he might kiss her, now he knew he wouldn't. He said: 'I know you're winding me up.'

'Do you? Look, here's that handkerchief. It's even quite clean – thank heavens, Otto never blew his nose on it.'

He wiped the blood with it, wishing he had another to use as a bandage, but this one would have to do. Then he rolled the messy thing into something like a bandage and tied it carefully round her arm. She pulled her sleeve down and put her arm into her jacket with a little shudder. Then she leaned towards him again, took his face between her hands – he could hardly believe it was happening, she was going to kiss him on the mouth.

Only she didn't. At the last minute it was his cheek she kissed, but quite near his mouth. He felt his face go hot, he was blushing, and wished he could stay cool. Then he heard the fighting getting nearer, louder, and the air darkened again. He had the stupid idea that another Hanno was fighting and dying out there.

He remembered the Jew again and started to talk to her about him: it came out in a rush, like a confession. 'Effi – I was in town, once, with my mate Emil and – some other boys.'

He still couldn't talk about Wolfgang.

'It was when the Jews were still around and an old Jew came along with an armful of books, he had a yellow star on, so we knew what he was. And we'd had a lesson in school about Jews, that day. So we started to yell at him. There were people standing there who could have told us to stop, but they didn't and Emil slapped his behind. The Jew just stood still and shivered, he didn't move. He dropped all his books and Emil kicked them into a puddle. The others laughed. But I walked out on them.'

She drew away from him. The closeness that had started him talking was gone, but he carried on even though he thought he was making a fool of himself.

He said: 'The teacher had told us Jews were bad, he said they had to be chased out of Germany, but – that man didn't look like the pictures in our schoolbooks, with those hook noses and blue chins; I've never seen any people like that. He was just an old man with white hair. And it felt wrong when Emil slapped his behind. Kids shouldn't slap old men.'

'Were you sorry for him?'

'I felt ashamed. My mates were laughing at the Jew because he didn't dare move or pick up his books. Then I went home all on my own. I thought *they* were cool, I thought I was just like a disapproving old woman. I couldn't help it, though. Anyway, it didn't make any difference when I went away. They didn't stop.'

Wolfgang had come home furious with him, he'd said Hanno had let them all down. They'd fought. He'd given

Wolfgang a black eye. Then they'd more or less agreed to forget all about it.

Effi pulled her knees up to her chest and didn't say anything.

He said: 'Emil's in the Black Forest now. His father got taken prisoner in Normandy and his mother took him and his little brother to stay with his uncle and aunt; they've got a farm there. I wonder if he went into the Home Guard.'

It had always been the three of them, the Frisch twins and Emil Honecker. They'd done everything together. Then it had just been Hanno and Wolfgang. Now it was only Hanno.

In a hard voice, Effi said: 'What do you think happened to the Jew?'

'They were all deported, weren't they? To be resettled in the east.'

'Your teacher didn't like them, did he? Do you think they were sent to nice places? Wherever they went, it'd be filthy. Like the ones in the camps in Germany, being starved and worked to death.'

'Weren't they criminals? Communists and left-wingers?'

'And Jews. Did nobody from your town ever talk when he came home from the Front in Russia? About masses of Jews having to dig their own graves and take all their clothes off and be shot? And they were so good, they did as they were told, maybe they thought they'd be let off then, maybe they believed in miracles like Hitler does.'

He said: 'I did hear that, but I thought they must have been conspiring against us with the Communists. Or why would they have killed them?'

Effi asked: 'Aren't you hungry? Did they teach you

how to do without food in the Hitler Youth? That would have been useful training.'

They ate a wing of duck each.

Effi said: 'There's not much food left. We'll have to find some other Germans.'

'We already met one. He wanted to shoot us.'

'I hope we never meet him again. Real civilians, that's what we want. We could barter.'

'What have you got to barter with?'

'Good fags. I was holding on to them till the war ended, but it's no good if we croak from hunger here.'

There was a noise of small hooves. Another herd of deer running away from the fighting.

He said: 'We're not out of food yet.'

'If we wait till we've nothing,' said Effi, 'we'll starve.'

In the end the other Germans came to them and they weren't much nicer than Otto. They were two soldiers, ordinary ones, ragged and bloody, but not badly hurt. She could hear their breath heaving as they came through the trees. They headed straight for the refuge.

'You should have kept your gun,' said the little weaselly one to the big ginger-haired one.

'Morning,' said Effi. 'Dangerous out there, is it?'

Swine, she thought, don't answer me, will you? Just come in, flop down, keep talking to each other as if we weren't here. But she made room for them. So did Hanno, because the gun was law, it had been Russian law half an hour ago, now it was German law because Weasel still had his. He lay on his side and clutched it to his belly.

'No, I shouldn't have kept my gun,' said Ginger to Weasel. He had a rash of freckles over his face and blood smeared on his cheek. He put his head down and panted. 'My war's over, mate.'

Effi hated the smell of him, pig-meat, she thought, that's what he is, a great big heavy carcass, and then: some people are really hard to like.

'Ordinary folk like us,' said Ginger as if he'd heard her thought. He rolled over onto his back. 'It's always us who get it in the neck. Little people. And their wives.'

'You be glad you've still got a wife,' said Weasel. 'My Trudchen ran off to live with a butcher in Hamburg, roast meat every Sunday, then she got roasted in the big fire-bomb raid. No Sunday lunches for her any more.'

'Kids?'

'No kids.'

'I've got kids,' said Ginger. 'I don't know if I've got a wife. The Ivans have probably had her by now.'

'Where do you live?' Weasel asked Ginger.

They weren't buddies then, they must have just met up. 'Halle.'

'No, that's all right, the Amis are there. They reached the Mulde three days ago.'

'That's what the army bulletins say –' Ginger groaned and shifted himself. 'Bullet in my shoulder at Bialystok,' he said, 'never been right since. Can you believe anything they tell you?'

Effi asked: 'How far is it to the Mulde?'

'You'll never get there, girlie, don't bother,' said Ginger. 'The Ivans'll get you first. We had our fun in Russia, now they're bringing the party back to our house.' To Weasel, he said: 'Our Colonel rang Headquarters at Zossen, someone picks up the phone, the Colonel starts off, saying, We've lost the rest of our unit, what are we meant to do now? Ivan's here, says the voice on the other end. You know what you can do with yourself. It was a Russian. They're in Army Headquarters. It's over, brother. Do you know you can get drunk on fuel oil?'

Weasel said: 'Where d'you think you'll get fuel oil from?'

They'd have to get away from this pair. They'd attract the Ivans.

'What's going on out there?' she asked, because she really wanted to know.

'Well, kids,' said Weasel, 'the heroic army of General Busse – heard of it? We were coming to save Berlin – is lying around the autobahn, smashed into pieces by the Reds. The Reds like the autobahns, they're very grateful to us for building them a nice four-lane ride all the way to the capital.'

'Have you got any food?' asked Hanno. 'We've run out.'

Weasel laughed. 'We've been fighting for you all the way from Russia, now you want food as well? Forget it, kid.'

Effi didn't want to offer him fags for food: if he knew she had fags he'd just take them, she'd swear. Ginger yawned, groaned, and closed his eyes.

They each had a rolled-up blanket on top of their packs, they probably had chocolate and porridge in there, more bread, sausage maybe.

'Go to sleep,' said Weasel to Ginger. 'If the Ivans come to get you, at least you'll have slept first. But keep hold of your pack, you don't want the kids to nick it.'

'If they nick my pack I'll crack their heads together and watch their brains spill out.' He meant it, too. Just like that swine Otto.

'Nah,' said Weasel. 'I'll stay awake. They won't try anything.'

In her head Effi heard Pierre saying, 'Sometimes, kid, you have to steal from the undeserving.' In her head she could see him standing in the ruins of a Party fat cat's house, holding a jar of caviar and grinning because a Jew was going to eat it.

Ginger was snoring already. Weasel put his head on his own pack and wrenched his eyelids open, but he dropped into sleep almost as quickly as Ginger. If I give them a while to get properly away – thought Effi. It wasn't her fault, after all. Weasel had put the idea into her head.

Hanno was sitting there with his eyes wide open, he'd had the same thought. She shook her head at him, keep still, boy. She'd do it better, she was lighter and had deft girl's fingers. She crept carefully round Ginger, ducking her head away from the curving pine branches.

It was a good thing she was thin, there was such a narrow space between the two men, but she went up like a worm, inch by inch: elbows – her arm was hurting, though – hips, knees, feet. At last she was face to face with the pack. She pushed herself up on her knees, put her hands out, picked it up and slung it round her shoulders so that it was hanging on her front. Then she backed away. This time it had to be on her knees with her head right down, dreadfully, scarily slowly, so as not to make a sound. The length of a tall fat man. It felt like a day's walking.

She was halfway back when Ginger opened his eyes and made grunty stirring noises. Hanno sucked in his breath. She went cold, time slowed down and then she knew what to do.

'It's all right,' she whispered, 'go back to sleep.'

Ginger turned on his side and went on snoring. Now his fat arse was poking out and she had to wriggle past it; it'd have been funny if he wasn't so dangerous.

She looked at Hanno again. He gathered up his milk pail – the water swished around inside and dribbled over the lip – crawled with her to the edge of the shelter, stood up next to her. They walked away, away from Weasel and Ginger, away from where you could hear the fighting. Effi kept the pack on her front, she wouldn't slow down for anything.

Chapter Eight

They'd walked for half an hour. Effi felt bad. OK, Ginger was a swine, but she'd taken everything he had left. And for herself. She and Pierre had always done like Robin Hood in England, taken from the rich to give to the poor. They came to a thicket of young oaks and there she stopped. She sat down.

'Can we empty his pack out and get rid of it?' said Hanno, sitting beside her. There was an edgy note in his voice. 'I don't want to carry army stuff.'

'Wouldn't help your undercover action?' He didn't respond. She told herself she'd taken the pack now, it'd be suicide to take it back to Ginger and crazy to waste it. She pulled the blanket loose from its straps. 'That blanket's good, we've got to keep that. OK. What's inside? Oh, God, cigarettes. Gold. One for us now, Hanno boy, what d'you say? And more matches, I was getting short of matches. Oh, lordy, chocolate. And a tin of sardines. I wonder where he rustled those up. And his bread.'

'We're thieves,' said the boy.

Sharply, she said, 'He's a German soldier. *He* was a thief. They went out to steal things from foreign countries; look, Hanno, everyone in Germany's been eating stolen goods since the war began.'

He didn't answer but she could see she'd shocked him. She'd insulted his father's memory, she shouldn't have said that. Or maybe she was glad she had. She didn't know.

She went on emptying Ginger's pack. There was his stinking underwear, she threw that on the ground. And then she felt the harmonica at the bottom of the pack. Oh, sweetheart, she thought, I lost you when the house was bombed, now you've risen from the grave.

'A mouth organ,' said Hanno, brightening up.

'Hands off,' she said. 'It's mine.'

It was even a chromatic harmonica, it'd play any key she wanted. For a moment she felt bad again for taking it, but Ginger couldn't have been a jazzman. Probably he'd murdered a Jewish jazzman in Russia and stolen the harmonica from *him*. It made her feel better to think that.

Hanno said: 'But girls don't play the mouth organ.'

'Maybe your sister doesn't play it, so what? And it's not a mouth organ, it's a harmonica. Mississippi saxophone, even.' She blew through the harmonica and wiped it to get Ginger's spit out. It moaned with relief. She tried it out, very quietly, just a few notes here and there, and then there was a piece wanting to come, 'Body and Soul'.

'What are you playing?' he asked. Then: 'It's good. I can't play anything like as well as that.'

'Thanks.' He *was* nice, policeman's kid or not.

She played with the theme, improvising, the way she used to play with Pierre. Him on the piano, they'd accompany each other's solos, listening hard for the way the music had to go, and Aunt Annelie would come down into the cellar and say: 'Hot Club of France, is it? Pierre, the way you've got that child talking, I don't know what her father will say.' Then she'd laugh, because she didn't think it mattered how you talked and anyway Effi had picked up a nice Berlin worker's accent to go with Pierre's jazzman slang. And Pierre would tell them for the hundredth time how he'd heard Larry Adler play the harmonica in Paris with Django Reinhardt and Stephane Grappelli. He'd heard the best musicians, Pierre had. Duke Ellington, Louis Armstrong. *He* was good. She'd thought they'd perform together and Papa would be in the audience.

She stopped in mid-note.

'Let's have that fag,' she said, and lit up. It was bad tobacco, but it'd make her feel better. Papa, she thought, Papa.

She asked Hanno, 'Which way is the Mulde? Where the Amis are?'

He stared at the dirty sky, then pointed at a brighter part where the sun must be. He said: 'The same way as Leipzig and Frankfurt.' Suddenly his face hardened, his cheekbones stood out. He said: 'I feel like a coward. I ought to go back and fight.'

That made her angry. It wasn't just that she'd be on her own. She didn't want him dead. After all, she'd kissed him back there. Though she'd half-wished she hadn't when he started saying the Jews and the comrades in the camps were all criminals.

'Go on then,' she said. 'Go and get killed with the rest of them. How many boys have already died for nothing?'

A huge shudder went through him. For a moment, he looked half-crazed, the way he did when he first came to the farm. Then he grabbed Ginger's empty pack, threw it down on the ground again, and kicked it away.

'Give me the fag,' he said.

She passed it over. 'The fighting was bad,' she said, 'was it?'

He smoked. He didn't answer. Then he gave a quick,

miserable shrug of his shoulders. 'I liked you playing the harmonica. It was jazz, wasn't it?'

'Jazz isn't for nice Hitler youths; where did you hear it?'

'Emil had a record,' said Hanno. But he was thinking about the bad stuff, she could tell. Wasn't Emil the one who'd hit the old Jew? Hanno's friend who went to the Black Forest. Oh, it was too complicated. She wanted to cheer him up, anyway.

'Who was the artist?'

'Louis Armstrong. I don't know how Emil got hold of it, but we listened to it once, then his father – he was home on leave – found out and broke the record to pieces. He said didn't Emil know the Negro music was forbidden? He said if anyone heard we'd all go to youth concentration camp.'

'Smashed one of Louis's records? Idiot. But that's the crazy world we've been living in. The thing about jazz,' she said, 'when you do a solo, that's something special, you don't follow the music line, you dance around it. If you like jazz, you like to have fun. That's why our leaders don't like it. But you'll be able to listen when the war's over, you'll be in some peacetime club with traffic outside and lights in the streets, there'll be no more Hitler Youth and no more Gestapo, and Louis will tour Europe again. Pierre said he would.'

'Who's Pierre?'

How could she have let his name out? Quickly, she said: 'You'll be sitting there with a nice beer, smoking and talking about anything you like. Listening to a band. Dating a nice girl.'

'I might be drinking with you – are you a nice girl?' That was better.

She said: 'I'll be in America. I'm going to be a star, I'll have a lion with a diamond collar, and drive a pink limousine and sunbathe on the beach and have a long gold cigarette-holder.'

'How will you get to America?'

'Not telling. When I make my first film, you'll come to watch me in the cinema, then you'll know.' She started to play the harmonica, 'They Can't Take That Away from Me'. She said: 'I want to smoke again, kid. Thanks.'

He passed the fag over, sat on the ground with his arms wrapped round his knees. She watched him through the smoke.

He said, 'Who is that Pierre? That's a French name.' She reminded herself that his father had been a policeman. Fraternizing with the foreign slave labourers had been a crime in the glorious German pirate Reich. And she was a criminal, she'd broken the Nazi law over and over again. The Nazis were so loud about their ideas, it got to you sometimes. Once she'd been smuggling food to a Jew in hiding, suddenly she'd felt almost wicked. She'd got herself through by saying, I'm Red Riding Hood, taking food to my Granny, the Nazis are the wolves, and I've got to make sure the story goes right, no wolves eating Granny this time. It was stupid and childish, but it worked.

She couldn't tell him the truth, but suddenly she felt a whole malicious story make itself up inside her head. How would he take it?

'Pierre was what you'd call a volunteer – a slave labourer, I call it - but he got away from the factory and stayed in Berlin pretending to be German,' she told him. 'He'd used to be a jazz musician. My aunt Annelie took him in. She bought stolen goods and sold them on.'

'I thought she had a bar.'

'Use your imagination. She did both. Pierre didn't have a ration card so we used to burgle houses during the air-raids, when everyone was in the shelters. We pretended to be wardens.' That was good, she'd make it better. 'We got jewellery as well as food, I used to sell it to a Nazi high-up who was saving up to run away. Schulz, his name was.' That was good. 'And Aunt Annelie taught me how to pick pockets.'

He stared at her. What would he say? Suddenly she realized she was really angry. Was it with him, or with herself for stealing Ginger's pack? She didn't know.

She said, 'Look, kid, I told you, Germans are all thieves now. Our men took all the food out of Russia, didn't they? Didn't matter because the Ivans were supposed to be sub-humans. Only now it turns out they can thrash the master race.'

His jaw clenched. He reached out and yanked at a young oak-branch, wanting to break it off, but it only bent over, then hung there crippled, refusing to come away. He stopped trying and looked at his hands.

'We'd better move,' he said. 'The soldiers might come after us.'

At noon they came out of the forest onto a side road. Down it tramped a line of refugees – children, women, old people; riding wagons, pushing handcarts, bicycles, wheelbarrows even, carrying rucksacks; thin tired cows with their udders swinging, goats in the same state, dogs with their mouths open.

A lone soldier came past without his gun. He was trying to get civilian clothing from a woman who had three small boys behind her on the wagon.

'I haven't got any,' she kept saying. 'You'll have to ask someone else.'

'You must have something laid by for your husband,' said the soldier, whining and pawing the wagon. 'Think how useful an army greatcoat would be to him.'

'He's got one,' said the woman. 'He probably wants rid of it as much as you do.'

Hanno looked at her face. It was savage with fear.

'Push off,' she said. 'Take your filthy hands off my wagon.'

I was lucky, Hanno thought. I found a dead man to strip.

'Which way is west?' Effi asked.

Again, he looked for that slight brightness in the grubby sky. Then he pointed to the right. The way everyone else was going.

'Do you want to go west?'

She hesitated. 'I want to go where the Amis are. What about you?'

He knew he wouldn't do any werewolf action. It was over. The soldier had said it. The Russians had answered the phone at army headquarters. He said, 'I'll go to Frankfurt, to my mother and sister.'

He thought of all the times he used to come to Mother with his hurts, when he was a little kid. Being without Wolfgang was the worst hurt he'd ever felt, and it'd break her heart when he brought it to her.

They went down to the road and joined the refugee trek, just behind a wagon that had a skinny cow attached behind it.

'Mother and Heide might have been walking like this. If they hadn't got train tickets,' Hanno said.

'Train tickets? They were lucky.'

'Did you go away on foot with your aunts? How did you come to lose them?'

'That was just a story for Braun, or Otto, or whatever he's called.' She hesitated. 'I might as well tell you. The aunt in Grunau's a fairy tale but don't contradict me if I talk about her to any more bullies. Or tell anyone else about the stolen goods. Aunt Annelie was killed in an air-raid in Berlin. Pierre died, too. I don't want to talk about that.'

'How did you get out of Berlin? They said nobody was allowed to leave any more.'

'That Nazi bigwig I told you about, Schulz, he took me in his car.'

'Why did he do that?'

'He used to take a fatherly interest in me. He's dead too. A Russian plane machine-gunned his car. It turned over and threw me clear. He burned up in it.'

'Did you care?'

'Of course I did. I meant to travel to the Amis in comfort. No, I did care about him – a bit. I don't know why. He wanted to adopt me once, only I didn't want to be his kid, I wanted to stay with my aunt. I liked the life of crime.' She grinned.

He said, 'You know, my father – I could never believe what Otto said. My father was the law in our family. "Eat your dinner up and don't complain. You've got to go to the Hitler Youth, you have to do your duty. What sort of mark is this? You know you've got to pay more attention at school." He was always going on at us like that. Were you really a burglar and a pickpocket?'

'Does it make you hate me?'

'I hated that soldier. I'd have taken his pack if you hadn't.'

She said: 'The army got better food than the civvies anyway. We were just evening up the score.'

They fell silent and kept on walking. The road was old and broken up by frost, slippery with horse and cow droppings. It was far harder going than the sandy tracks they'd been following through the forest. After an hour or so it felt as if they'd been walking the road for always. It was as if the trek had its own life that had swallowed him and Effi and everyone else, taken their thoughts and even their fears, so that they had to plod wearily onwards towards a safety they wanted and yet couldn't imagine with the noise of fighting all round them and planes in the further sky. It was there, that was all, and they had to reach it. His legs ached and soon his shoulders started to ache too. He was so tired, sometimes one foot would slither or he'd find his ankle going over in a pothole, but his army boots saved him from more than a wrench. In front of him the cow's bandy legs moved resignedly onwards and her udder swung, but it didn't look as if she had much milk to give. Maybe he was wrong. He didn't know anything about cows.

The girl started to sing something he'd heard her singing before. Some popular song. Only the words sounded different.

'What's that?'

She pulled the harmonica out and played the melody.

He said, 'Oh, I know that. It's "Keep My Picture By You".'

'No, it isn't. You'll hear when we get to the Amis what it really is.'

'What were the words you were singing before?'

'English. I suppose you learned Latin and Greek at school.'

'My sister learned English and I got her to teach me some. I didn't like Latin and Greek.'

'OK.' She put the harmonica away. She sang:

> I'm lost and broken-hearted
> lonesome, weary and blue
> and I'm writing these words, dear, to tell you
> you're the Queen of my heart
> and I'll always be true.
> I said words that should never be spoken
> I behaved as if I didn't care
> and then you looked at me
> and all I could see
> were the raindrops shining in your hair.

He asked her: 'Where did you learn those English words?'

'I got the sheet music from Herr Schulz; the fat cats could get anything they wanted, even if it was forbidden. I got a couple of Louis Armstrong records from him, too.'

Could, she'd said. Yes, it was over. There was a new world coming, a world without the Party, a world where he wasn't a twin any longer. It felt as if he'd have to learn a new language before he could live in it. 'Did you learn English at school?' he asked her.

'Yeah. I learned it at school.'

There she was walking beside him with her black curls and her eyes and her smile going up at the corners of her mouth. Her lips had been soft when they'd touched his cheek. He remembered the feel of her back against his, the bone of her spine, the tiny movements of her body even while she lay still. She was supposed to be a bad girl, a delinquent – he didn't care. Maybe he even liked the idea? She talked as if she knew all about the world that was coming. The peacetime world. Was it really going to be the way she said? He imagined himself with long hair flopping into his face and a loud, checked English jacket, the kind of boy Emil's father went on about when he took the Louis Armstrong record away. There were kids like that in Hamburg, Emil's father said, they were a disgrace to the Reich. So what? Wolfgang had been a credit to the Reich, he'd had to die a hero's death – but he'd really wanted to have fun and be alive. Hanno was fed up with destiny and duty and loyalty, all they seemed to mean was killing and dying. Now he wanted to dance with a girl in a satin dress. With Effi in a satin dress. Effi, he said under his breath, liking the feel of her name on his tongue.

'What's that?'

'Nothing.'

A shell exploded, perhaps a kilometre away, and another, and another. You could see trees exploding. The refugee column started to hurry. Effi tripped in a crack. Hanno put his hand out and saved her from falling.

'Thanks,' she said. He hadn't noticed how pale she was.

'How's your arm?' he asked her.

'Sore,' she said. 'It makes you tired.'

She started to sing, she had a rough, strong singing voice, she could make it miaow like a cat's.

> I'm tired of thieving
> tired of lying.
> Take me to the Promised Land.

It was evening, the fighting had got worse and worse around them but it hadn't come to the road they were on. Lucky so far, thought Effi; how long will it last? There was a nasty taste in the air, the wind was blowing it through a clump of last year's dead bulrushes, and straight into her mouth.

'I need another drink,' she said. 'Pass me the water, Hitler Youth.'

He rounded on her, furious. 'Don't call me Hitler Youth!'

'All right,' she said. 'Swing Boy, I want the water.'

'There's not much left.'

'We'll have to get some more. This countryside's full of drainage ditches.'

'Dirty water,' he said, worried, 'and no chance of boiling it.'

She said, 'If you drink, you might get dysentery. If you don't drink, you're bound to die of thirst.'

'OK.'

They both drank a mouthful out of the milk can.

Half an hour later the column slowed down, wagons and walkers had to wait, go forward a few paces, wait again. The woman with a bicycle who was walking just behind them called out to the man who was driving the cart ahead.

'What's going on?'

'I don't know,' he shouted back.

It came to Effi that it might be the Ivans up ahead, taking things off people and dragging the women away. But there'd be screams then, surely? The stopping and the starting set her nerves whining; it was much worse than the plodding trek.

'Are you all right?' asked Hanno.

'Just tired.'

Her arm was burning, and she wanted a proper drink of water. She wanted Pierre. She wanted him to come and pick her up and carry her to bed where Aunt Annelie would tuck her in. She shivered.

The column moved again and they saw what had slowed it down. There was a drainage ditch running under the road and people were getting water from it, hustling each other with their bottles and cups. Their wagons and carts were blocking the road.

'I'll get the water,' said Hanno.

She said, 'We'll both go.' But she flinched from the thought of those elbows and shoulders hitting her bad arm.

'Don't be a fool.'

'Swing Boy,' she said, 'if you want to run errands for me, I'll be kind and let you.'

He shoved his way in and came back with the milk can full.

The water was full of silt. Effi tried to gather it under her tongue and spit it out afterwards, but she ended up swallowing most of it. Anyway, it was good to drink. Hanno went back and filled the milk can again. The women were good at pushing and shoving but he was better, he seemed to be enjoying himself. Well, the old women were always complaining about the Hitler Youth, saying they were taught not to stand back for their elders.

A tall woman with a blue and white checked scarf tied round her head gave Effi a push from behind. 'Hey, Fräulein,' she said, 'standing about in everybody's way.'

She'd hurt Effi's arm after all. Effi realized she needed to bad-mouth somebody, and God, who was meant to provide, had provided this sour-faced cow. It'd be blasphemy to throw God's gift back at him.

'Too stupid to find your way round me, then?' she answered.

'I never heard such cheek. Berlin brat. If you're too lazy to fetch water, you shouldn't block other people.'

Ma Headscarf had a milk pail in her hand too, a bigger one than Effi and Hanno's. There was a kid behind her, putting her thin face out to watch her mother arguing, and Effi caught sight of her stockings, blood all over them. Oh God, she thought, she's been raped.

'Come on, Barbara,' said Ma Headscarf. 'We haven't time to dawdle like this little trollop.'

Effi stared at the poor raped kid.

Hanno came back: 'What do you want?' he asked Ma Headscarf.

'She doesn't want anything,' said Effi. 'Except to mind her own business.' She saw a tiny shiver go through Ma Headscarf – was she afraid of Hanno? Then the dame stuck her nose in the air as if Effi and Hanno smelt bad, but she was the smelly one, they'd washed yesterday – snorted and hunched down to dip her milk pail in the ditch.

'Let's go on,' said Effi. 'I don't like her, she's like the nurse who came in when my mother was really ill. She even looks like her.'

'What did she do?' Hanno asked.

She shouldn't be talking when she was so tired, especially not about this, but she couldn't stop, somehow.

'She wanted to keep me apart from my mother – it sounded OK, because of the infection, but if I was going to get TB I'd already have got it. Schmidt, she was called. There are some names you never forget, aren't there? Usually the kind you'd rather forget. She just hated to see me sitting beside my mother. Her face used to go sour enough to make a jazz band lose the tune. And then I got a cold and started to cough and Schmidt said I'd caught TB. She said it just to punish us. I had to keep telling my mother I really was OK. And then my mother died. She died really peacefully in my arms. At least the nurse was out of the room then. She came in and said: "That's what happens when I turn my back just for one minute." And I had to go to hospital and be X-rayed. I didn't want to go. They dragged me off as if I was under arrest.'

'What was it like in hospital?'

'Vile.' Now she ought to stop. But she went on. 'The nurse said my mother and I must be part Jewish because of our black hair and black eyes; she said Jews carried TB. And there'd been a kid at my school who really was part Jewish. Claudia. She went to hospital for an operation and they killed her there.'

Would he say it was just criminal kids who were killed? He didn't say anything. He was frowning again, then he looked away from Effi.

She said, 'I kept thinking about the hospital doctors giving Claudia something – like a drink – and then she was dead. I was so scared, Hanno, I thought they'd do that to me. I think it was the first time I really knew I could die myself – my mother had died, hadn't she? It felt like a horrible insect crawling round in my stomach.'

He put his arm round her. He patted her shoulder, rather clumsily, but it helped. They were together, a double act. It was OK. She laughed.

'I told you I'm going to have a pet lion. I'll take it around with me like a dog and it'll scare bad-tempered dames shitless. That'll show them. Hanno, boy, one day they'll all come to see me in the movies, maybe even that Nurse Schmidt, and that cow back there with the checked headscarf and her poor little kid, did you see her stockings? I'll make them all smile, I'll be the biggest star –'

Judy Garland. Marlene Dietrich. Effi Mann.

Chapter Nine

Ida Rupf noticed the two children cheeking Magda at the drainage ditch. Dear God, she thought, where were their mothers? Children shouldn't run round like that with no one to keep an eye on them. The girl was a baggage, but the boy was nice-looking. If her little Hans had grown up he might have looked like that boy. Well, she had troubles enough of her own.

Was it only yesterday it had happened? The Russian soldiers, shouting in a German she could hardly understand, but it had been clear what they wanted. How any of them would get over it, God knew – and little Barbara was only twelve! And Lisbeth Czekalla, dear God, who was expecting a baby. The only saving grace was that the other Russian – an officer, she thought – had come and put a stop to it. But they'd helped themselves to half the food – perhaps they'd thought they were being kind when they left a few sacks for her and her family. And they'd taken her horses. She kept trying to see their backs and their two pairs of ears, instead of the Czekallas' unsound beasts. But wishing wouldn't bring them back, they were gone, poor Fred and Botho whom she'd reared from foals. Now the Russians would be taking them into battle, and they'd never done anything heavier than draw guests to and from the station in the fly till she'd had to harness them to a wagon to escape.

It had been Magda who'd wanted to come. Ida had always wanted to stay put at home; it could hardly have been any worse if they'd done that.

She set her teeth. There was no point in regretting what she'd done, she'd had enough of that in her life already. As for Barbara, it'd be up to Ida to stop Magda getting at her with some religious nonsense. Telling her that how she couldn't get married in a white dress, or even worse, that no respectable man would ever marry her. Magda was quite capable of that, and why, Ida couldn't understand, because surely she loved her daughter? People shouldn't have strong beliefs, Ida thought, faith made you merciless.

It was different with grandmothers, children told them things they wouldn't tell their own parents. Only just now Barbara wasn't telling anything to anyone. She hadn't said a word since it happened.

I want to be at home, Ida thought, with everything going right. She'd go home one day, though. She had the title deeds to her house in her pocket. Even if now she had to ride in a wagon with Lisbeth Czekalla and her vile husband and be grateful to them because if Lisbeth hadn't been Magda's best friend she'd never have taken them up in her wagon and they'd all have had to walk. The Czekallas' horses didn't look as if they'd last much longer anyway, that was why the Russians hadn't taken them, and the cow was in the same state. She'd have felt sorry for Czekalla, coming back from Russia so badly injured, if he'd ever been a likeable man. She did feel sorry for Lisbeth, having all the work to do and Czekalla to live with on top of that. At least he didn't hit Lisbeth any more, she was stronger than him since his wound, even with the baby coming.

*

Effi was struggling, and Hanno was worried about her. It was only a little wound, but pain dragged you down, he knew that. She was so pale her dark eyes and black hair looked like ink on white paper. And she was hungry. They were both hungry. They'd eaten Ginger's bread, it hadn't gone far, neither had the chocolate. There were still the sardines, but you had to keep something in reserve. It would soon be dark. The trek was thinning out, nobody wanted to stay on the road at night, even though they'd been safe on it so far. The fighting hadn't come to this part of the forest, so they'd try to find shelter there.

The wagon ahead of them had a couple of knobbly sacks at the rear. It was turning, following a small line of others into the forest.

'Potatoes,' he said, and Effi nodded. 'Shall we go after it?'

'Yes.'

It was good to be walking on a forest track again. There were birches and pines growing on either side of it and the air was better.

'Cigarettes for potatoes?' he asked. She nodded again. He could see she was all in. He said: 'I'll do the trading.'

There was a place where a lot of wagons had come to a halt, a clearing far enough away from the road to feel safe. People were unharnessing their horses and tying them to birch trees for the night. The horses were lucky, they could eat grass, and they got going at once. As they moved the halter-ropes slid up and down the white peeling bark, nudging it off the pink fleshy lower layers.

There was a man leaning on a tree, drinking from a schnapps bottle and complaining to his flimsy pregnant wife while she milked their cow. 'Why on earth did we have to take that Rupf woman up with us?' he said. 'Just because Magda Lehmann's your friend. We should have left the old woman behind, you don't like her either, but you had to start off, Oh, Fritz, she's Magda's mother. And those sacks of food that she won't be sharing with us, oh no, not Ida Rupf.'

The wife carried on milking as if she was too tired to do anything else. Hanno spoke to the husband, who gave him a long stare.

'Why aren't you in the Home Guard?'

'Why aren't you?'

'I got half my lung shot away in Russia.'

Effi was shaking her head slowly from side to side. I've got to leave it, Hanno told himself. Keep cool.

'I've got cigarettes to sell,' he said.

An old woman turned round from beside the nearest wagon and came hurrying up to him. She had a pair of expensive-looking silver foxes' heads round her neck and her grey hair was tied up in a silk headscarf. Her coat was dirty, but good.

'You've got cigarettes?'

She smiled at Hanno and a gold tooth winked as she bared it. 'What will you take for them?'

'I'll buy a fag,' said the man quickly, shoving his bottle in his pocket. 'As long as they're real tobacco.'

'Army issue,' said Hanno, and the man laughed sharply.

'You can have a potato for a cigarette,' said the old woman, 'and an apple. Will it do?'

Hanno shook his head. 'You'll have to do better than that.'

'All *he'll* give you is a drink of milk,' the old woman said.

'Milk's fresh,' said Hanno. 'Warm.'

The old woman said, 'Their cow's diseased. And he won't save the cigarette, I know you, Czekalla, for all you've only one lung to smoke it with.'

'I take you with me out of the kindness of my heart,' said the man. 'Now all you do is hurl abuse at me.'

The old woman laughed rudely at him. 'You took me because your wife told you to. You have to do as you're told now, Czekalla, and serve you right.'

Hanno said: 'Why should I care what you do with the cigarettes? We want two potatoes and an apple.'

'Four potatoes, two apples,' she said quickly, 'for two cigarettes.'

Hanno looked at Effi. They knew it was a good bargain, and they'd get the milk as well.

'Magda!' shouted the old woman. 'I've bought some cigarettes.'

The woman who came was the woman who'd scrapped with Effi at the drainage ditch. She came slowly, pulling her feet as if they didn't want to obey her mother. She had the child with the bloody stockings with her. Hanno tried not to look at the child, maybe nobody looked at her any more, she'd be invisible till she changed her stockings, but probably she didn't have any more stockings with her.

The old woman went back to the wagon, came back with four potatoes and two apples and handed them over to Hanno. There was something about her – the jaunty tilt of her head when the deal was done – that Hanno couldn't help liking. She stuffed the cigarettes away in her own pocket and he wondered how many times they'd change hands before anybody smoked them. The man Czekalla didn't smoke his cigarette either, maybe only because of what the old woman had said.

The daughter, Frau Magda, darted a poisoned look at Effi.

The milk was thin, but comforting. They drank it at once. There'd be fruit and raw potato afterwards.

'Ida Rupf,' said the old woman to Hanno. 'From the Giants' Mountains in Silesia.'

Hanno said: 'I went there on holiday once.'

'Really? Where did you go?'

'A place near the Snowcap.'

'I live near there,' she said proudly. 'I own a hotel.'

'You owned it,' said Czekalla. 'The Ivans have it now.'

'I have the title deeds. I'll go back. I've got a chestful of silver buried in the garden. I'd be there still if you and the other men had fought the Ivans properly. How is it, just tell me, that our men could go to Paris in a week, but they never took Moscow?'

The headscarfed Magda was running a rosary through her fingers, but now she stopped. 'Just remember,' she said, 'before you say any more, Mother, that my husband's out there and he's doing everything he can to stop them.' There was an angry sob in her voice

Her mother opened her mouth to say something, but Czekalla interrupted her.

'You don't know what you're talking about. It's another world out there; the Ivan's not made like us, he's a monster, he can stand anything.' He got his schnapps bottle out again. 'Why didn't you send us better clothes for the winter, tell me that? If you'd collected more wool, maybe less good men would have frozen to death. They'd have been here to keep the Bolsheviks off you.'

But we did collect, thought Hanno. Wolfgang and Emil and I used to go out day after day, doing the clothes collections for the troops. Much good it did. He saw out of the corner of his eye that the raped girl had sat down on the ground and was pulling the petals off a dandelion, he loves me, he loves me not.

Czekalla's wife grabbed his arm and jerked her head towards the child, who took no notice. Too loudly, she said, 'You brought me chocolates from Paris, and the silk stockings, it was good when you came back from France.' She put her hand on her stomach, as if the baby was crying inside there and she wanted to soothe it.

Frau Rupf wanted to laugh the whole thing off, but she wasn't a tactful woman. 'You pleased your wife once, then, Czekalla.'

'Sneering at me,' said Czekalla angrily, 'you filthy old hag. We burned their villages down and drove them into the minefields, thousands of them we shot and strung up – you've no idea how many there were – he's treacherous, the Russian, drinks it in with his mother's milk, the women and kids are worst of all. I've had to execute girls and boys no older than this pair here.'

Hanno remembered Otto, and he shivered.

'Who told you to behave like that?' said Frau Rupf. 'You might have guessed they'd come here and take their revenge.'

'You always know better than anyone else, don't you? Who d'you think told me what to do? The officers, and who gave them their orders? Our great military leader Hitler, who turned out not to know his arse from his elbow, led us into a war we couldn't win – now he'll put a bullet in his head, it's all the same to him what happens to the ordinary folk.'

Frau Rupf said: 'And he had a bee in his bonnet about the Jews.' Then she looked as if she wished she hadn't said it.

Frau Magda clutched her rosary. 'The Jews killed Jesus.'

'That's why you didn't care about the Steinbergs at your church,' said Frau Rupf – and still she looked as if she wished she could keep quiet, but she kept on, 'they'd been converted, they loved Jesus, but that didn't stop the police rounding them up.'

'Why bother about the Jews?' said Czekalla. 'We've got enough on our plates.'

'You said they lived like pigs out there in Russia,' said Frau Rupf. 'You came home and told everyone what a good idea it was to kill them. But the Steinbergs used to have a nice clean house and Herr Steinberg was the best doctor, he was so kind to everyone, especially to – to the children.'

The horses' big teeth tore at their evening meal of grass. You could see flashes in the sky and hear explosions, but in between the explosions you could hear the birds singing here. Hanno wanted them to shut up and stop arguing.

Effi sat down by the little girl. 'Poor kid,' she said. 'I bet you're tired, aren't you? Fed up with them shouting at each other?'

The girl was at her second dandelion, tearing the petals out and throwing them away. When Effi spoke to her she looked up at her for a moment. Her eyes were blank and dazed.

'Come on,' said Effi, 'let's make a chain.' She picked a yellow flower and split its stem with her fingernail, then threaded another through the green stem.

Frau Magda burst out crying, putting her hands over her face so that the tears dripped through her fingers. She pulled her headscarf off her dirty head and wiped her face with it. 'Can't you let anyone have a moment's peace?' she asked her mother.

Frau Czekalla put her hand to her face and said: 'You hear terrible rumours about the concentration camps in Poland. They say they were gassing millions of Jews –'

Everyone fell completely silent. It was a bad silence, it felt as if it'd go on for ever, then Frau Rupf said loudly: 'There's no point in thinking about rumours, we hear too many rumours, we need to keep our spirits up, after all. I wish I could listen to the BBC, then we might find out what's really going on.'

Hanno noticed that another man had come up to join their group. He was standing quite still, listening. He had silvery-white hair and was wearing a smart suit underneath an open overcoat with a fur collar, a Homburg hat and walking boots that looked odd underneath his grey trousers. He'd put a small suitcase down on the ground beside him. He had wolf eyes, triangular, savage, somehow. And he was quivering slightly. He was a frightened wolf in smart civilized clothing. But not a fighting man, like Otto. He was a professional man, maybe, something like a doctor or a lawyer. He was watching Effi as she made the dandelion chain for the little girl.

'I have coffee,' he said. His voice trembled ever so slightly and then he started. He leapt round to his left. Hanno's heart bumped and he looked to see what had scared the man so much, but there wasn't anything. The man turned back, took a deep breath and pulled the edges of his coat round him. 'My name is Hungerland,' he said. 'I would exchange coffee beans for food if you were prepared to accommodate me.'

Effi had finished the dandelion chain, and she put it on Barbara's head. Effi and the child looked at each other for a few moments, then Effi laughed and the girl gave her a shaky smile. Effi took the harmonica out and played it quietly, something quick and cheeky. 'It's OK,' she said to the girl, 'just forget the bad stuff and think about the future. The kids didn't start it, nothing we could have done, nobody ever asked us. But one day you're going to get on a train to Paris. There'll be peace then. You'll stay in a smart hotel and wear nice clothes and drink coffee on the Champs-Elysées.'

'I was meant to be a big landlord out in Russia,' muttered Czekalla. 'That was what they promised me, but things never go the way they should.'

'That Czekalla,' said Hanno to Effi. They'd found a sheltered spot among a stand of pine trees and were sitting down eating slices of raw potato, after that they'd share an apple.

'What about him?'

'He reminded me – when he was talking about what he'd done in Russia –'

'No,' she said. 'I want to sleep well tonight, and I won't if I have to think about Otto.'

'OK.' But he still wanted to bad-mouth Czekalla. 'When he asked me: why aren't you in the Home Guard? I've had a skinful of people like that going on at me. You know, one day I'd been fire-watching on the roof all night and as soon as we got to school they marched us down to the railway station to move these huge spools of wire from the works in our town, a bomb had wrecked the freight tracks at the factory and we had to roll them half a kilometre and then get them up a ramp to the trucks. It was three hours of punishing work, and then we had to go back to school. The teacher started on at us, why hadn't we learned our Latin verbs? Emil stood up and he said: "Excuse me, sir, we've been too busy labouring and fire-watching." So he says: "Listen, Honecker, just because you've been trying out a man's job doesn't mean you can fool a real man." So I stood up and I said, if he was a real man, why hadn't he been down at the wireworks with us? I got the cane.'

She laughed. 'That's what you get for being a good boy. You should have said you wouldn't go to the wireworks.'

He grinned. 'It was better than Latin verbs.'

She was looking better now she'd had something to eat, and could rest.

'Czekalla's a little swine,' she said, 'but it's the man with the coffee I really don't like. Hungerland – what sort of name is that?'

'He's mad. He was looking at things that weren't there.'

'Yes, but what sent him mad?'

'Maybe he's had a bad experience.'

'Or given someone else a bad experience. Killed someone who didn't deserve to be killed, a lot of people maybe.'

Hanno remembered the story she'd told about hospital.

'That girl was killed just because she was part Jewish?'

'She had one leg shorter than the other, too. But being part Jewish must have made it worse.'

'There was a big row about the killings in the hospitals, wasn't there? Some priest preached against it from the pulpit. I remember thinking how glad I was there was nothing wrong with any of us. At least they stopped it.'

'They said they did.'

He said, 'It shook me up to think about it too. But in the end, you just got on with your life. Only – Effi, my father came home for the last time at Christmas, he was really tired all the time and he kept shouting at us, but we went for a walk, once. It'd been snowing, it was really beautiful.'

It had been the three of them. Father and his two boys, one either side of him. He remembered the pines clumped with snow and the birch-stems looking yellow against the cold whiteness. They'd walked along a forest path. It was very quiet and the sky was grey with more snow to come.

'We hardly talked. We were just together. But he said: "When this war is over, all I want to do is to forget."'

'Yeah. There'll be plenty who want that.'

Hanno pulled his mind away from the memory of Wolfgang on Father's other side.

'But I want to understand. What do you think he was talking about? Did he do the kind of thing Czekalla did? Killing kids in Russia?'

'Are you sure you want to ask, Swing Boy?'

'I can't ask, can I? He's dead. Anyway, he fought in Russia, in the winter. In temperatures of forty below zero. They didn't have warm clothes and the fuel froze in the tanks' engines. Men were falling apart from frostbite. That must have been what he meant.'

But he was shivering, as if the Russian cold was blowing round him.

She wiped her hands on her skirt. 'It's what happened to that poor little Barbara that's bugging me. The Russians didn't do anything to Czekalla, did they? They took it out on her, what did she ever do to them? Look, I told you, I want to sleep well tonight. What do you like doing as well as listening to Louis Armstrong?'

He hesitated. 'I like whittling wood. Carving things.'

'And here we are with all this wood round us. You could borrow my knife, it's good and sharp.'

He said, 'I'm too tired.'

'You won't be one day.'

They lay down under two blankets tonight. Back to back again.

Hanno was carving wood with an enormous chisel, he was carving men, women and children, it went really fast and as soon as each figure was finished it became a real live person, a Jew, they were all leaping out of the big piece of wood he was working on and marching up to a huge pit that other Jews were digging out of the ground. One of them was the old gentleman Emil had slapped. The old gentleman had to take his clothes off before he was killed, and he was trembling. Hanno felt how much he didn't want to die, as if he was the old gentleman, and then suddenly he was there, taking his clothes off, and a German police officer stepped behind him and put a gun to his neck. He felt a terror that was cold, cold as ice. He looked down into the pit and saw Wolfgang lying dead there already. He turned round to face the officer who was going to kill him and saw that it was Father – or was it Otto? It was both of them together. 'I have to kill you,' said the police officer. 'You deserted and stole from a German soldier, you're an enemy of the Reich.' Then he was furious, ragingly angry, he turned round and fought the officer, the gun went off but it was Father who fell into the pit, and Hanno was shouting: 'What did Wolfgang do wrong? Tell me that.' Father wouldn't answer, he was dead. Hanno shouted: 'I hate you, I hate you, I hate you.'

He thought he was awake. He was still angry with his father. Effi had gone from beside him. He pushed himself up on one elbow and saw her stealing from the other refugees, who lay asleep on the forest path, a little way apart from each other, bleached by the white moonlight.

He couldn't see what she was taking, only how graceful she was, silent and clever. She seemed to know when her victims were going to turn over. She moved with them as if they were partners in a dance, as if this was some slippery music she was making with them. When she'd finished she lay down with Hanno again, facing him, and started to stroke his nose, his eyes, the place where his moustache was just beginning to fuzz. He lay still, he didn't dare move, but just when she kissed him he woke up properly.

Chapter Ten

It was very early morning and the air ought to have felt fresh and clean. It didn't. A terrible stink had come down with the dew. Effi wasn't in his arms, she was curled up with her knees against his side. Her cheeks were pink now, and she looked very young. The other people were asleep in their wagons, not on the ground. It must still be very early in the morning but you could still hear the noise of battle – had they been fighting all night? The outside of the rough grey army blanket was damp and cold.

A squirrel came bouncing across the branches, sending woody scraps down on his face. Effi stretched and woke up.

'How's your arm?'

'Better. OK, it hurts a bit, but I slept well, that helps. Those are planes I can hear, aren't they?'

'Yes. Not close, though.'

'Good.'

They drank some of the water from their milk can and ate half a potato raw, sliced thin. It'd have been horrible if they hadn't been so hungry.

They were rolling the blankets up when the old woman got down out of her wagon and went into the trees to do her business. Coming back, she called out to them.

'Good morning. Are you off already?'

On the off-chance, Hanno asked: 'Have you got any sausage? For another fag?'

Frau Rupf hesitated, then she winked at Hanno – she had a soft spot for him, he did right to be cheeky. Stealthily, she walked to the wagon, fished about among the sacks, did something in there and came to him with her hands behind her back. She winked again.

'Which side?'

'Either,' said Hanno. He wasn't going to play children's games.

She showed him a good piece of sausage, about two centimetres thick, ten centimetres wide, real meat, pocketed with fat. Worth a fag, there was enough for him and Effi both. But old Rupf wasn't after cigarettes this morning.

'Give me a kiss.' Her voice had gone soft, sentimental. He kissed her old dry cheek, thinking he was only doing it for the meat, but then he found himself half-liking her. She had guts.

'Now go away,' she said. 'I don't want my daughter to know what I've been up to.'

They ate the sausage on the way back to the westward road. It was wonderful.

'I'm not going to look like that when I'm old,' said Effi.

'How can you get out of it?'

'Face-lifts.'

There were hardly any refugees on the road yet, but after a while they heard an engine running behind them and turned round to see a big silver car, dulled with dirt. There was a woman in the back wearing furs, you could see her felt hat inside the ruff of fuzzy darkness, a curl of smoke, a pair of made-up eyes. The driver blew his horn at them.

'Lucky bitch,' said Effi. 'Look at the fur coat. Sable. One day I'm going to have a coat as nice as that. Hey, d'you think it's Eva Braun?'

'No,' said Hanno. 'They'd get her away by plane.'

'Of course they would. So this is some Party fat cat's moll, isn't it? I bet she's got a nice lipstick. You know, Hanno, we ought to get ourselves some wheels. You know you love me –'

'Do I?' There was something like a flash, a rush of voltage inside him, but he wasn't going to show it.

'Don't you? Well, never mind. Look, get a gun from somewhere, there must be plenty lying around. Hijack me that car. Or the next one that happens along. You fiddled a chunk of sausage, after all – the car would be child's play. You don't need a gun, just find another old woman to kiss. Don't make that face. You did well.'

Hanno looked ahead of him at the changing pattern of cracks along the road. On the outside he was jaunty, pleased with himself for wheedling the sausage out of the old woman, but inside he was all anger and confusion. He'd said last night that he wanted to understand, and then he'd had that awful dream about Father – and now he was remembering how Father had got angry with Mother at Christmas because the dinner was late, then he'd gone into the kids' bedrooms and shouted: 'What's all this filthy mess?' Just because Heide had left a pair of socks on the floor, and Wolfgang had rumpled up his bed after Mother had made it. He'd given the boys a clip round the ear each and told Heide to stop snivelling.

It was always bad when Father came home on leave; they'd got used to living without him, and maybe he knew himself he didn't fit in any more. Hanno used to count the days till he went back to the Front. It shouldn't have been like that. It should all have been like that walk in the snow. Only it wasn't.

He said to Effi: 'What was it like, being a criminal?'

'It was hard work, kid. You had to look out for yourself all the time.'

'Yes, but you didn't care about anything – wasn't that good?'

'I cared about myself, and my friends.' Her mouth went up at the corners and he wondered why. She said: 'At least I didn't have to be a good Nazi girl, so I saw what other people were shutting their eyes to. And did whatever I could get away with, like listening to the BBC. Did you?'

'In the end we all did, never mind that we might have got into trouble for it. Everyone wanted to know how far the Russians had got.'

The road came out of the woods and met a bigger highway that had once been lined with trees, but only their stumps were left. The trees had been made into a barricade to stop the Russians. It hadn't worked. You could see the smashed-up bits of it alongside the road for about half a kilometre. There had been a trench behind the barricade, too, but the Russians had filled it up with a mixture of wood and earth. You could see the tank-tracks going over it, and then the tyres of the fur-coat woman's car. It made it easier for them to walk, anyway.

The village came next. It had been destroyed. Blackened spars poked up from the house roofs. One of the houses was still smoking. The church tower was a stump. There were dozens of dead German soldiers lying around. The tanks had rolled over some of them. The stink of explosives was strong here; that was a good thing, because you didn't smell the bodies. Hanno looked away from the corpses on the road and saw a dead soldier in a house doorway. It made him think of Wolfgang, though he tried not to.

There were still dead soldiers lying on the road when they got out into the countryside again. About half a kilometre from the village centre there was a house that had lost part of its roof. A little man came out of the front door, bright and chirpy as if he hadn't slept in a ruin, knotting a striped tie in front of his chin.

'Good morning!' he said. 'It was lively here last night. But I made it through in the potato cellar. No potatoes, that's the only trouble. Inhabitants fled. Don't blame them. But what's a man to do when he sees a lot of tanks coming? He dives for the nearest shelter, that's what he does.'

The little man was male and had four limbs, so he should be in the army, but there was something about him that contradicted the whole idea of the army. He dragged a handcart out of the door behind him: it was made out of an orange box mounted on the wheels and pushing handle of a pram. Behind the handcart came a large dog on the end of a piece of string. The dog tried to run towards a dead soldier who lay a metre or so away.

'Cornelius!' the little man said angrily.

The dog was a long-legged comedy of an animal, muddy-cream-coloured with a curling tail, a pink-brown muzzle and tangled floppy hair. He fought and whined till the little man slapped him, then he gave in, but you could see he didn't understand. The little man fetched out a raggy grey handkerchief and wiped his face with it. 'Of course,' he said as if he was ashamed of himself, 'of course the dog was interested. He's hungry, like the rest of us, but there are decencies, aren't there? My name's Sperling, by the way.'

He started to walk along the road beside them.

'Hanno Frisch,' said the boy. 'My friend's called Effi.' He didn't know what her surname was.

'Effi Mann,' she said. 'Are you short of food?'

'Well,' said Sperling, 'Fräulein Effi, can't be wasteful with what we've got, can we? And he's always been a greedy mutt.'

Cornelius wagged his tail, grinning.

Sperling said: 'So, kids, the thousand-year Reich is over already. It only felt like twelve years. Doesn't time fly? Well, everything's short at the moment: it's such a short distance between the Eastern Front and the Western Front, the fare has gone down to ten pfennigs. Thanks for laughing, pretty Fräulein, that'll be another ten pfennigs for the joke – you might as well, after all, you won't get anything serious for hard cash, not nowadays.'

'Are you from Berlin?' asked Effi.

There was a rattle of wheels behind them.

'Soldiers,' said Sperling, smiling, nervous now. 'Trouble.'

But the little cart, drawn by two hairy ponies, went past them without stopping.

'On the run,' said Sperling. 'I'd really like to get off this main road, it's too serious for me.'

'I think we should head for those woods,' said Effi, pointing ahead where the land sloped upwards again.

Now other refugees were coming up behind them, going at a good pace and overtaking them. Hanno saw the Czekallas in their wagon with the old woman, her daughter and granddaughter, and the man in the Homburg hat was riding too. Probably he'd bought the ride with coffee beans. He saw them with his sideways glancing wolf-eyes but he didn't greet them.

'I'm not from Berlin, no,' said Sperling. 'I'm from Zossen, I was a ticket clerk at the station there. I always fancied a career in cabaret but the times weren't right for the sort of jokes I wanted to tell. Couldn't go into the army, you know. Chronic bronchitis.' He coughed at the thought of it. 'They tried to get me in at the end, though. They were sending people out in wheelchairs. And I saw the Home Guard commandant going to the graveyard with a spade – this is God's truth, I swear – I said to him, Where are you going, Herr Kommandant? and he says to me, "Oh, just digging out a few more slackers, some people'll bed themselves two metres down to get out of doing their bit." But he had to stop halfway down the first grave because the Russians were coming.'

Hanno had heard this joke before, but Sperling told it well.

'You're right,' said Effi. 'You should have been in cabaret. Maybe when the war's over there'll be an opening for you.'

There was a faint grumble in the sky, planes coming. Russian planes, there were no German planes, no Luftwaffe left. It was the worst possible place, flat fields all around, no cover at all.

'The ditch,' shouted Hanno. 'There must be a ditch.'

There was, and they got down into it. Hanno just remembered to keep the milk pail upright so that the water wouldn't spill out. Luckily there was no water down here to speak of, only a damp silty bottom. The planes came down low. Hanno put his hands over his head; somehow he felt safe with his hands over his head, and he shut his eyes tight. Please God, he found himself thinking, please. He heard bullets bouncing off the hard surface of the road.

Ida Rupf and her family ran for the ditch, too; Herr Hungerland ran with them. There was no time to do anything about the animals. Ida felt the silt seeping into her clothes, felt it squish between her fingers as she tried to grab hold of it, she wanted something to hold. She found a tree-root and grasped that. Then she was calling out, she was ashamed of herself, for her mother, for Felix. She wanted Felix. She couldn't believe it. After all those years.

The planes went away. She was still alive. She had to get out of the ditch.

One of the Czekallas' horses was dead and the other bleeding to death because they'd got him in the throat. The wagon was keeling over, one of the big rear wheels had gone. The air was full of flour from a burst sack, so everything, even the horses, was covered with white powder. She couldn't help thinking about Botho and Fred, maybe they were lying like this. Oh, please, God, no. She'd rather the Russians kept them than that they were dead.

Magda started to scream. 'Oh, Lord Jesus. Oh, Lord Jesus.'

'Calm yourself, girl!' she said.

Magda was screaming about Czekalla and Lisbeth, who hadn't got to the ditch. They lay dead on the road. The cow was still alive. The spray of bullets had pushed Czekalla across the road; his schnapps bottle lay intact a short distance away from his corpse. Herr Hungerland was alive, he'd come out of the ditch with his smart clothes plastered in mud. The rest of them were just as filthy.

Magda went to pray over Lisbeth. She even prayed over Czekalla, but not so long.

There was no discussion about what they had to do next. They all knew. They'd have to work quickly, though, nobody wanted to stay here in the open, after what had happened. They started to rifle the wagon for what they could carry away with them. Barbara worked too, wordlessly, her grey eyes darting here and there. She reached for the boy baby doll she'd got for her third birthday, held it close to her for a moment, then saw her mother looking at her. Magda didn't say anything, but Barbara put the doll back again. Poor child, thought Ida, poor child. But Magda's right.

'Empty half the potatoes and the porridge,' she said, 'and we'll carry the sacks with the rest.' It made her feel better to give orders. She put her silver-fox heads round her throat, she wasn't leaving *them* behind, even if they made her sweat in the daytime, and she'd keep her coat too. 'And the sausage,' she said.

Magda said: 'Give me the knife. I'm going to get some meat. And we'll take that cow along with us and have her milk.'

Ida looked at the horses. They were both dead now, but for the life of her she couldn't face chopping them up for meat. She scolded herself for weakness. Anyway, Magda was going to do it. But when Magda got to the horses she hesitated, wondering how to start. Then Herr Hungerland walked over to stand beside her, putting his hand out for the knife.

'Let me,' he said. 'I have some knowledge of physiology. I am a doctor.'

The planes were gone, still Hanno wasn't sure if he could open his eyes or get up. Then he heard the dog whining, looked and saw him nudging Sperling, who had a bloody hole in his belly.

'Poor Cornelius,' said Sperling, and managed to grin. 'You got some water, kids? I'm dreadfully thirsty.'

He was going fast. Hanno got behind him and held the milk pail to his mouth. He managed one gulp. Hanno stroked his thinning brown hair and his temples, Effi came alongside him. She took his hand and crooned over and over again: 'Poor Sperling, poor darling.'

Sperling opened his eyes wide and again he managed the grin. 'Give me a kiss, will you?' he asked Effi. 'Cheer a poor man up on his death bed? Oh, and listen, take the dog, kids. And the cart, if it's still alive.' As if the cart had been keeping him company. Effi bent over and kissed him.

'I love you,' she said, 'just remember that where you're going.'

'Listen,' he said, 'have you heard this one? There was a Russian, a Frenchman and a German, all standing in an aeroplane, waiting to jump – give me another kiss, Fräulein Effi –' his voice was quiet now, and slurred. 'And a bit more water, Frisch. Don't think I don't appreciate you looking after me, like a brother, Frisch, only if Fräulein Effi gives me one more kiss I'll just go from her arms to the angels' and I won't notice the difference –'

He was gone. It was too late for any more kisses.

They laid him out in the ditch with his arms by his sides. Hanno shut his eyes and fastened his chin up with the necktie. The dog sniffed his master, crying. Then Effi took a few handfuls of silt and scattered them over his face.

'He's buried now,' she said. 'Poor little arsehole, with his jokes, why did it have to be him? Is his cart still alive?'

'I don't know,' said Hanno. 'Yes, it is.'

'And we've got to take the dog. It's a sacred trust.

Though I don't know why we've been burdened with an extra mouth in these times.' She said this in an old woman's voice, disapproving, sad. 'Come on, mutt.'

Hanno stood by Sperling. He didn't want to leave him. He'd already left Wolfgang.

'Hanno,' said Effi, 'can't you help me catch this dog?'

Hanno looked up to see Cornelius duck away from Effi with all the hair on his spine standing up.

'He doesn't want to go with us,' said Hanno.

'OK,' said Effi, 'if you're so ungrateful, mutt. We'll just take the cart.'

But when she got near the cart Cornelius sprang forward, jumped on top of it, and growled at her.

'We'll have to bribe him,' said Effi, and fetched the sardine tin out of her bag. 'Let's hope there are some goodies in the cart to make up.'

'You're giving the sardines to the dog?'

'Not all of them.' Effi put the key into the tab of the tin and turned it back, singing, 'Dinner time, Swing Boy, dinner time, dog.'

As soon as the dog caught the sardine smell he was there.

'We'll have some first,' said Effi, 'show him who's boss. Two each for us, the mutt can have the last one and lick the tin out.'

Hanno saw the sardines under the curling lid, saw dark rich flesh looking out from under the fragile silver skins. Somewhere there were heavy engines in the further sky. He saw big planes, bombers, saw smoke go up where they were dropping explosives – maybe on civilians, maybe on the army. There he was standing on the open road, in danger. But he had sardines to eat. They tasted good. And Sperling had said: 'Like a brother.' And his own brother was dead. These were all things that he couldn't fit together in his mind.

He watched Effi put the tin down in front of the waiting, panting dog. Cornelius slobbered his tongue into the opening, getting the single sardine she'd left him and every last drop of oil: he didn't notice when she got hold of his string lead.

She tugged at him as soon as he'd finished. He put his hind legs forward and skidded along the road. You could hear his nails on the rough surface. Effi swore, using words Hanno had never heard, some of them sounded French, some English, only one was German. It made no difference to the dog. She slapped him. Suddenly he jerked forward and jumped onto the cart again. He sat there. He wasn't growling now.

'Jesus,' said Effi. 'Some dogs pull carts, we've got to push a dog. Little Sperling was a joker all right.'

Chapter Eleven

Effi said: 'I feel as if he was still there.'

'Who?' asked Hanno.

'Sperling. How can he have left so quickly? We'd only just met him. Hey, maybe his ghost is sitting on the cart, cracking jokes we can't hear. I'd better not die, Hanno, it must be awful, out on the street, playing to people who don't even know you're there.' He didn't answer. 'Do you know I'm here, kid?'

'What?'

'Oh, forget it.' She thought, It's not just Sperling that's bugging him.

'Look,' he said, 'this dog weighs a ton, do we really have to drag him? Is the cart worth it?'

'How should I know?' she said. 'I haven't had the chance to look inside.'

At the next turn of the road, they found the family from the night before, only now the Czekallas were dead and the old woman was standing in the lopsided wagon with little Barbara, unloading it. The man Hungerland was cutting meat out of one of the horses, only every now and again he'd whip round and stare at whatever ghost was stalking him. Ma Headscarf was crying as she packed meat away in sacking. And now the dog was off the cart, he snatched a big piece of meat out of Ma Headscarf's hand and ran to the other side of the ditch to gobble it up.

Ma Headscarf, holding the rest of the meat high up in the air, screamed at Effi: 'Where did you get that cur?'

Effi asked Hanno, 'Is this another of Sperling's jokes? Not in good taste, is it?'

'You're shameless, both of you,' said Ma Headscarf. 'People are dead here – you don't care about that, do you?' She bent down to pick another piece of meat off the ground.

Effi got her knife out. Poor Ma Headscarf, she thought. It's tough losing your friends, and the Czekalla woman didn't seem to have been such a stinker as her husband. 'Come on,' she said, 'why grudge the poor dog a treat? There's plenty for all of us.'

Hungerland said to Ma Headscarf: 'There's another piece of meat here, if you're ready for it.' He stared at Effi for a moment. I don't like you, she thought. I don't like the way you look at me.

'If anyone has a right to those horses it's our family,' said Ma Headscarf, wrapping the next piece of meat up in the sacking and keeping an eye out for the dog. 'Poor Lisbeth and I were at school together, she'd have wanted me to have them.'

'Auntie,' said Hanno, cheeking her, 'are you going to carry two whole horses all the way to the Mulde?' So he'd snapped out of his brooding. 'I'll get the meat,' he said to Effi.

Only Ma Headscarf wasn't charmed with him the way her mother was. 'Oh, go ahead!' she shouted, in tears again. 'Help yourself to all our food while you're about it, why don't you?'

Effi gave him the knife. We've got to eat, she thought.

'It's an outrage,' said Ma Headscarf, but she went back to packing the meat away. The old woman called to Effi.

'Come here,' she said, 'Berlin baggage.' She pointed. There were potatoes on the road that she'd shaken out of the sacks to make them light enough to carry. 'You can have those,' she said. 'Share them with the boy, though.'

Effi said: 'We share everything.'

'Do you now?'

Effi grinned at the Rupf. 'Not that, no.'

The old dame grinned back. She said: 'If you find anything else lying about, you can have it. There's more than we can carry on this cart. Only do it quietly, so that my daughter doesn't see you.'

Effi picked up potatoes. She found half a sausage that had rolled away from the cart. She stuffed it inside the waistband of her skirt. Then she saw a heel of black bread and a linen bag of dried apple. With the potatoes, that was enough to be going on with.

'What have you got there?' bellowed Ma Headscarf.

The old woman said: 'Magda. It's only some potatoes that we can't carry.'

'They're thieves,' said Ma Headscarf. 'They must have stolen that cart.'

'The cart was willed to us,' said Effi. 'By a dying man. So was the dog.'

Hanno started to laugh. Effi saw that the dog was beside him, sitting up to beg. Of course, Sperling had taught him tricks. Hanno gave him a scrap of meat and he gulped it down, then got up on his haunches again. He was a sight, with his front paws dangling in the air.

Ma Headscarf stared at them, poison in her eyes. The old dame grinned again, *she* was cool, and little Barbara didn't react at all. Hungerland jumped and then shot one of those furtive looks over his shoulder. As if his ghosts might be laughing at him. Then he looked relieved, as if he'd seen them and discovered that they weren't after all.

'I've got as big a piece as we can carry,' said Hanno when he'd stopped laughing. 'I need something to wrap this in.'

'You'll get no sacking from us,' said Ma Headscarf quickly.

'Here you are,' called the old woman. She threw a thin bundle of folded paper at Effi, who caught it. It was Czekalla's family tree. He'd traced his ancestors back two centuries, all Aryan of course. Pure German. The name sounded Polish, but that didn't matter in the crazy Nazi world. After all, there was even a story that Hitler was half-Jewish. None of it made sense when you really got down to it, except that National Socialism had all been about killing people. They'd done a good job there. Anyway, the Czekalla pedigree was nice stout paper; it'd wrap the meat up nicely.

They put the meat in Effi's bag because Cornelius could have got at it if it had been in the handcart. As for him, now that he had a full belly, he let Effi take his string and lead him away from the dead horses.

As they went off, Ma Headscarf and her mother started arguing and shouting at each other. Ma Headscarf was angry with the old dame for giving food away. You could hear her shouting about 'thieving vagabonds'. Then Effi and Hanno turned off the road and into the forest and the voices died away.

The track went uphill and down again. After something like half an hour's walking there was an explosion ahead of them. The shock of the blast made them stagger. Then the trees came to an end in a swampy field full of bulrushes, and on the other side of it the battle was going on in another wood. When the next blast came it spat leaves, dirt and a few splinters in their faces, grazing Effi's forehead. They threw themselves down, even the dog knew what to do.

'We'll have to go back,' said Hanno into her ear because of the noise. 'Sooner or later they'll stop fighting there and we can cross.'

'OK,' she said, 'let's find a nice thicket and look through this cart. I want to see what Sperling left us. Hey, we could even light a fire and cook meat and potatoes. If an Ivan flyer sees smoke he'll only think one of his mates has dropped a bomb in the woods. I'm so hungry, my God, I'm surprised I didn't grab a chunk of meat back there, the way the dog did.'

He said: 'I'm so hungry I could eat a tree if it was stewed long enough.'

'I'm so hungry I can feel my stomach sticking to my spine.'

'I'm so hungry I could eat a horse. And I'm going to eat a horse.' He grinned, but not quite as if he was happy.

'Ma Headscarf wanted a whole horse. Poor woman.'

'How come you're sorry for her? She doesn't like you.'

'She's in a nasty situation, and maybe her husband's dead. How's she going to hear about it, if he is? Nobody will know her address. Do you think the Allies will set up an information centre for Germans when the war's over?'

'I don't know. I feel bad about eating the horses. They just had to do what they were told till the Ivans killed them.'

'That's what it's like to be a domestic animal, kid. Oh, I feel sorry for the horses, too. But they're in horse heaven, they don't need their bodies any more, and we're hungry.'

They left the track. It was hard to push the cart, though the undercarriage had been part of one smart perambulator once upon a time and it was well sprung. But sprawls of bramble lassoed its wheels and every now and again it'd drop through a drift of dead leaves into a sudden dip in the ground and stick there. The trees were young pines growing close together, and they didn't always want to let the cart pass between them. In the end they found a small clearing surrounded by horse-chestnut saplings and scrub. The spot felt as safe as you could ever feel these days.

'I'll get some wood,' said Hanno. He still had to talk loudly to be heard, even back here.

Effi tied the dog to a tree trunk. Then she started to clear the sandy soil, brushing leaves and sticks into a heap for kindling, making a circular wall of earth for a fire-place, with gaps every now and again to let the air through. Hanno had gone out of sight and she listened out for his foot crunching on sticks. She couldn't hear him though, just the fighting. She thought, supposing something bad happens to him?

And she was remembering all the bad stuff, Sperling dying, Pierre dying, Aunt Annelie's body, Mama, even old Schulz inside the flames of his posh Merc. That was the second Merc he'd lost when he'd been travelling with Effi.

She shouldn't have thought that, now her mind was running unstoppably to the worst memories, she was right back there in Mama's bedroom in Wannsee, Mama was coughing and making Effi learn Aunt Annelie's address off by heart because she was going to die. She said: 'Tell Schulz you want to go to Annelie. No one else. Schulz will take you there.' It was the last thing she said before she stopped breathing. Effi knew Aunt Annelie, they'd met up with her a few times, always in cafés in the middle of Berlin, because Aunt Annelie didn't trust Anna the maid. It was always a bit stiff because Mama was a Wannsee lady and Aunt Annelie was working-class to the bone. They respected each other, though, and Mama trusted Aunt Annelie.

Schulz was away when Mama fell so very ill; he was in Vienna, he didn't even know what was happening. Effi had asked Anna to telegraph to him after Mama died, and Anna just said: 'That's not for you to decide.' She must have sent the telegram, though, because after Effi had been three days in that foul hospital one of the nurses came in and told her she was leaving. 'A gentleman called Herr Schulz has come for you,' she said, putting Effi's clothes down on the bed. Gooing, the way Anna used to. Schulz was waiting outside the ward. He'd been crying. He told Effi her lungs were OK. Then they got into his Merc and the driver took them to his plushy house and Schulz sat her down in the salon and said he was going to adopt her.

'No,' she said. 'I have to go to my aunt.'

'Your aunt,' said Schulz. 'You're too young to under-stand why that's a bad idea.'

'Mama said I had to go to her.'

'You're a well-off child,' said Schulz – as if that would make her want to stay with him. He explained to her that now she owned the villa and had a lot of invest-ments, he was her trustee, he said, he'd make sure she was comfortable.

What did Effi care about a lot of investments? And she didn't want the villa, she felt as if it had killed Mama and Grandmama. She wanted to go to Aunt Annelie and she kept telling Schulz so, till he gave in. He took her back to Wannsee and Anna had to pack up the things she wanted to take with her. Only she looked under the mattress for Papa's photograph and it had gone. She turned round and saw Anna in the doorway. Watching her. She knew Anna had got rid of the photograph. Luckily Aunt Annelie had one, too, or Effi might have forgotten what Papa looked like.

The car was driving up Schönhauser Allee when the air-raid siren started. Effi, Schulz and the chauffeur had to get out of the car and hide in the public shelter. It was the first big raid on Berlin, but they didn't know how bad it was going to be.

The roof kept shaking with the blast and the light bulbs went dancing around all over the place. Everyone was so scared; later on they were still scared but they found ways of coping with it, they'd breathe in special ways, they'd knit. This time was the worst. Schulz sat there in his sharp suit, drumming with his thumbs on his sleek trouser legs, you could see how uncomfortable he felt with all the workers around him in their shabby clothes. When the all-clear sounded and they came up into the open, half the street had been wrecked. There was smoke billowing everywhere and the sky was red with fire.

'It's not safe to go on,' said Schulz.

Effi said: 'It's further to go back.'

The chauffeur said: 'Didn't there used to be a Jewish cemetery up here?'

Schulz looked at him as if he was mad. 'Where's the car?' he said.

A block of masonry had fallen on the bonnet, at least that time Schulz was still alive to create about it. 'My

God, child, have you any idea how much that model costs? I knew we shouldn't have come.'

Effi only said: 'We'll have to walk.'

She did mind that Schulz was dead. OK, he'd wanted to get Mama away from Papa. He'd probably written dozens of letters to artists telling them they'd have to ditch their Jewish wives or husbands if they wanted to keep working. But he'd never been a complete swine like Otto – please God she'd never meet Otto again. Schulz had got her to Aunt Annelie even though he didn't want to. He used to come to see her in Prenzlauer Berg now and again and she wasn't sorry to see him. He'd got her out of Berlin in the end.

'It's all crazy,' she said to the dog. 'None of it makes sense.' He whined, sniffing after the meat in her bag. 'Sit down,' she said to him. She was glad he was there, though, and now he did as he was told. She hadn't expected that. His eyes, with their pale lashes, were watering with his desire for meat. 'You've eaten,' she said to him. 'We haven't.' He looked ashamed of himself, lay down and poked his nose towards his big hairy paws. It was all done for effect, of course. All she had to do was to speak kindly to him and he'd be up and capering again. One of his feet was twitching, and his wet spongy brown nose was moving. If he could talk he'd have been asking her if she'd heard this one? Just like poor little Sperling.

Hanno was back, and he had a good armful of wood. They built the fire together. The kindling burned pale and fast, then, as they loaded it down with thicker sticks and chunks of wormy tree-branch, it settled down to a darker, fiercer heat. They got two potatoes out and set them in the embers. They'd be black and sooty by the time they were ready. They put all the horse-flesh in the pot to roast because they both knew it'd keep better once it had been cooked. The brown smell of meat crept out between the pot and the lid.

'Someone could smell that,' said Hanno.

She said: 'You've got to take a risk sometimes.'

He shrugged his shoulders. 'What's in the cart?'

She showed him the dried apple and the sausage, then set it aside where the dog couldn't get it. He reached into the cart and fetched out a bundle of clean underpants, a shirt and a pair of trousers, all rolled up tight. There was a rolled blanket and a small cushion decorated with a cross-stitch heart and the words 'From Liesl'. There was a half-loaf of bread, one of the blue-stripe sausages that was so full of cereal it was really bread, a pot of rhubarb jam and a bottle of white beer.

'More fags,' said Hanno. 'Two packets. And matches again. What's this?' It was a cash box. He opened it up. 'No money in here. Ticket blanks. For the railway, of course, that's where he worked, isn't it? And a lot of big rubber stamps with dates and places. I wonder why he brought those with him.'

'Ask the dog,' said Effi, 'maybe Sperling told him. I wish I could make tickets that'd get me on a train. All the way to the west. Here, let's share one of those fags.'

He pulled one out and lit it at the fire, then passed it to her. She held it out between her two fingers, imagining it was at the end of a long holder. Then she took a breath of smoke and felt good. When she'd had enough, she passed it back to him.

'We'd have done OK,' she said, 'even if we hadn't got the horseflesh and the potatoes and sausage. Now – well, we won't eat it all at once. It's a shame that Ma Headscarf got so angry with us – what was the point? You know what's wrong with me? In spite of everything I know, I still really want to believe the world's good.'

The wood burned apart on the fire and the pot started to slip sideways. Hanno rescued it with a piece of wood he'd set aside to use as a poker and got it sitting nice and steady again.

'Can I have the knife?' he asked.

'You've got it, kid. You were getting the meat with it.'

'So I have. I wanted to try something with this.' He pulled a piece of wood from his pocket.

'It's half rotten.'

'That's why.' It was a big knot of wood with a little bit of splintered straight stuff at either side of it. He got the knife and started to cut the soft brown rotten wood away from the sound white stuff, holding the round edge of the knot against his palm.

'What kind of wood is it?'

'Pine, I think. I just – I like the shape of this.' His head was bent and intent, and his hands were different, suddenly, very careful and clever. He'd made a good job of bandaging her arm, too. Suddenly she wanted to kiss him again.

And then it hit her, a real slap in the face. Here she was letting herself get sweet on him, but he didn't know who she really was, and she'd no idea what he'd say if she told him.

'What are you making?' she asked. Though that wasn't what she really wanted to know.

'I don't know. It's just a shape, not a thing. I just want to see what's left in the wood when all this rotten stuff comes out.'

'It's a nice curve. Like a wave in a picture.'

'Yes, or – I don't know.'

'Like music. You just hear a line in your head, then you want some more to go with it. That's what my father used to say.'

'Your father, did he used to be a musician?'

Oh, God, what could she say now? And what was wrong with her, that she kept giving things away?

'Yeah, he was in a military band. The trumpet. He used to write some of the music himself.'

'Cool.'

'D'you like brass bands?'

'Yes.'

'You're good with your hands.'

'At school they got angry with me because I used to doodle on my exercise books. I got beaten a few times. Wasting paper, didn't I know there was a war on?' He frowned. Staring at the wood, pushing the rotten stuff out with his knife, he said: 'I used to like going scouting at weekends. And the solstice bonfires, and the torchlight processions we used to have, with all the singing and the banners. It made you believe in it all.'

She was glad she hadn't kissed him now. She didn't say anything.

He said: 'I didn't like my sports teacher. He taught us to box. He'd be standing there, shouting. "Come on, come on, I want to see blood." There used to be this really weedy boy at school. Jürgen Markus, the English teacher's son. And the sports teacher, Keller, last year he put me opposite Markus and told me to hit him. "Go on," he said, "he's easy to knock down." I looked at Markus, and I couldn't.'

'Because he was so weedy?' She didn't want to hear this stuff, it was like the story about the Jew – was he blaming himself for sometimes feeling sorry for someone?

'It's not as easy as that. Old Markus was quite big in the Nazi Party, locally, and Jürgen used to hang around in the playground and listen to what the kids were saying about their parents, then he'd tell his father. A lot of people hated them both. He got Hans Nagel's mother three years in jail for listening to the BBC. That's one of the things I didn't like. All the sneaking. You always had to be so careful what you said. Then all of a sudden, just after Easter, Markus wasn't there, some enemy he'd made in the Party had denounced *him* and now he was in a concentration camp. So Jürgen was on his own, and that was when Keller gave him to me to hit. Look, he was a filthy little rat. I ought to have been able to hit him. Then suddenly Keller hit me, and he shouted: "Do you want to hit someone now?" I was really angry then, I hit Jürgen and made his nose bleed. Keller asked me what was wrong with me. I didn't know. Look, I don't want to talk about this kind of thing.'

She hadn't been listening properly anyway. Why should she care about him? He was just some boy she'd run into on the road. It was Papa she cared about, and cared about reaching. She thought she'd tell a story to let him know she was tough. 'Do you remember when they bombed the zoo in Berlin?'

'I heard about it.'

'Well, next morning I was pretending to queue for cakes in one of those smart cafés on Kurfürstendamm – I was getting ready to take a purse out of a smart dame's handbag – and one of the tigers pushed his way inside.' It was a story everyone had been telling in Berlin, she hadn't actually been in the café but that didn't matter. 'Everyone raced for the door into the kitchen, but the tiger just started to eat a cake off the table and then it dropped dead. One of the lady customers said that showed what sort of a cake they served in the joint. Then all hell broke loose, the café owner was screaming that he'd sue her, and she was refusing to give her name and address. It made it easy for me to get the dame's purse. There were crocodiles and snakes swimming in the canal outside.'

Hanno said: 'You know, my brother –'

'Didn't know you had a brother.'

'I don't want to talk about him.'

'You started.'

She ought to want rid of him. To be right away from him, away from Germany too, in America with Papa. Yes, if wishes were horses, beggars would be parading into Moscow.

She said: 'Look, I know what. Let's make ourselves some tickets.' She fetched the stamps and ticket blanks out of the cashbox. 'One for me, one for you, one for Cornelius. Where can we go?'

The stamps had a wheel at the side: when you moved it, you got different stations. 'Cologne,' she said, 'Düsseldorf, Essen. All those places are bombed to bits. How about Göttingen? There's a famous university there, isn't there? We could study, you and me.'

She'd learned to hide what she was feeling, it was good to see she hadn't lost the knack. She wasn't going back to liking him, hadn't he said he believed in the Nazi stuff? Neither was she going to listen to the little voice that said she wasn't being fair to him. It was all too much, too difficult, and now she noticed how sore her bad arm was again.

She moved the wheel back. 'I know, Frankfurt am Main. Where your mother is. And the Amis.' She stamped three ticket blanks. 'And it has to leave from somewhere.

A place round here. Where are we, anyway? Here's a stamp for a place called Kummersdorf, how about that? I'm sure we're near Kummersdorf. Village of sorrows, Kummersdorf's everywhere nowadays. Now the date. The train goes tomorrow. At twelve. The blanks all say "Valid one month from" – I don't know what date it is.'

'Nor do I,' he said. 'Maybe the twenty-fourth?'

There was an enormous explosion: the whole wood shook and the dog started howling. God, it was dark!

'Shut up,' she said to the dog. 'You must have been in air-raids before now.'

'Ammunition going up,' said Hanno. 'Your turn for the fag.'

She sucked smoke in. 'Thanks, sweetie. Listen, what date should I put on these tickets?'

'April the fifteenth,' he said. 'Leaves us plenty of time. There's another stamp, look. It says "Express" – that's what we want.'

'An express train to get us out of this mess, that'd be something.' She passed a ticket to him. 'Last express train out of Kummersdorf. Don't lose your ticket, or what will you show at the barrier? Look, I'm going to make a ticket for the kid, Barbara. I promised her she'd be all right. I won't give tickets to Ma Headscarf, though. I don't want her on my train. Oh, why not? The kid's probably fond of her mum. And the granny's sweet on you. We don't have to share a compartment with them. Maybe I'll let them all ride the train. Louis Armstrong did a song like that. Pierre taught it me. But I won't have that Hungerland on board. He's creepy. He can walk. I ain't joking, I'm a tough guy.'

Another big explosion, but it felt better when you had something to do. She made three more tickets and handed them to Hanno. He put them into the cart. She fetched out her harmonica and played a high, sharp note like a train's whistle, then set the harmonica to repeat a set of metallic short phrases. The air was full of engine noise, Effi sent the locomotive hustling along the track, making it whistle again. She stopped, looked at him, raised her eyebrows.

'Brilliant,' he said. But he was still a scumbag Nazi kid. He said: 'That's a man's jacket, isn't it?'

She snatched the fag from his mouth. There wasn't much of it left now. 'Smart boy. It used to belong to my Uncle Max. Aunt Annelie cut it down for me.'

'What happened to him?'

'He was a con man. He used to sell audiences with Hitler to people up from the country. He even made special badges for them to wear – eagle, swastika, the lot. At first he just gave his suckers directions and then vanished, then he started getting too interested in the whole thing, telling them fairy tales he'd invented about what'd happen when they got inside. He spent too much time with them, they got to remember his face, so the police caught him. He died in the camp. Poor Uncle Max.'

It wasn't a bad story considering she'd just made it up.

Chapter Twelve

'All right,' said Hanno suddenly. 'I'll tell you about my brother. He was my twin, he was half an hour younger than me. We were both supposed to be cheeky, but he was cheekier. My mother used to say I was the quieter one. He liked the Louis Armstrong music too; I can remember how he danced to it. When I was being caned for cheeking the teacher about working down at the wireworks he said in a really loud voice, "We thank Hanno Frisch for giving our teacher this much-needed exercise." He got the cane too.'

She said: 'And he's in Frankfurt. With your mother and your sister.'

'You know he's not.' He sat quite still, staring at the ground. 'They got him in the chest; at least he died straight away. I put him down behind a wall, but I didn't bury him. I stayed with him a bit, then I ran away. I don't even know where it was that he died. I wish I'd buried him.'

'You've confessed,' said Effi quickly. It was no use asking him what he'd have buried the kid with, he'd never listen. 'Just say six Aves and four Glorias.'

He put his hand on his own chest. You could see he was afraid of crying. 'We weren't religious, my father left the church. Are you a Catholic?'

'My father wasn't, but my mother was, so I had to be. Aunt Annelie wasn't. I went back to confession a year ago, just for fun.' That was all true, at least.

'What did you confess?'

'Oh, the usual rubbish, but the priest wanted to know if I'd had any thoughts. I said I was always thinking. No, he said, not ordinary thoughts. Sinful thoughts about boys. Dirty old man. I said I wanted to be a nun and I never went back. This fag's finished. We ought to save our fag-ends, we can make roll-ups with the tobacco if we can find some paper.'

'You didn't tell him about the stealing?'

'That wasn't a sin, it was my job.'

'What happened to the Frenchman? Pierre?' Hanno asked.

'The police hanged him.'

A muscle tightened in his cheek and he turned his face away. 'Do you think the food's ready?'

The meat was tough, but that was good because they mustn't eat too much of it. It took longer to eat when it was tough. They drank all the gravy. The potatoes were white and soft inside their charred jackets.

Cornelius laid his head on Effi's foot now, eyes rolling up like a saint gazing at God.

'You've had,' Effi told him, putting the pot with the rest of the meat back in her bag. 'I'm a tough guy, it's no use coming begging to me.'

Hanno threw dirt on the dying fire. Then suddenly there were tears running down his face, he was sobbing and shaking all over as if it was really hard for him to cry. The dog went to him and nudged him with his wet nose. There was no need for her to try and comfort him, then. He had Cornelius. But he didn't take any notice of the dog. She couldn't let him just sit there on the ground and cry like that, it was awful. She went over to him and put her arm on his shoulder. He clutched her and cried. That was bad, she wanted to cry too – but no, she thought. I won't cry till I find Papa. Then the boy had his arms round her, they were close together and he wasn't crying so hard. Her bag was getting wedged between them and hurting, but she pushed it to one side. They were holding each other tight, they were kissing each other, mouth to mouth. His body was close to hers, his hand was against her back, this is so nice, she thought, you could forget about everything else.

And then suddenly she remembered everything. She felt sick and angry, ragingly angry with herself, with him. He was a policeman's kid and the police had killed Pierre. And he was stuffed full of Nazi lies. The Nazis said the Jews wanted to destroy Germany. They said all the enemies were Jews, the Russians were Bolshevik Jews, the English and the Americans were Jewish fat-cat businessmen. Every bomb that fell out of the sky was supposed to be Jewish. What would he say if he knew she'd helped hide Jews from the police and get them out of Germany? He'd say she'd helped kill his twin brother. She shoved him off her, rolled away from him and stood up. He sat there with his mouth open. She hated his stupid face.

She said: 'Let me tell you, Hitler Youth. You're nothing compared to Pierre. Listen, one night we did an apartment, it was the only thing standing in a whole block, and there were fires everywhere, it was as hot as hell. The people had a Steinway grand in their best room, all black and shiny, and there was a white vase on it with violets, but they'd wilted in the heat and they were plastered flat to the side. And Pierre said: "Look, forget about work for a moment. I'm going to play that piano." So he played "When the Saints Go Marching In". I sang, and he played, and all the time I could smell the violets, even though they were really dead, and I was sweating in torrents, but I could sing all right because they'd got their windows so well taped up they hadn't broken and there wasn't any smoke in the place. I'll swear Pierre played better than he'd ever done in his life. And I knew I wanted to be a singer more than anything, more than I wanted to live, maybe, even though that doesn't make sense. Then the piano started to go out of tune. It sounded all right at first, just as if he'd changed key, but it got worse and worse, and in the end he stood up. He said: "You're a professional, kid, you've got what it takes. Now let's get out, this is the hottest club either of us will ever play." That was Pierre, he was really something.'

She thought, I want to go back to Berlin, I have to go back and find him, it was all a mistake, they didn't string him up after all and he's waiting for me there, looking round, shouting, 'Effi, how can I go back to Annelie without you?'

The boy started to say something, but she didn't want to hear it. She ran away, on and on into the woods, tripping over tree roots and brambles. Once she fell and grazed her hands. She got up and went on running, she didn't know where she was running to, she didn't care, the wildness was howling inside her and all the while she knew Pierre and Aunt Annelie were both really dead and she kept on running.

Hanno stood up. Mechanically, he started to pack everything into the cart. He thought, what did I do wrong? The dog whined.

'Shut up,' he said. He stared at the ashes under their cover of sandy soil. He'd have to go to Frankfurt, wouldn't he? Mother was waiting for him in Frankfurt. And Effi didn't want him any longer. She'd said he was nothing.

He sat down again and clutched his arms round him. Now he was crying again; it was horrible to cry, it felt as if the sobs were breaking him apart. There was a cold touch on his forehead. It was the dog again, nosing him. He stopped crying. Now the dog got up, tugging at the string. The dog knew what he wanted to do. He wanted to go after Effi. Maybe only because she had the meat. Hanno felt empty and hopeless. Then he felt it in his gut that he must go after Effi, it was like the shape that was left after he'd scooped the rotten stuff out of the pine-knot, the thing that had to be. He picked the pine-knot off the ground and shoved it in the cart, somehow he didn't want to leave it behind. He stood up and wondered which way to go. The dog knew.

He ran forwards with his nose on the ground.

Effi stopped still when she heard the voices ahead of her. The wildness all drained out of her and she listened. They were women's voices, but that didn't mean they weren't Russians – there were supposed to be women with the Russian army, people said they were terrible, brutal women because they carried guns. No, these women were talking German. It was the old dame talking to Ma Headscarf. She mustn't let *them* see her in a state. I'm all right, she told herself, I'm going to get out of here on a luxury train. And she wouldn't let herself miss the boy. Good riddance.

You'll be OK, she told herself. Don't think. Sing.

> I've nothing to eat
> not a crust, not a bone.
> Lost everyone I know,
> but I'm happy all alone.

Her voice was coming on, there was a note in it, Pierre said so – well, it came from Mama. Mama's voice growing again in Effi's body. So she wasn't alone, she'd better remember that. She fetched the harmonica out and improvised as she strolled ahead. She'd go and see Ma Headscarf and annoy her.

'Oh, it's you,' said the old dame. 'What have you been up to?'

Ma Headscarf snorted. Old Hungerland was there, too, but he was busily tidying all the leaves up on the ground under one of the trees, laying them in lines and throwing little twigs or broken leaves out of the way. He was forcing himself to concentrate on them but you could see his eyes twitching, wanting to look over his shoulder at his ghosts, who must be people he'd murdered or betrayed.

'Oh,' said Effi – you got used to shouting, but once the fighting stopped they'd have to be careful and talk more quietly – 'I've just got myself a ticket for a train to Frankfurt and as soon as the fighting's over I'm on my way to catch it.'

'Aren't you ashamed of yourself?' Ma Headscarf wanted to know. 'Telling lies like that?'

Effi started to whistle. Hungerland looked up at her for a moment and a cold shiver ran down her spine. He made her think of Otto; he'd kill her too. But not in the same way. She remembered the way he'd cut the meat out of the horses. He'd kill coldly. But she wasn't going to let him scare *her*. She was Effi Mann.

'A whistling woman,' said Ma Headscarf, 'and a crowing hen –'

'Deserve to have their heads cut off,' said Effi. 'Yes, I know the saying. The Ivans' ammo makes more noise than I do, anyway. Why bother?'

The old dame was peering behind Effi, into the trees.

Effi asked her: 'Are you looking for your little Hitler Youth, do you want to give him some more potatoes?'

And all at once the dog was there, jumping at Effi, licking her face, almost knocking her off her feet. Oh no, she thought, now it'll get complicated again. And he'll be angry, but he's no right to be, he doesn't own me, nobody does.

She grabbed the dog by the collar and made him sit. 'Nice dog, isn't he?' she said to the little silent Barbara. 'Come and give him a pat.'

Hungerland spoke, with a creepy kind of eagerness in his voice. 'A train? Where is it departing from?'

'Kummersdorf,' said Effi. 'Tomorrow at noon. The tickets are hellishly expensive but I had my mother's diamond ring and I swapped that for mine.'

'She's telling lies,' said Ma Headscarf. 'There is no train.' No wonder the kid didn't bother to talk, her ma was the sort who'd shove anything you said back down your throat.

'I don't care if you believe me or not,' said Effi. 'We bought our tickets from a man, but he's flitted. *I* don't want you on my train.' She did the whistle again, went on to the chuff-chuff notes. She had to play loudly because of the noise. Pierre said you have to know how to do a train if you play the harmonica, the audience loves it. But this audience wasn't loving it. It was getting up their noses. They were standing by the track, watching the carriages shoot past, no chance of hitching a lift, and there they were on their two feet without so much as a handcart.

'Oh, give our ears a rest,' said Ma Headscarf, 'for pity's sake.'

Effi stopped playing. She got her ticket out of her pocket and waved it around. Hungerland stood up and took a step towards her.

'Let me see those.'

Effi shoved the ticket back in her pocket and set the train running again. And here was Hanno, pushing the cart.

'Hello, sweetie,' she called out to him.

He gave her a dirty look, and Ma Headscarf scowled. Frau Rupf's face went soft, my Lord, was she sweet on Swing Boy. The dog, who was determined to make a carnival out of everything, started jumping at Hanno as if he hadn't seen him for hours.

'*She* says,' Frau Rupf looked at him, you could see her thinking, Now this nice lad's come we'll get right to the bottom of things. 'The girl says you've bought tickets for a train to Frankfurt.' Effi set the train going on the harmonica again but she backed out of Ma Headscarf's reach because the look on her face said she was the earboxing type and any moment now Hanno was going to tell them it was only a wind-up. She whooped through the harmonica, it wasn't really a German train at all, it was an American train with a cowcatcher in front and a big fat funnel, riding endlessly across a sea of waving grasses.

They were all staring at Hanno, Frau Rupf, Ma Headscarf, and Hungerland. Hanno didn't say anything. He frowned.

'Well,' asked Ma Headscarf, 'are you going to tell us the truth?'

As if she had a right to know – who did she think she was?

'I don't know –' said Hanno.

'What do you mean,' shouted Ma Headscarf, 'you don't know? You know it's all a lie, don't you?'

'Let him speak, Magda,' said old Frau Rupf, fiddling with her fox-heads. That had been quite a nice fur once.

Hanno shook his head at Effi. 'You promised to keep it quiet.'

All right, thought Effi, we'll wind them up a bit longer.

Hungerland jumped in feet first. 'Can I find this man who sold you the tickets?'

Well, thought Effi, thank you, Sperling, this is your work. And for a moment she saw him; he was standing behind Hungerland, killing himself laughing.

'Herr Doctor,' said Ma Headscarf, 'don't take any notice of them.'

So Hungerland was a doctor, was he? Again, Effi felt the cold shiver down her spine and she remembered the awful nights in the hospital after Mama died. Anyway, this doctor was going to look a nice fool in the end. Hanno would laugh in his face.

She played the train music again, as quietly as she could and still be heard, the track was a kilometre or so away and the trains were rattling along there. The dog was sitting aside, grinning as if he was master of ceremonies (and now for the famous double act, Effi Mann and Hanno Frisch).

'Sweetie,' she said, 'I'm so sorry I let it out, but look, it's no use anyone trying to buy tickets unless they have the sort of valuables the man's interested in.'

'I've nothing at all,' said Frau Rupf, but she put her hand to her waist. There must be something tucked away inside her corsets. 'The Ivans took my gold watch. It's a shame, my sister-in-law lives near Frankfurt. Is this man genuine?'

'Well,' said Effi, 'it could be a con trick, but I don't think so, and I've seen through some con men you dames would have trusted your little boy to.'

There was another huge explosion, but that wasn't what made the old woman shiver.

'What sort of man is this?' the doctor asked.

Hanno looked innocent. 'He's in the woods,' he said, 'a big man in a suit.'

Ma Headscarf got her rosary out and started telling her beads, but no Aves, Paternosters or Glorias, instead train tickets, suits and con men. Dr Hungerland coughed as if he was going to speak, but instead he started to mess up all the leaves he'd been arranging so carefully, and again he coughed, and again, and, at last, he spoke.

'I have – I have something that might be of interest to the man. If he could be found. If you could take me to look for him – or go on my behalf, maybe –'

He really was crazy or he'd never have been taken in. Now was the time to tell them, laugh at Hungerland, and run off. But Hanno said: 'You'd need to make that worth our while.'

'I have this,' said Dr Hungerland. 'It might satisfy you.'

He fished in his pocket and brought out a gold cigarette case. He passed it to Effi, who found herself turning it over to see the hallmark. Inside there were three cigarettes and a message engraved on the underside of the lid: *For Doctor Hungerland, with heartfelt gratitude. The Brandt family.*

'I am an able physician,' he said. 'I saved this child from scarlet fever and she suffered no complications.'

'Never mind that,' said Hanno. 'Let's see what you've got for the fare.'

The doctor coughed again. 'I think it would be better for us to go aside.'

Now the three of them were walking away behind a tree trunk and the doctor was bringing a little leather pouch out of a body-belt inside his shirt – he had horrible grey hair on his chest – and opening it for them.

'Diamonds,' he said. A plane screamed in the sky right overhead. They just had time to flinch before it was gone.

'How do we know they're genuine?' asked Hanno. And Effi thought, what's the boy up to, does he really want diamonds?

The stones were lying in Hungerland's palm like drops of water, only you couldn't cut facets in water. They were cold and starry, lovely diamonds – one day, thought Effi, someone will give me diamonds like that. Then she heard Sperling, as if he was just behind her, 'Fräulein Effi, Frisch is getting them for you now.' Laughter in his voice. Part of her screamed with laughter too, because the boy thought she was a criminal, was he doing this to impress her? Or even to get back at her for the things she'd said to him?

Maybe Sperling was the Devil. He might be; it was easier to believe in the Devil than it was to believe in God, nowadays.

Dr Hungerland got a pair of horn-rimmed spectacles out of his pocket with his other hand.

'My reading glasses,' he said. He pushed them at Effi. She didn't want to take them, because they smelt of him and felt like him, but she did, and he scratched one diamond across the glass surface. There was a small chiselling sound. He tested the second diamond, and the third. His hand quivered as he did it. He was bricking himself with terror all the time, she thought, a filthy terror that made *her* feel dirty when he was so close to her.

She looked at Hanno, but he wouldn't meet her eye. There was a stubborn look on his face. She thought, You've only yourself to blame, Effi – if you hadn't run away none of this would have happened.

Hanno said, 'All right, they'll do. I'll take your glasses, though. So that the man can test the diamonds for himself.'

'Not both of you,' said Hungerland at once. 'The girl can stay, you can go. I don't want you both disappearing and leaving me without my ticket.'

Wonderful, thought Effi, now I have to stay with this lot. Well, she'd keep the dog, she didn't think he was much of a fighter, but it'd make her feel better. And there were the others, they'd dilute Hungerland's company. It was coming to something when she was glad to be with Ma Headscarf.

Chapter Thirteen

Hanno walked away into the woods, making sure he knew where he was going: no sun to help him, but there was a broken tree; here there was a stand of old oaks and one of them had a stump of a branch reaching up at the side of the main stem. He squirrelled the details into his head, making a map there – that was something useful he'd got from the Hitler Youth, anyway. Now he wondered where Kummersdorf was exactly. He thought it was somewhere south of Berlin.

Somewhere in the woods there was a non-existent man selling non-existent tickets. Hanno kept on walking as if he really expected to find him. He almost shouted for him. That was stupid, though. He stopped when he reckoned he was half a kilometre away from the others. He stood under a smaller oak and looked up at the trunk straining up into the dark sky. Tiny red leaves were just beginning to come out on the branches. He sat down, elbows on his knees, hands dangling. He shouldn't go back at once.

Now he had time to wonder why the joke about the train had turned so serious, and why he was sitting there with three diamonds and a pair of reading glasses in his pocket. He'd give Effi the diamonds. That'd show her.

He was really a criminal now – this went far beyond the theft of the soldier's pack. What would Wolfgang have thought about it? He might have thought it was a cool stunt – but no, Hanno realized he had no idea what Wolfgang would have thought. He'd moved on into a world that Wolfgang had never imagined. He'd set foot in it the moment he'd gone on the run and broken the oath he'd sworn to Hitler. Obedience till death.

But Hitler had been a bad leader; they were all saying that now. He'd led Germany into a war that couldn't be won. Why had they all followed, then?

He remembered the heavy, limp body that had been all that was left of his twin brother. And Sperling, alive and joking one moment, bleeding to death the next. And the old Jew on the street, having to be frightened of a lot of little boys. He remembered those rumours about Jews being gassed – he thought they came from the English radio. Mother said they were lies. She said in the First World War each side had lied about awful things that the others were supposed to have done. It made him feel confused, all the same, because now everything was so different from the way it was supposed to have been.

Not Germans, he said to himself. Germans wouldn't murder all those people. But a cynical voice came back at him from inside his head: Why not? You know what they said about Jews. You know what happened in Russia. You know what they were doing to the sick kids in the hospitals. And it made him feel ashamed to remember how Emil had hit the old Jew in Sternberg – and then he thought of Otto and how he should have known Otto was a murdering brute. Why? Because murder and brutality had been going on in the background of his life. He'd known it, but he hadn't noticed it. Maybe because all the grown-ups went along with it. It felt as if it hadn't been possible to notice it.

He said aloud to himself: 'They should have stopped it before Wolfgang had to go out and die.' And then, as if his father could hear him: 'Why didn't *you* stop it?' And he thought about the boxing lesson, and Keller shouting: 'Do you want to hit someone now?' His head had still been swimming, but he'd hit out. Yes, he thought. I want to get back at someone. At a grown-up. A horrible grown-up like Otto. Only he's not here, so Hungerland will do.

What was it Effi had said? You danced around the music line? He remembered Louis Armstrong doing that on his trumpet. Now he'd made his own solo out of the train-theme she'd played on her harmonica. He tried to grin. Then his thoughts started to lecture him: OK, how far would you go, Johannes Frisch? Would you cheat the old woman and her daughter? And the poor kid who doesn't speak?

He was going to do it – that was all. No point in arguing.

He'd have to score the glasses again, as if he'd done it for the man. He stood up and got the pouch and the glasses out of his pocket, brought out a diamond and scraped it across the glasses again. Hungerland had scratched the left lens so he scratched the right one. Then he put the glasses on to see what he'd done. The scratches flew across his vision like insects and the lenses reshaped the world, pulling everything sideways, widening the oak trunks, stunting their upward growth. It made him feel dizzy. He took a step and tripped over a tree-root. The open pouch tumbled out of his hand along with the loose diamonds. He picked up the pouch. It was empty. There was a lot of grass here and he couldn't see where the diamonds had gone.

He took the glasses off. He shouldn't have mucked about like a silly kid, now look what had happened.

He crawled forward on all fours, searching the ground, his eyes picked up clover, dandelion and grass, and the greyish sandy soil underneath – and he saw a white gleam under a ragged leaf of dandelion. He put his hand out and found the small faceted hardness of a diamond. He grabbed it at once, afraid it'd escape again. He put it back in the pouch. He went on looking and at last he found the second stone. He went on hunting. He was looking so hard at soil, grass and leaves that when he shut his eyes for a moment they were still there. He might have to go back with only two diamonds, well, that would do, surely? But he wanted the third one, he didn't want to tell Effi he'd lost it. And there it was, sitting on a clump of dry grey moss.

He stood up, holding the pouch, and someone came behind him. A hand took hold of his shoulder.

'What are you doing, boy?'

It was Otto.

Ida Rupf watched the girl. She was sitting with her eyes half-closed, one hand on the dog's collar, the other on the side of the cart. She'd been pretending to doze for the last half-hour, but she was awake and alert, watching for the boy's return.

'Don't worry,' Ida said to her. 'He'll be back soon.'

'I'm not worried.'

'Dear God,' said Ida, 'you're so young to be in love.'

'In love, Granny? Not me.'

It was odd how nice it was to have the Berlin brat call you Granny when your own granddaughter was sitting there saying nothing and looking at nothing.

'You don't fool me, you baggage,' said Ida.

The girl said: 'My aunt said you always knew when you

were in love because when he looked at you your heart raced and your knees went weak. The war does that to me, so how can I tell?'

Ida said, 'You've all had to grow up too quickly, that's the trouble, you boys and girls. With this terrible war – and now the Russians have come to tear the last of your innocence away. God help you.'

'I don't want to talk about the Russians.'

'You're probably right. Better not. But you've no respect nowadays, in my youth we really *were* young. We were innocent, so we respected our elders and did as we were told.'

The girl smiled, dear God, she was pretty when the corners of her mouth went up. 'More fools you.'

'Cheeky brat,' said Ida. 'There was a time in my life – in 1904, I was nineteen then – when I didn't want to do as my father told me. I did in the end, though. I don't know where I'd be now, if I'd followed my own way.'

'It was a man,' said the little baggage, 'wasn't it? Someone you wanted to marry. Does *she* know?' She jerked her chin at Magda, who sat against a tree, snoring a little, with Barbara close beside her. The cow, which Magda had tethered to the same tree, was eating grass just behind them.

Ida said: 'You're too clever for your own good. No, she doesn't know. And I might never have had her. Or my little Hans. He died, the poor child. He was so sweet. He looked like that boy. What are your names?'

'I'm Effi, he's Hanno.'

'Hanno, it's the same name as my child. Is he called Johannes?'

'How should I know? I met him on the road, I'm not his godmother.' Mockingly, the girl went on: 'I know what *your* name is. Ida Rupf, and you own a hotel in the Giants' Mountains. Near the Snowcap.'

'Cheeking me again,' said Ida, 'but I do own that hotel, and maybe after the war you might marry someone rich enough to bring you there. Because I'll go back. I've got the title deeds to the house in my pocket, and I've got all the silver buried in the garden.' But her mind went running round the garden now, trying to remember where she'd buried the silver. Under the roses, maybe? 'It was such a rush when we left,' she said aloud. 'I'd never have believed we'd have to leave like that, dear God, we had people in the hotel who'd been evacuated there, away from the bombing. So many things have happened that we can hardly believe.'

The doctor said, 'I have to get that train.'

'Where do you come from?' Ida asked.

'From Sterbin. I was senior paediatrician at a hospital there.'

'Saving kids' lives,' said Effi, half-jeeringly, and Ida wondered why. 'Earning gold cigarette cases. Have it back, by the way. I don't need it.'

'Why not?' he asked. 'It was your payment for getting me the tickets.' But he took the cigarette case and put it away as if he had a right to it. He noticed that there was blood on his fur collar from the horses. He pulled the collar to his nose and sniffed fastidiously at it, then let it drop and dusted his two fingers together.

'You can have this one on me,' the girl said, grinning. 'I'm a kind person, I go around doing good.'

'I have always been a compassionate children's physician,' he said. 'I have always striven to prevent unnecessary suffering.' Then his shoulders shuddered together and his hand flew to his throat as if he was pushing something away from it. His eyes shot to the right, again. 'I have problems with my nerves,' he said. 'War service.'

'You just said you ran a kid's ward?' asked the girl. Magda gave a loud snore and woke herself up; she looked startled, and Ida remembered how she used to bawl in her cot in the mornings when she was a small child.

The girl said, 'I was in hospital once. I hated it. I hated the doctors.'

'Children don't always understand what is good for them,' Dr Hungerland said.

'They made me have a bath as soon as I got there, as if I was dirty.'

'Maybe you were,' said Magda, sniffing.

'And they made me stand against a horrible cold sheet of metal and they all went out of the room as if it was too dangerous to stay in there but I had to stay and there was this horrible whirring noise.'

'A chest X-ray,' said the doctor. 'A necessary investigation.'

'They didn't explain anything to me. They didn't talk to me. They just said: "Breathe in" or "Breathe out".'

'What would you have understood?' said Hungerland. 'Children have to obey.'

'They gave me a drink of hot milk every night and stayed till I drank it. I used to think maybe it was poisoned, they were so keen for me to drink it.'

The girl looked straight at Dr Hungerland and he looked back at her. Then he gave one of his ghastly twitches. Ida felt a pain at her heart. Keep quiet, she told herself. Stay out of this.

Magda knew what was in her mother's mind, and she didn't want it even thought about. Magda was ashamed of her poor little brother. She said loudly: 'Tell us about your war service, Dr Hungerland.'

He was relieved. He took a deep breath. 'As the Front drew nearer, the hospital was evacuated, and we treated wounded soldiers. Although I am a physician and not a surgeon I volunteered to remain and serve my country. In fact, I had always believed I could have become a surgeon, I have a steady hand – at least, I had a steady hand. It was the experiences of the past few months that attacked my nerves.' He gave the girl an offended look. 'I was dealing with more soldiers than I could count. There was no time to count. I was dedicated, I never spared myself. I'd have to deal with a wound full of splinters, then a case of pneumonia. I am not as young as I was. In the end, they said to me: "Dr Hungerland, you are too dedicated, you have exhausted yourself. And now the Russians are coming. You have to accept that you can do no more here." And of course, if the situation had not been so chaotic, arrangements would have been made – maybe a ticket for the train was sent to me, but didn't reach me.'

Magda put a hand on her heart. 'Did you ever treat a soldier called Lehmann? From Silesia?'

'My good woman,' the doctor said, 'how do you expect me to remember? I might have treated fifty Silesian soldiers called Lehmann.'

Magda said, 'It's my husband. He doesn't know where we are, I haven't any way of finding out what has happened to him.'

Now Ida's heart hurt for her daughter, and yet she said: 'Magda, pull yourself together. You mustn't give way.' You couldn't be sweet and kind to Magda, it didn't work, she hated it. She was like Rupf. If you put your hand on her shoulder, she'd shrug you off.

'I sympathize,' said the doctor, but not as if he meant it. 'My son-in-law is in the army. A colonel.'

He sat up and pushed his chest out to let them know he was an important man and everyone connected to him was important. As if he wasn't on the run. He was mad. Mad people always had delusions of grandeur, he'd be telling them he had royal blood next. And now he jumped again, as if the thing he was afraid of had come up behind him to stop him boasting. Is there a train? thought Ida. Once upon a time I might have believed so, just because the doctor believed it. But it's a long time since I believed doctors knew best. And the girl gave the doctor his cigarette case back. As if she had a conscience about deceiving him. Oh, dear, I'd rather not think the boy was lying. Not just because I'd like to get on a train, I'm wearier than I've ever been before in my life. No, it's because he makes me think of my little Hans. Only he's got good strong legs, he's healthy.

The doctor said: 'If my wife had been alive I would have evacuated with the hospital. But she left me ten years ago. Pleurisy.' He said it as if she'd let him down by dying.

Ida thought, And what's come over him all of a sudden that he won't stop talking? Really, it was better when he kept his mouth shut.

He went on: 'My only daughter lives in Lindau, on Lake Constance. She has two girls and a boy. Fine, healthy children.'

'In Lindau,' said Ida. 'I suppose the Americans are coming to Lindau.'

'I believe so,' he said, and jumped, so that Ida thought a detachment of Russians were coming, but there was nobody. He leaned over to her and whispered: 'Do you see eyes?'

She didn't like this. 'I can see your eyes,' she said, 'and I can see through my own.'

'No,' he said. 'Look behind me. There are at least a hundred pairs of eyes. One can see them most clearly at night, but even in the daytime – they follow me everywhere, but perhaps if I board the train I can leave them behind.'

There was a sound of boots tramping among the trees. Maybe the Russians were coming now after all. But it was the boy, and with him a big man, so it looked as if the story about the train might be true after all.

Otto, thought Effi. Oh no. This is where it gets really nasty.

'This is the man?' asked the doctor, standing up and holding his hand out to Otto. 'The man who's selling you my ticket? Hungerland,' he said. Otto took the hand and gave it a sharp tug, no more Heil-Hitlering nowadays.

Ma Headscarf said, 'Is there really a train leaving Kummersdorf for the west tomorrow? And you have tickets for it?'

Otto couldn't be drunk now because you could see his mind going clicketty-click, fitting everything together. Easy for him, with Ma Headscarf feeding him the lines. Hungerland was putting his hand out again, Otto was digging *his* hand into his pocket and pulling out the ticket Effi had made for Hanno. Effi knew what else he had in there. The gun. And probably the diamonds, too, because Hanno had a furious, miserable look on his face. This *was* the Devil at work, a fiendishly clever director who'd engaged Otto to star as the man with the tickets. Hot as hell, this show was, and the Devil must be laughing his head off at the rest of them.

Otto gave the ticket to the doctor, who stowed it quickly in his own pocket. Hanno walked away from him and came close to Effi, but Otto kept his eyes on him and his hand on the bulge in his pocket.

Hungerland asked: 'Will you show me which way to go?'

'You paid well,' said Otto. (So he had got the diamonds from Hanno. Poor Swing Boy.) 'I'll take you to the train. We can leave as soon as the fighting finishes over there.'

'What kind of train is this?' asked Ma Headscarf. Nothing more from her about there not being a train, she was gaping at Otto as if he was Jesus Christ come to be her saviour.

'It was meant for a few selected high Party officials,' said Otto, 'but some of them weren't able to leave Berlin, so we have some tickets to spare. At a price, though,' he said, and his eyes ran over the women.

'Mother?' said Magda Headscarf to the old dame. Otto looked warningly at Hanno and shoved his hand in his pocket again. Fine policeman *he* was, the best con man of all. And he wasn't about to let Hanno or Effi give the game away.

The old woman looked at Hanno too, and then she said roughly, 'I haven't got anything.' She knew – old Rupfi had rumbled Otto.

Ma Headscarf hadn't, though. 'Mother –' she said again. She believed Otto, just because he was a big evil-looking man? You'd think she'd have learned after twelve years of Nazi rule. 'We could go to Aunt Dorothea, as you said.'

Hanno whispered to Effi: 'He made me give him the diamonds. And the ticket. He came back here with me to find out who I got them from. I couldn't stop him.'

'He's evil,' Effi whispered back. 'But at least he hasn't killed you yet.'

Otto gave them a threatening look. They'd have to be so careful now.

Ida Rupf asked: 'Where is Kummersdorf?'

'South-west from here,' said Otto, promptly.

'We can go there,' said Frau Rupf, staring at him, 'and see if there really is a train.'

'Stupid old woman,' said Otto, laughing at her. 'You'll have to get your ticket before they'll let you within half a kilometre of it.'

'All right,' said the old dame, pulling herself up. 'We'll go to within half a kilometre and see the guards. Then I'll buy a ticket.'

You could see Otto's mind working: She'll get so tired by the end of the day, she'll be ready to drop, *then* she might change her mind and buy a ticket without expecting to see the guards. But if he wanted her valuables, why didn't he just shoot her now and get them? He could make her take her clothes off first, the way he probably had with Jews in Russia, and go through them when he'd finished her off. Maybe it did make a difference to him that she was Aryan. He'd have shot an old Jewish dame without thinking twice about it.

He said, 'We'll all go together to the train.'

So that was it. No chance of Hanno and Effi sneaking off yet, that'd give the game away. And what did he mean to do with them when he'd fleeced Frau Rupf? It wasn't fair, anyway, she'd started to like the old woman.

The doctor put his hand on his suitcase. 'I am ready to go,' he said, trembling slightly. 'As soon as the way is clear.'

*

Hanno walked with the others across the swampy field with the bulrushes. The track ran across a dyke, so their feet stayed dry. Otto was walking at the back, watching everybody. Frau Magda, beside him, was saying something about 'a comfort to have someone who knows the way'. The cow plodded resignedly along, and little Barbara went with her pale face and her closed lips, staring down at the ground. The wood ahead of them was a mess of smashed and smoking trees.

'Do you think this is safe?' Effi whispered to Hanno.

'It's gone all quiet over there. Look, anywhere we go is dangerous when we're with him.'

She said: 'He can't threaten us directly because we're supposed to want to get on the train. Is this just about getting the old dame's valuables?'

'How should I know? I hate him.'

'I'd say we look for a place where we could slip away, but I want to warn the old dame. I don't want him fleecing her.'

'I want to get the diamonds back. They were my loot.'

She shook her head. 'I don't care about them.'

'Why not? Have you got the cigarette case?'

'I gave it back to Hungerland.'

'Why?'

'Too complicated to explain, kid. Look, what matters is that we're together.'

Hanno stared at her. She liked him after all. He'd hoped so, she'd looked a little bit pleased when he'd found her after she'd run away. For a moment, he didn't care about the diamonds, but they were for her. And he remembered Otto, his gun in his hand, making him hand over the diamonds: right, boy, I'm taking everything now. Laughing at him. And there'd been nothing he could do but obey. His stomach tightened and he clenched his fists.

In front of them, Hungerland was saying to Frau Rupf, 'And of course, I was presented with a decoration by the Führer in person – you, boy and girl, keep your dog under control. He keeps knocking into my legs. And slobbering on my coat.'

Cornelius growled at him.

'Dogs are degenerate,' the doctor said to Hanno and Effi, telling them off. 'What is there to associate an animal like this with the ferocious nobility of the wolf?'

'Our Dr Hungerland sees eyes,' said Effi to Hanno. 'Come on, Cornelius, you don't want to waste your time on him.'

'Eyes?' said Hanno.

'Hundreds of them. Hanging in the air. He told the old woman, but she didn't ask him whose eyes they were.'

'*Is* there a train?' Frau Rupf asked Hanno.

Otto said, 'Careful!' Hanno knew what he meant, and he went on, for the benefit of the others: 'We don't know what we might find in the woods.'

The doctor continued with his lecture. 'When the dog is bred for selected characteristics,' he said, 'such as a long body, like the dachshund, or floppy ears like the spaniel, it not only brings with it associated health problems – ear canker in the spaniel, back trouble in the dachshund – but also behavioural problems. If you breed a dog to have floppy ears like a puppy, its nature will remain juvenile for the whole of its life. Subservient, foolish. At least the Alsatian or the husky are physically close to the wolf.' And on he droned, you wouldn't have thought he had the energy to talk so much.

Chapter Fourteen

The wind had been blowing towards the wood, so they'd picked their way about fifty metres in among the wrecked trees before the smoke from the battle got really thick; then it got worse with every step. Hanno remembered the smell and hated it: spent explosives, burned-petrol fumes, and something worse. It caught in his throat, he was coughing, they were all coughing. They all stopped still. Cornelius whined and dragged on his string. They were looking at broken trees and a fog of smoke.

'They've been using phosphorus,' said Otto grimly. 'But we have to go through here if you want to reach the train.'

The doctor put his suitcase up in front of his chest and went ahead of them all. At least he wasn't talking any longer. Hanno heard men crying out. Wounded men. Frau Magda heard it as well, and her hand went to her heart for a moment, then she took Barbara by the hand and walked forward, tripping over a tussock of grass. Frau Rupf shrugged her shoulders and followed her.

'Move,' said Otto, behind Hanno.

'If you say it's safe, Herr Major,' said Effi in the silly-girl voice she'd used with him before.

'Don't fool around,' said Otto. They walked forward. It was horrible to feel him behind them. But maybe they could get away in the smoke, find a broken piece of wood, he'd hit Otto over the head with it and get the diamonds out of his pocket. That'd be better than just escaping. He didn't want Otto to get away with it. He wanted to punish him.

They went gingerly along the track. And there was a German corpse: fair-haired, blood-soaked, and another whose head was too much of a mess to see what colour his hair had been. Frau Magda stared at him, then looked quickly away. We're crazy to come here, thought Hanno.

They almost fell into a sandy crater, then there was a rearing broken tank, an armoured car, a fallen helmet like a blackened cooking-pot and a bare-headed dead soldier. They had to go round dead horses and broken carts, and a pram, just like the cart, with a lot of bundles spilled out of it. A woman and a child were lying there dead. Nothing to do for them. They walked on, coughing, eyes streaming. Most of the time Hanno and Effi had to carry the cart between them. Cornelius kept close to Effi with his tail down between his legs. The cow didn't like it either, she kept stopping and mooing and Frau Magda had to drag her along. Now suddenly there were grey men leaning against grey metal, splashed with blood. Other men writhing on the ground. The cries were animal or babyish, any language or none. And there were Russians right here, Russians who had come to the wounded with stretchers. When little Barbara saw the Russians she let out a scream. Her mother seized her and clapped her hand over her mouth. Barbara twisted herself free, dropped to the ground and screamed again, hunching herself into a ball.

There were four Russians and they all had guns. The doctor was standing quite still now, with his shoulders hunched. Hanno turned round to look at Otto and saw him in the same posture, scared rigid, the filthy coward. Frau Magda had put her hands over her face. Frau Rupf was shaking. Hanno reached out to Effi's arm and felt a small, stiff tremble going through her. Cornelius growled.

'Shut up,' said Hanno to him. That was the last thing they wanted, the dog starting a fight with the Ivans.

I can't do anything, he thought. I couldn't do anything for Wolfgang, I can't do anything against Otto. If I tried to fight the Russians off they'd kill me easily and do what they wanted to the women anyway. Fighting doesn't work. So what does? Maybe nothing? I don't want this, he thought. I don't want it.

But the Russians hadn't grabbed the women, one of them was down on one knee, talking in a heavy, halting German, asking if Barbara was hurt?

Frau Rupf spoke up, looking straight at the Russian. 'She's terrified,' she said. 'Your comrades did shameful things to her. You can't make that better, can you?'

The Russian flinched, and stood up. 'The child should not have to suffer,' he said. Then he spoke angrily to the other three in Russian. One shook his head, the second said something roughly – and Hanno thought he half cared what had happened to Barbara, half thought it didn't matter so much, because she was a German child. The third fingered his gun, then shrugged his shoulders. The two German men stayed still, trying to behave as if they weren't there.

Hanno could hardly believe that the Russians were being kind. The one who spoke German talked to them again and said they were good Russians, they wouldn't harm women and children. Or civilians. Hanno wondered if the Russian he'd killed had been a man like this, not a rotten raping swine.

Effi turned to him and grinned. 'They're OK,' she said, and then he thought he heard her say, 'Red brothers,' but he wasn't sure.

Now he realized his knees were shaking, he was more scared than he had been, now that she was safe – but what did 'safe' mean, with Otto breathing down the back of their necks?

'I wish I spoke Russian,' said Effi. 'I could tell them he was a Nazi. They could take him away from us.'

'He'd use his gun. We'd all be caught in the middle of a shooting match.'

And they'd take the diamonds away. But he didn't say that to Effi.

The Russian was waving them to go on, they were on the move again, the Russians were going back to their work among the wounded.

Frau Rupf said, 'They're not all monsters, thank God. And there was the man who came – that time – and made them leave us alone, and left us some of the food –'

Barbara had got up and was standing by her mother, who said, 'Mother. Supposing Lehmann was here? My husband,' she explained to Otto. It looked for a moment as if she was going to go out there and search the wood for him, but then she shook herself. 'No,' she said in a hard voice. 'We must go on.'

They kept going among the wreckage of machines and soldiers and trees. There were bits of branch lying around here that would have done fine to hit Otto over the head with, but he kept too close behind them for Hanno to do anything. Then suddenly they were back in untouched woodland – though the air was still full of smoke – and shortly afterwards they found a narrow path that widened into a track. There was a bank of pale soil to one side of it, with young birches growing along the top. They turned a corner and found several broken trees tangled up with the burned wreckage of a small plane. The tailpiece lay on its own, pointing towards them.

'Magda,' said Frau Rupf, 'I must rest. Just for a few minutes.'

She sat down on one of the wings and peered into the plane.

'The pilot's in there,' she said, in a crackly, tired voice. 'Burned to a crisp. Maybe the boy should run back and tell the Ivans, so that they can come and pick him up. Bury him.'

'What do you think we are?' asked Otto. 'The International Red Cross?' He'd straightened up now; he was a big bully again.

Effi sat down on the track and took her harmonica out. She played a strophe and stopped. The dog flopped at her feet.

The doctor said, 'I don't like these delays. We should push on.'

There was somebody coming up the path behind them, Hanno heard footsteps on the soft ground, firm footsteps, but not heavy enough for military boots. Cornelius started to bark and a middle-aged man came into sight, sweating inside a heavy grey coat and a felt hat. A much younger woman followed, she had smooth blonde hair and she was wearing smart clothes and walking boots. Each of them was carrying a handsome leather suitcase. They stopped and stared angrily at the crashed plane.

'Always some hindrance,' the man said, over Cornelius's barks. 'And where are you people from?'

'From Silesia,' said Frau Magda, then turned to Effi. 'Can't you shut your cur up?'

'Be quiet,' said Effi, putting her hand round Cornelius's muzzle, then letting it go. Cornelius tried to bark again, so she held his mouth shut again. Squashed growlings came out of it.

'So far?' said the woman. 'Did you walk all the way?'

'We had a wagon,' Frau Magda said. 'The Russians machine-gunned it from a plane.'

'I have come from Sterbin,' said the doctor, picking up *his* bag as if he wanted them to notice how nice it was. 'I was a senior physician at a hospital there.'

'We're going to the west,' said Frau Magda. 'All of us.'

Otto didn't say anything. Neither did Frau Rupf, Hanno, Effi, Barbara, or the cow, but Cornelius kept growling from between Effi's hands. As if he was still upset after the meeting with the Russians.

Hanno remembered the two men as they'd stood in front of the Ivan with their shoulders hunched. He thought, I'll always remember that, and then, One day I'll do a picture of it. No, a sculpture in wood, rotten wood with decaying knots in it. Or twisted metal. That's what I want. To be a sculptor. It was such a crazy thing to decide in the middle of war and chaos that he almost laughed out loud at himself, but his hands moved, almost of themselves as if they were already shaping his material. He wondered how you worked in metal. Didn't you make a clay mould first?

'We came from the village,' said the man. 'The Russians are there, but I brought my wife away.'

'We've just met some Russians,' said Effi, letting go of Cornelius again and giving him a tap on the muzzle. He was quiet now. 'These ones were OK.'

'You should be careful,' said the man, 'they're unpredictable. Of course, in our position –'

The woman gave him a look and he shut up.

'Little Nazi fish, were you?' asked Effi, and Hanno saw old Frau Rupf smile. She was OK, the old woman. She'd told the Ivans what she thought.

Frau Magda kicked at the ground. 'We've got to get moving.' Half-angrily, she said to the doctor: 'You've got your train to catch.' Emphasizing the 'your', and staring at her mother.

'What train is that?' asked the smart man, frowning.

'A train to Frankfurt am Main,' said Ida Rupf. 'It's supposed to be leaving tomorrow at twelve. But haven't the lines all been blown up?'

Frau Magda broke in: 'But, Mother, the gentleman knows all about it.'

'What *is* your name?' Ida Rupf asked Otto.

'Mickel,' said Otto. Hanno wondered how many passports he had in his pocket.

'Really?' asked Effi. 'I thought the gentleman's name was Braun.'

'No,' said Otto. Of course, Effi was safe to cheek him a bit. She'd said it, he wouldn't threaten them outright, because that would spoil his con trick. They were supposed to be going willingly to the train. Otto just said, 'Fool of a girl.'

'I could have sworn it was Braun,' said Effi. 'Or maybe Wagner? But you're right, Herr Major, I'm just a silly girl.' She giggled. Ida Rupf and Frau Magda both stared at her, at which she shut her mouth and pulled an exaggeratedly demure face that made the old woman grin. 'I'll believe in this train when I see it,' Frau Rupf said.

'Oh, no,' said the smart man. 'I heard about this. There's a line the Führer needs. To move important papers out. And staff.' He nodded. 'Isn't that right, Helga?'

His wife nodded too. 'You're right,' she said, 'there was definitely talk about a train last time we were in Berlin.'

'There you are,' said Frau Magda to her mother. 'We must press on.'

'We've got to press on anyway,' said the old woman, sighing, pulling her fox-heads straight and standing up.

And Effi thought, Why is it that con men always have luck? It must be that the Devil loves a con man. Like Hitler – he was the top con man after all. Telling the Germans they were the best people in the world, saying they'd win the war. Saying he was a peace-loving man. When the good generals tried to kill him last year, he just happened to walk away from the suitcase with the bomb in it. The war could have been over then, but no, he was kept alive. Well, Hitler was after people's souls, not their money. And then they went to hell. Of course the Devil was interested. And Satan's good at improvising, better than the best jazzman.

When you improvised, Pierre had explained to her, there was a set pattern of things you could do, so the other players knew how to go along with your music. The Devil had used Major Mickel-Otto to pick up Hanno's con man theme, now it was easy for him to bring this pair in, just because they were so full of themselves.

She saw Ma Headscarf look at Helga and the man, and she knew she resented Frau Helga for having a nice hair-do and looking so chic. But she wanted to believe them, because she wanted to believe in the train. She was part of the Devil's improvisation too.

'What are we waiting for?' asked the doctor, putting his suitcase down again, fetching out a handkerchief, wiping his face, then giving that start again. The hundred eyes were still watching him. Whose eyes were they?

'Where are you going?' Frau Rupf asked the couple.

'I don't know,' said the man, and suddenly the sweat was dripping on his face. 'I believe the Russians are everywhere.' (That was true, there was a poor burned-out Ivan pilot right behind him.)

'You could buy a ticket for the train,' said Mickel-Otto. 'I can arrange it for you.'

'Darling Liebfried,' Frau Helga came in, plaintive as a cat, 'the suitcase is so heavy. Wouldn't it be worth it to try?'

'Of course,' said her darling, with a nice sour note in his voice, 'there are always special arrangements for the real high-ups.' He unbuttoned his coat and pulled his silk tie loose, now he wasn't so smart any more. 'It's difficult,' he complained, 'trying to decide what to bring with one. At such short notice. I couldn't leave a good winter coat for the Russians. Where is the departure point for this train?'

'Kummersdorf,' said Mickel-Otto.

'As long as you have enough tickets for all of us –' Ma Headscarf started.

But Herr Liebfried was faltering all of a sudden. 'I don't like the sound of Kummersdorf,' he said. 'I heard the worst of the fighting is in that direction.'

'There's serious fighting everywhere,' said Otto, quickly.

'Yes, but we want to get away from it, and in Kummersdorf – in my position one hears things – that is I used to hear things –' He pulled at the knot of his tie again. Keep going, thought Effi, in half an hour you'll look like a tramp.

His eyes went to his wife as if he expected her to save him. But Frau Helga only said, 'You know best, darling.'

His voice went up half an octave. 'These are all impossible decisions.'

Frau Helga was still in love with her sugar daddy: 'I'm sure *you* know what to do, Liebfried.'

'You can believe me,' said Herr Liebfried, pulling himself together. 'Kummersdorf is not the direction to take. I had good sources. Even if the train departs, I am afraid the line may be broken. Granted, it was the source of a considerable security operation, but in this dark hour, when all we fought for is falling apart –' Liebfried was good at the wailing notes, you could almost feel sorry for him.

'Did you fight?' asked Hanno.

Liebfried opened his mouth, but Frau Rupf said to Ma Headscarf, 'Do you hear him?'

'Mother,' said Ma Headscarf, 'we're going in that direction already.'

'Towards the worst of the fighting?'

'The fighting is over,' said Otto in a false, reliable voice, like the wolf's when he was sweet-talking Little Red Riding Hood. 'And the line is safe, I'll guarantee it.'

'And what if your guarantees are nonsense?'

Major Wolf turned on her and spoke in his own threatening voice. 'Aren't you tired, Granny? Aren't your legs ready to give way? So you might as well bring out whatever you've got hidden in your corsets, because you'd die before you got to the west on foot, so it's worth it to take a chance on the train.'

'I won't die,' said Frau Rupf.

Ma Headscarf said, 'And Barbara? How do you expect her to get that far? Not all the Russians we meet will be good men.'

Liebfried said to his wife, 'I'm afraid we had better avoid Kummersdorf.'

Frau Helga gave a little squeaky sigh and took hold of her heavy suitcase.

'You wouldn't sell your handcart?' she wheedled Hanno – that cat really knew how to get a sweet note out when she wanted to.

'It's not for sale,' said Hanno.

And Liebfried and Helga went off down another track with their suitcases, heading away from Kummersdorf. But maybe Otto wasn't taking them towards Kummersdorf either? Surely he wasn't crazy enough to go into the hottest fighting? Didn't he want to get to the west as much as they did?

Ida stopped, put her sack down, picked it up again. She wouldn't give that man a chance to jeer at her again. As she walked on she started to wonder again where she'd buried the chest. No. She mustn't. She needed every last bit of energy to walk. If only Magda wasn't such a fool! But since she was, Ida would have to go with her. Magda was her daughter after all, her own flesh and blood. And there was Barbara.

The smoke was thinning, that was one good thing.

Then the boy, Hanno, said to her: 'We could take your sack from you and carry it in our handcart. It'd be safe there.'

She gave it to him. She felt so relieved her head swam for a moment. It was so much easier to walk now. He was a good, kind boy.

'You'd better not steal it,' said Magda harshly.

'You'll get it back,' said the girl Effi. 'Trust me.'

Mickel – or whatever he called himself – laughed. But he was probably so lost to all decency he couldn't believe in a simple act of kindness. Did the war make him into a brute? Ida thought. Or was he always like that? Czekalla now, he was bad from the start; the war only gave him scope for his badness.

'You have got a ticket for us, Herr Major, haven't you?' Magda asked. How could she trust a man like that better than she trusted her own mother?

The doctor said, 'I hope too many riff-raff won't be coming on the train.'

Ida started to laugh. She could feel the man's angry eyes on her, but she kept laughing. And then, as if the laughter had released something inside her, and partly because she was angry too, angry with Magda for being such a fool, she started to talk to the girl about Felix.

'My young man,' she said, 'the one I started to tell you about, he was a poet and a journalist, he worked for some literary magazine. And of course he had no money. But he had beautiful dark eyes and a lovely voice – and his smile!'

Effi said, 'Did it make your heart race and your knees go weak when he looked at you?'

'Oh yes, and more. My father had a guesthouse up in the mountains, just a quiet little house and modest prices. Felix came there in Maytime, when all the birds were singing. I used to run away from my parents and we'd go for walks together. Even when he wasn't there – I'd lay the table for breakfast and kiss the plate and cup and knife that he'd soon be holding. I never stopped thinking about him, he was the air I breathed. When I put my head down on my pillow at night the pillow felt like his cheek against mine.'

Magda was listening, but she didn't say anything.

'And you wanted to get married,' the girl said.

'We wanted to get married. I didn't care how little money we'd have. But my father threw Felix out of the guesthouse. He hadn't told me but he'd already made arrangements with Rupf. Rupf wanted to marry me, too; Rupf was much older, he had a big hotel and plenty of money. I don't believe he ever loved me, but I was really pretty in those days, though you wouldn't believe it now, and he thought I was a good investment. That was the way Rupf's mind worked. I'd help him with the hotel and bring in customers.'

'So they made you marry the old man. Was he ugly?'

'Not terribly ugly, but not good-looking either. He had a square head and his hair was cut short like a brush. A pair of droopy moustaches and a round face. I always thought he had a face like a clock, the moustaches were the hands at twenty past eight.' Ida laughed again at the memory of Rupf's face. 'He'd been married before but his wife had died with her first child and he'd lost the child too. Diphtheria. My parents wore me down, God forgive me. They said they'd never speak to me again if I married Felix. They said we'd starve, and it was true he didn't really earn enough to keep a wife. My mother took to her bed and said I was making her ill. And she told me I could never be happy with a man like Felix.'

'Why? Because he was a journalist and a poet?'

'Because he was Jewish.' She was in tears, she couldn't stop herself. But Magda came and took her by the arm.

'Now, Mother, you give me those pearls, so that I can buy tickets for the train. Or else I'll never speak to you again.' To the man, she said, 'They're good pearls, worth a fortune.'

'You're just like your father,' said Ida.

'I want the pearls,' said Magda.

Ida sighed. 'There isn't a train, Magda.' But she was so tired, and she could see the man's eyes on her, gleaming like her pearls, which were what he was thinking about.

Maybe she should give them to Magda. They'd been a present from Rupf, after all, and Magda was Rupf's daughter.

'What was Felix's second name? Did he get to be famous?' the girl asked her.

Ida didn't answer. She was almost done.

The girl said, 'Well, you've taught me something. I'm never going to have regrets like that. I'll marry who I want no matter what anyone says.'

Later, the wood came to an end, fields and reedy fen stretched out ahead of them and the track joined a narrow road bordered with poplars. Ida saw the ends of brick houses and barns. They came into a tiny village, and it was all in one piece, nobody had been fighting there. The houses had neat little gardens divided by little walls into raised beds that were full of bachelor's button daisies, red and white, and a few late tulips. But there was no sign of life, no people, no chickens or cows. There were padlocks on the doors of the farm buildings. Either everyone was hiding from the Russians or they'd run away. It frightened Ida.

They tramped through it, forward and on. Just wearily putting one foot in front of another. Even the dog looked as if he needed a rest.

Chapter Fifteen

They'd gone back onto forest tracks. It was getting late, soon it would be dark.

'How far is it to Kummersdorf?' asked the doctor.

Otto said, 'We'll be there tomorrow morning.'

Sooner or later they'd have to stop and rest, and once it was really dark, thought Effi, Otto would realize that he couldn't keep an eye on her and Hanno. If they ran off, it'd be hard to keep fooling the rest of the party. He didn't know that she was hanging around because she wanted to warn Ida Rupf, though he might guess that Hanno would keep near him because he wanted the diamonds back.

On cue, he stepped forward and grabbed Hanno's shoulder.

'You two will walk with me,' he said. 'Right in front of me.'

'Watch it,' said Effi. 'You'll make the old dame suspicious.' Then she cursed herself for forgetting to act like a fluffball.

'You know I've got a gun,' said Otto. 'Any funny business and I'll use it.'

Or even without funny business. He might just suddenly decide, the way he had in the stable, that the nicest thing would be to start killing. Maybe he'd only do that when he was drunk. You had to look on the bright side.

*

Effi said to Hanno, 'It's my turn to push the cart.'

Their hands touched as she took hold of it. Hanno's hand was cold. Ahead of them, Frau Magda went, not speaking to her mother. Little Barbara was still keeping her eyes on the ground. The cow walked and mooed slightly, she'd need milking soon. They'd have to stop for that.

'What is Otto up to?' Effi whispered to Hanno. 'OK, he'd have taken the diamonds from you whoever you were; after all, he's got his retirement to save up for – but your train scam?'

She wished then that she'd kept her mouth shut, because Hanno looked angry.

'Be careful,' she hissed.

'What are you two whispering about?' Otto wanted to know, and he felt in his pocket – nothing subtle about this cat. He could never be a jazzman.

Hanno said to Otto, 'You said my father did something criminal. What was it?'

Shut up, Swing Boy. And yet she understood why he wanted to know. She would, really, if it was her.

'You don't want to know, boy.'

'I do.'

'Why should I tell you, just to please you?' Otto laughed.

Hanno said, in a scornful voice, 'You were making it up. It never happened.'

Otto laughed again. He didn't say anything. Hanno made himself look as if he didn't care, but of course he wanted to find out and Otto knew it.

'Are there sleeping arrangements on the train?' asked the doctor. 'Will I be able to lie down?'

'It depends how many other passengers there are,' said Otto.

'I paid you well,' the doctor said.

'So have all the rest,' said Otto, impatiently. 'You should be glad to get a seat on the roof.'

'No,' said the doctor. 'I mustn't go outside. The eyes will follow me if I'm outside.'

'The eyes?' asked Otto. 'What eyes?'

The doctor didn't answer.

Old Ida said to her daughter, 'You know you're a fool, Magda?'

'When we stop to rest,' Magda said, 'you can give me the pearls.'

Effi thought, It must be so tough, losing your twin. I don't know what that would feel like. Like you'd have to start all over again being someone on your own. Only he's not alone, he's got me. And I've got him, and I do like him. We've been through a lot together. The old woman said I was in love. These days, you're so busy, how are you supposed to have time to be in love? But I want to go to sleep beside him all on our own. Then when we wake up he might put his arms round me and I might kiss him. It was nice when I kissed him before. It was bad afterwards, though.

'Will there be water on the train?' the doctor asked. 'I would like to shave.'

Effi thought about the little fuzz on Hanno's upper lip. She wanted to finger it. She wanted to forget about Otto. I've got to be careful, she thought, I can feel the wildness again – and careless means dead. Like Pierre, God rest his soul. No, not rest, that wouldn't do for Pierre. God ought to let him play jazz up in Heaven for ever. And Aunt Annelie can sit there with a nice glass of white beer, listening to the music. Pierre wouldn't like it if Aunt Annelie wasn't there. God'll have to let her in even if she is an atheist.

But Hanno was OK. Even those Russians had turned out OK: that was good –it proved the Nazis were wrong when they said the Ivans were all monsters. They were good and bad, like anyone else, and later on some of the ones who'd raped and machine-gunned refugees might be sorry for what they'd done. When they had time to think about it. The old dame was OK because she'd loved a Jew.

'Dishonesty,' Otto said to Hanno. 'Your father was dishonest. Corrupt.'

The cow mooed again, softly, as if she was afraid to make too much noise.

'You mean he took bribes?'

'Yes,' said Otto. 'He took bribes from criminals. Then they could get on with their crimes undisturbed. He was a menace to honest Germans.'

What did Otto mean by honest Germans? Maybe Hanno's father had done some crimes. From the Russian or Jewish point of view, anyway. Nothing worse than what Otto had done, she'd swear. She started to sing, ever so quietly:

> Nobody knows the trouble I've seen,
> Nobody knows but Jesus.

Suddenly, Cornelius jerked forward; there was no holding him. He dragged Hanno forward – oh, God, was Otto going to get his gun out? He didn't, thank God, but he went running after Hanno; they were all running now, even the old woman, who was so tired, even the moaning cow on the end of her string, Ma Headscarf, little Barbara, the crazy doctor. The dog went off the path in among the pines and the dead needles slithered under their feet when they followed him.

There was a row of trees and beyond it more trees, but between them there was a narrow railway cutting. The dog tore the string out of Hanno's hand and vanished over the ridge. When Effi got to the edge of the cutting she saw the humped dark roof of a railway carriage – no, two railway carriages, standing on the single track.

'Is that the train?' asked Hungerland. 'Will they bring the locomotive in the morning?'

Cornelius's pale fur made him easy to see in the failing light. He was peeing on the wheel of the train, then he put his front paws on the metal steps to the carriage door and barked. Otto stood still on the edge of the cutting, staring down at the train. Then he was on his way down the steep slope, slithering a little on the sandy soil. Cornelius turned round and barked at him again. He wanted to get into the train, he thought Otto was just the person to open the door for him. Now the doctor followed Otto, having a hard time with his suitcase and his long coat round his feet, half-sliding down the slope. Little Barbara went after him. Then her mother, letting go of the cow.

'What is this?' Ida Rupf asked.

'It's the Devil's joke,' said Effi. 'If you go on that train you'll disappear and never be seen again.'

'You could be right,' said Frau Rupf, 'but my daughter and my granddaughter are down there, and even if Magda's angry with me for loving a Jew it's my duty to be with her.'

'Is that all you've got left?' Effi asked. 'Duty?'

'And wanting to live,' said the old woman. 'That's the strongest thing, you'd never think so, but it is.'

'I'll help you down,' said Hanno.

'You're a good boy,' said Frau Rupf.

Hanno laughed suddenly. 'It's our train,' he said. 'We conjured it up when we made the tickets.'

'He'll hear,' whispered Effi, and they both looked at Otto, but he didn't seem to have done. He was trying the carriage doors, first one, then the other. They were both locked.

'I heard,' said the old woman quietly. 'What's *he* up to? No, don't tell me. He's dangerous, isn't he?'

'Yes,' said Hanno.

Cornelius stood beside Otto with his tail wagging, whining a little. What was there inside that he wanted so much? Now Otto got his gun out of his pocket after all. He fired it once: the shot echoed in the cutting, an explosion and the smash of the lock breaking.

Effi and Hanno only just managed to fit the handcart through the carriage door. It was dark inside the train, but Effi got her little lamp out. In its dim yellow light they saw elegant leather armchairs, a chair and a solid walnut desk for someone to write at, a walnut dining set. Polished wooden floors. Dr Hungerland slipped off his coat with its astrakhan collar, put it carefully down on the floor, sat down in one of the armchairs and started to ease his boots off.

'The furniture has been polished,' he remarked. He approves of the housekeeping, then, thought Effi. Then he said, 'Pull the blinds down. I don't want the eyes looking in from outside.'

Otto did as he'd asked. Of course it made sense to pull the blinds down. If you were inside, with a light on, you had to have a blackout: Effi could only just remember when things were different. There were little lamps with parchment shades, but they must work off the train's own electricity, so it was no use trying to light them. Pity.

Otto sat down himself now, looking the premises over. Of course this was some Party high-up's carriage, some real top brass, maybe even Goebbels or Göring, or Himmler. Everyone knew they had these luxury trains. There was something about all the luxury that made you feel safe, that was the weird thing. Maybe that was why they'd done all those crazy and monstrous things and kept on about the final victory when it was only a ten-pfennig tram ride between the two battle fronts, as Sperling had said. They'd done themselves so proud they thought nothing could touch them.

Otto stood up.

'We'll go and see what's in the other carriage,' he said. 'Bring the lamp, girl.'

The whole party except the dog went, Effi felt like the conductress showing them the sleeping arrangements, because that was what was there, four bedrooms, all really nice, goosefeather quilts and pillows, white embroidered cases and a little cut-out in the middle of the quilt covers to let the nice red quilt peek out from underneath. Beyond there was a bathroom with a little tub and a shower. The blinds were all down here already. Hungerland pushed ahead of them into the bathroom and tried the taps, but no water came out of them. Probably the water needed an electric pump too. Effi shone the lamp on a shelf with a pile of white linen towels, another with four thick white bath towels.

'Excellent,' said the doctor. 'The accommodation is suitable for a man of my standing.' He squeezed his way back along the corridor and must have found his coat and his suitcase in the dark, because he came back with them.

'Give me some light in this bedroom,' he said to Effi. She shone the lamp for him and saw him dump them on the bed: they put mud on the white quilt cover, but he didn't care. He opened the suitcase: he had neatly folded clothes inside and a lot of tissue paper. He fetched out a pair of red leather slippers and a shoehorn, unlaced his walking boots, eased them off with the shoehorn, and put on his slippers. He took his hat off and laid it on the bed next to the suitcase.

'I would so much like to shave,' he said.

Three bedrooms left, thought Effi, one for the old dame, one for Ma Headscarf and Barbara, one for Otto. That leaves me and Hanno out. Oh, well. Maybe we can push a couple of armchairs together.

'Back to the other carriage,' said Otto. Swine, she thought. I hope you burn in hell.

'Tomorrow,' said Dr Hungerland, trotting along after Otto, 'the driver will arrive with the locomotive. Once it is attached, the water will function, and I shall wash and shave. And at noon we shall be on our way. Perhaps we could persuade the driver to leave sooner? I would make it worth your while – looking at Otto. 'I have other means.'

More numbered Swiss bank accounts, thought Effi.

'You old fool,' said Ida Rupf, 'what makes you think this train will move?'

Effi saw Ma Headscarf put her hand over her mouth.

'Who's an old fool?' Otto asked Ma Headscarf. 'The doctor, or your senile hag of a mother?' Jeering, he was good at that. Well, it was the Nazi tone. At least he wasn't beating the old dame up, or torturing her. Yet.

'You have no faith,' Ma Headscarf said to old Ida. 'I've known it for years.'

'This is the train,' said Dr Hungerland, 'and tomorrow it will move.' He glanced at the windows, reassuring himself that the eyes couldn't look in at him through the blackout blinds. He sighed with relief.

Two of them with faith, thought Effi. Well, I have faith too, in my own way. I believe Pierre's in a jazz band in the sky. Then she noticed a big paraffin lamp sitting in a corner, full of fuel and a tin can of paraffin beside it. Someone had been thinking of everything, though whether they'd been expecting Otto and Hungerland, Frau Rupf, Ma Headscarf, Barbara, Hanno, Effi, the handcart and the dog was another matter.

Otto saw it too. 'Light that,' he said to Effi. She turned the screw and struck one of Sperling's matches on the sole of her boot. The lamp flared and hissed and lit the room up properly.

There was a painting on the wall in a heavy gold frame. Two horses running across a field. On the desk Hitler's photograph sat, looking bad-temperedly at them, though no doubt it was meant to be a glance full of serious concern for Germany. Frau Rupf went to it, and put it face-down. Otto frowned, but he didn't stop her. There was another door, too, which they hadn't noticed. Cornelius was sitting in front of it, sweeping the floor with his tail. How long had he been there?

Hungerland sat down in the armchair again, crossing his legs. 'Is there any food?' he asked. 'Or do we have to eat what we have brought with us?'

'What food have *you* brought?' Frau Rupf demanded of him.

'Coffee beans,' he said.

'There's that other door,' said Otto. 'Where the cur is. Bring that lamp of yours, girl.'

Effi filled it up with paraffin from the tin first. Otto stood there tapping his foot. Then Effi came over with the lamp. Little Barbara came with her.

'Dinner, maybe,' said Effi to the child.

Frau Rupf came. So did Hanno and Ma Headscarf. Only Dr Hungerland sat in his chair with his legs crossed, waiting for the aperitifs.

It was a kitchen. The blinds were down in here, too. There was a clean cooking stove, a table built in against the wall, a sink with a tap, which didn't work either. There were three cupboards against the wall. Otto pulled one of them open and it was full of food. Frau Rupf gasped.

'Caviar,' she said, reverently, 'truffles, French champagne – my God, how many bottles are there?'

'About twenty,' said Effi.

Ida Rupf went on: 'Italian macaroons, three tins, one, two, three, four – five jars of bottled peaches, condensed milk, tins of black bread, a side of smoked salmon, my God, tinned salmon, chocolate, cognac, how many jars of coffee beans? Tins of new potatoes, peas and carrots, dill-pickled gherkins and marrons glacés. Three boxes. Real apple juice. One moment we're hungry and the next we have all this fine food in front of us. I can't believe it.'

'Touch it,' said Effi. 'See if it disappears in a fart of sulphur.'

But she fetched one of the bars of chocolate down and broke off a big piece that she handed to little Barbara. Barbara stared at it, sniffed it, then leaned against her mother and started to eat it. She didn't stuff it down but nibbled it in tiny bites, stopping to taste and enjoy before she nibbled another fragment. At her feet, Cornelius sat and dribbled.

'Have the whole bar,' said Effi to Barbara. 'It's yours. And the next one's for me and Hanno. You'll get some-thing, dog. Tough horsemeat out of my bag, that's what dogs like. Chocolate's for kids, right?'

Suddenly Otto said, 'Not another bite. Nothing for any of you till you pay me the fare.' He patted his pocket, where the gun was bulging. Now everybody saw it.

'Mother!' said Ma Headscarf, and her voice sounded almost relieved. She's OK with this, thought Effi, having someone bully her again. It's what she's used to.

Old Ida sighed. 'Very well. You'll all have to go out. I'm not undoing my corsets with people watching.'

Otto opened another cupboard, as if he hadn't heard her. There was a row of bottles of cognac. Oh no, thought Effi. If he gets drunk he might shoot us before we can get our dinner. She stuffed the bar of chocolate into her bag. She wasn't going to leave the bag down, though she'd give the horsemeat to Cornelius. She fetched it out and handed it to him. He ran away with it into the salon: she could hear him growling at Hungerland in case the doctor tried to steal it from him. Otto wasn't looking, he was undoing the cognac bottle. Effi whipped two tins of salmon off the shelf and slipped them in the bag to make up for the horsemeat. She'd have to find a tin-opener, too.

'Leave the room!' said old Ida sharply to Otto. 'You can fleece me of my pearls, but I'll get them out with decency. Or you can just take that gun out and shoot me. You should be ashamed of yourself.'

'Senile hag,' said Otto, but he herded them all out and then shut the door.

He stood in the salon tipping cognac down his throat, straight out of the bottle. Some of it ran down his chin and dripped on the floor.

'We can have a party,' said Effi. If they were in for it, they were in for it and she wasn't going to show she was scared. 'A party for Sperling and other loved ones we've lost. Are there any fags about?'

'Look in the desk drawer, boy,' said Otto.

Hanno pulled it open.

'Cigars,' he said.

'They'll do,' said Otto.

'And there's a wind-up gramophone here,' said Hanno. 'In the kneehole of the desk.'

'Are the records any good?' asked Effi.

'I can't see any. There are matches. And a little silver knife to cut the heads off the cigars.'

Otto went over and started the men's rigmarole of cigar-cutting and lighting. Effi remembered Schulz doing the same thing. Maybe the cigar would slow down Otto's boozing. Then the kitchen door opened and old Ida came out with a lovely string of pearls in her hand. Otto held out his hand for them. She dropped them into his palm.

'Now I've nothing,' she said. 'Nothing except my family and this boy and girl and their dog. And tonight's dinner. I've paid for it.' She laughed. Good for her. It bemused Otto. Probably he'd been hoping to see her cry. She went back into the kitchen.

'Nice silver cutlery,' she called out to them. 'Champagne flutes, a porcelain dinner-service – Dresden! Cut-crystal dessert dishes, here's a lovely damask table-cloth with napkins. And a carving knife and fork with bone handles, and a strop, everything right and proper.'

'As nice as in your hotel?' asked Effi.

'I'll have a cigar,' said Frau Rupf. 'After all, we've all paid our share, haven't we, Herr Otto?'

And Otto just handed the cigars out and a moment later they were all smoking except little Barbara, who was happy just to nibble chocolate. By and by Frau Rupf put her cigar down on a crystal ashtray she'd found, brought one of the damask cloths out of the kitchen and spread it over the table. Ma Headscarf fetched an armful of silver cutlery.

'Listen,' said Frau Rupf suddenly. 'I can hear the cow.'

There was a loud mooing outside the carriage. The cow needed to be milked and she was standing there asking them for help. Poor creature.

'You'd better go out and milk her,' Frau Rupf said to her daughter. 'For Barbara.'

'There's condensed milk here,' said Ma Headscarf. She didn't want to go outside the train.

'And there's tomorrow, and the day after, and a cow walks with milk inside her. You won't be able to carry all those tins.'

'Tomorrow we'll be on the train,' said Ma Headscarf. Her mother opened her mouth to contradict her, then she glanced at Otto and shut it again. The cow kept calling to them. Effi was scared then, because it was the cat that had got Otto going back at the farm, but he just snapped: 'Go and milk that beast, she'll bring the Russians!'

You couldn't tell who he was giving the order to, but it was Ma Headscarf who went. She took a silver champagne chiller for a pail.

Otto got up now, cigar in one hand, and started tapping along the walls with the other hand as if he was doing it for fun.

Effi nudged Hanno. 'He's looking for a safe. What do you think he means to do? Because now he's got the pearls there's no reason why he shouldn't shoot the lot of us.'

'Come here,' said Hanno. 'Look what I've found.'

He'd opened one of the doors of the enormous desk. There were records there, a rack of about fifteen in their brown paper jackets.

'What's there?' she asked.

He pulled out a record and whispered, 'It's something to do with me. I think so, anyway. He knows I don't believe him about Father and he wants me to believe it. He wants to hurt me, then he might start shooting.' Loudly, he said, '"The Blue Danube".'

'That sounds nice,' said Frau Rupf. 'Put it on.'

'Hang on a bit,' said Hanno. 'Let's see what else there is.' He whispered, 'We've just got to be on our guard, ready for anything.'

Effi crouched next to him. 'Maybe he wants dinner served up to him before he kills anyone. I'm going to act harmless, anyway. As if I was all carried away by the party.'

He went on pulling the records out one by one. His face was intent, then he turned round and looked at her and suddenly his eyes went all soft the way Pierre's used to when he looked at Aunt Annelie.

He loves me, thought Effi. Did my heart go bump because of that, or is it only because of Otto?

'We'll have this one,' said Hanno.

'Let me see.'

'You'll hear.' He held the record out of her reach with his hand over the label.

'OK,' she said, and started to wind up the gramophone.

'Don't look.'

Otto was patting the walls and keeping one eye on them both. She didn't care now.

Hanno put the record on. It was Louis. Nobody else had that croaky, wonderful voice, amused, tender, with a hint of a sadness he wasn't ever going to give in to, there was so much in his voice. And when he went on to play trumpet – Pierre used to say nobody else could give the trumpet that clarity and brilliance. It made you forget you were tired, all you thought about was dancing. Now Hanno showed her the label. Of course it was Louis. It was dangerous to make a noise, but you could only worry about so much danger.

Effi stood up and started to dance, held out her hand to Hanno. He picked up the rhythm easily. He was a really sweet mover. When she touched his hand a buzz went right through her – do I love him? she thought. Would it help if I had a daisy to pull the petals off? Dr Hungerland gave them both a bad look, but he didn't say anything. Then Frau Rupf shook her head and *she* was moving to the music while she set the table, even Otto was patting the wall to the rhythm of Louis's trumpet, and suddenly the little Barbara was there, though she didn't smile and she was clumsy, not quite with the rhythm, but she was dancing. Ma Headscarf came in with her silver milk pail, and stood there gobsmacked to see what her kid was doing.

'I know what,' said Effi, stopping still. 'I'm going to have a wash. So should you, Swing Boy.'

'In what?' he asked.

'Champagne. I bet it's really good for the skin.'

Chapter Sixteen

Effi fetched four bottles of champagne out of the kitchen.

'Two for you, Swing Boy, two for me.'

She'd almost forgotten they were in danger. She took him by the hand, picked up her lamp, and started towing him towards the bathroom. Cornelius, who'd eaten all the horsemeat, now got up, stretched, and made to follow.

'Not so fast,' Otto said sharply. 'You're not both going in there together.' His face was hard all of a sudden, watchful, but he kept on tapping the wall.

'One at a time,' put in Frau Magda, 'a boy and a girl in a bathroom together, whatever next!'

Hanno started to laugh, Effi laughed too. It was better than screaming, anyway.

Dr Hungerland said, 'Thank heavens that terrible noise has finished. How can there be such music on this train, degenerate, Negro music?'

'So you recognize Louis Armstrong?' asked Effi. 'What else is there, Hanno?'

Hanno put his two champagne bottles on the desk, crouched down behind it and started pulling out records.

'The Quintet of the Hot Club de France, Stephane Grappelli, Django Reinhardt and Larry Adler?'

'He plays harmonica,' said Effi. 'He's brilliant.'

'Then there's more Louis Armstrong and Benny Goodman. Goodman's Jewish, isn't he? They were such hypocrites, the high-ups.'

'Yes,' said Otto. 'The top brass thought they couldn't be corrupted. That kind of music – jungle music – it's not for Germans. Look at you all just now, dancing and drooling like black baboons.'

'It got to you, too,' said Hanno. 'Didn't it?'

Otto stared across the room at him with his glassy blue eyes. Hanno stared back. Careful, Swing Boy.

Otto said, 'I suppose you're glad we lost.'

'You were lying about my father,' said Hanno. It wasn't just that Otto wanted to hurt Hanno. There was some kind of duel going on between them. Otto was taking his time, why shouldn't he? He had a gun. Just as long as he didn't get too drunk. Maybe religion would help them all. Hail Mary, full of grace, keep this swine policeman sober.

'No,' said Otto.

There was a loud pop. Otto jumped and pulled his gun out. Cornelius started barking. Then Otto laughed, half-angrily. Frau Rupf had opened a bottle of champagne.

'We'll all have a drink,' she said.

'I want apple juice,' said Hanno.

'What a good boy,' said Frau Rupf, but Effi guessed why he was drinking apple juice. She thought the old dame guessed, too. He wanted to keep his head clear.

Frau Rupf said, 'Barbara can have apple juice, too, but I expect the baggage will want to drink champagne as well as washing in it. Go on, hussy, or you'll keep us waiting for ever for our dinner.'

So Effi went along the corridor with her bottles of champagne. Cornelius's head went this way and that, unsure who to go with but then he turned towards the food smell from the kitchen and decided to stay put.

*

Effi went into the little bathroom. It had its own toilet, best-quality paper too, and a sea sponge hanging from a chrome hook on the wall. She put the champagne bottle down on the floor and the lamp on the little shelf beside the sink. She undressed, throwing her clothes on the floor. They were stiff with dirt, it was so good to take them off. Now she popped the first cork and set champagne smoking and frothing into the sink. She got the sponge, wet it with champagne, and hopped into the bath where she cleaned herself off, especially her feet, they were filthy – and shivered with the cold of it. Grapes in the rain, she thought, somewhere down in France where Pierre was born. Only he said they don't make champagne in Alsace. They make sparkling wine on the German side of the Rhine. The British are on the Rhine now, and the Americans.

She imagined American soldiers laughing, taking her hand, pulling her along the street. Shouting: 'Bruno, here's your kid!'

Papa getting up from behind a desk. Papa with his arms spread wide. On the photograph he was wearing a linen jacket and a summer hat, but he'd be in Ami uniform. And Hanno would be there, too. She wasn't quite sure what would happen about Hanno. Papa would get in touch with his mother and his sister. Would he have to go away then?

Aloud, she said, 'Don't dream too hard, kid.' She opened the second bottle and poured it down over herself, cold as a rainshower, squeaked with the cold and saved a drop to drink. She dried herself with the fluffy towel that was hanging there. That felt warmer. She rubbed her hands down over her belly. It was hollow and hard. 'I'll make you bulge tonight,' she promised.

There was a little cupboard behind the mirror. She opened it. Treasure. There was an unused lipstick, nail varnish, a manicure set, a brush and comb and a new bottle of French perfume. The lipstick was bright red. The Nazis used to say the pure German woman shouldn't wear makeup, so which impure woman was going to use all this stuff? Magda Goebbels, maybe? Or fat Hermann Göring's floozy wife Emmy?

She combed the tangles out of her hair – it hurt, but it was so good to feel them coming out. Then she pushed her lips forward and outlined them in the dim yellow-amber light from the lamp. She dug the dirt out of her nails, fingers and toes, and painted them bright red too. She squeezed the rubber globe of the perfume bottle. It smelt good, even on top of champagne.

She didn't want to get dressed in her dirty clothes. Maybe there was something in the sleeping compartments that she could wear? She wrapped the towel round her and took her lamp out into the corridor. There were cupboards under the beds, men's pyjamas in three of them, in the fourth she hit the jackpot. A pair of white silk satin pyjamas, only a little too big for her, but the legs were short and she could tear the waistband open a little and make the elastic tighter. A white silk satin kimono, as well as satin slippers with swansdown trimmings, also too big, but she'd wear them.

Back in the bathroom, she bundled up her skirt, her shirt and knickers and put them in the bag with the cotton reels and Schulz's cigarettes. That bag was as fat as a beat-up featherbed now, but she had to carry it. She'd have to put the jacket on over the pyjamas to hide the bag. So she couldn't wear the kimono, pity about that, but the jacket looked surprisingly good. Now she'd go back to the party. She'd have to carry her boots in her hand, that wasn't very elegant, but it didn't matter.

Otto had given up tapping the walls and was sprawled in a chair opposite Hungerland, watching Hanno while Ida Rupf and Ma Headscarf set the table. They'd been hard at work: they'd found some candles and silver candlesticks, and there were thin slices of smoked salmon set out on black bread. Heaps of caviar glittered blackly in crystal saucers, and there was a serving dish full of new potatoes, peas and carrots. Who cared if they were cold!

'Hussy,' said Frau Rupf, setting down a dish of gherkins – you could smell their sharpness from three metres away. As for Hanno, the way his eyes opened wide you'd have thought Greta Garbo had come into the carriage. She thought, I was pretty before, was I, Swing Boy? Just look at me now.

Otto looked at her from his chair, his blue eyes cold and hostile. And Dr Hungerland looked. Intently, as if he could see right through the silk pyjamas. He wasn't just thinking dirty thoughts, though, there was something far worse going on inside his head. For a moment, she wished she'd put all her ordinary clothes back on. Then he shut his eyes as if he had a headache and kept them shut. She was glad.

Ma Headscarf looked too, and for a moment there was a yearning look on her face. And little Barbara came over to Effi and put her fingers on the pyjamas. They were rough and snagged the silk. She shook her head, thought for a moment, turned her hand over and stroked the silk with the back of it.

'Nice,' she said.

Effi grinned.

'Isn't it?'

Frau Rupf started to say something, then put her hand over her mouth. Ma Headscarf got her rosary beads out and started to tell them. Almost frantically, poor ugly dame.

'Hanno boy,' said Effi. 'Go and get washed. I'm hungry.'

He went.

'Your dog likes smoked salmon,' said Frau Rupf. Cornelius was her friend now, slavering next to her. 'I didn't give him too much, though. Dogs mustn't be spoiled, though they're always hungry. I wonder how much you'd have to give a dog before he'd stop eating? I think he'd burst.' She laughed, she didn't care about the dog or anything else, she was like a dog with two tails herself, because Barbara had spoken.

'I'm hungry,' said Barbara, as if there was nothing special about her talking. Her grandmother seized her and kissed her, then let her go.

Effi went to look over the records for herself. She found the Larry Adler record and thought she'd put it on, till she found another that made her whistle. It was 'Raindrops Shining in Your Hair'. Papa's music. The Nazis had bought it, just like they'd bought Louis Armstrong's black-man's music and Benny Goodman's Jewish music. There was another of Papa's on the other side, 'Riviera Nights'. She wound up the gramophone, she couldn't wait. She'd never heard the record before, and here she was going to listen to it in a Nazi fat-cat carriage before a feast of looted food, with battles going on all around her and a Nazi with a gun waiting to murder her, maybe.

> I'm lost and broken-hearted
> lonesome, weary and blue
> and I'm writing these words, dear, to tell you –

She was so proud, she wanted to shout: 'My father wrote those words *and* the music, and the Nazis bought *his* record, not the crappy German version about the soldier taking his sweetheart's photograph to the Front.' Of course, it wasn't Papa singing, but it sounded as if it was his voice, singing to her.

> I'm waiting for you now, my darling,
> I'm just longing to kiss you again
> To see your bright eyes smiling –

Hanno was back with his face all clean. OK, she still wasn't sure if she loved him, but it sure made her happy to see him come through the salon door. Now they'd eat, to the sound of Papa's words and his music. She danced to the table and snatched up black bread and smoked salmon. Did it taste good! But she thought, This is like me and Pierre in the burning house, I can't feel the flames this time, but they're all round us.

At dinner, Dr Hungerland said, 'I used to have good dinners when I visited other specialists in my field. When I went to Dr Pfannmüller's institution in Bavaria we had Château Mouton-Rothschild, duck with orange, crêpes suzette. Liqueurs and coffee. But I couldn't agree with his policies. I didn't believe in causing unnecessary suffering.'

Effi saw Otto nod to himself. Otto understood what bad business had taken Hungerland down to Pfann-müller's place.

She took a teaspoonful of caviar. The little black globes popped against her tongue. They tasted soapy, but she liked the popping. Cornelius, the gourmet dog, was walking round and gazing up at all of them, drooling.

Barbara gave him bread and a spoonful of caviar.

'It's good,' she said.

'The champagne's superb,' said Frau Rupf. 'Louis Roederer.' The dog whined, he thought he ought to have champagne as well as smoked salmon and caviar.

'Not for dogs,' said the old dame. 'A drunken dog – that would be a fine thing.'

Effi sipped the French champagne. It popped against her tongue in a different way from the caviar. When she was famous and had her tame lion and the pink limousine, she'd have champagne for breakfast every morning. And bath in it first. She could just scoop a glassful of champagne out of her bath and drink it then and there. And she'd have caviar in the soap dish. Only where would Hanno be? No, she wouldn't worry about that, she wouldn't worry about Otto either. Not at this feast.

'I'll give you a toast,' she said. 'I'm drinking to the dead.'

'To our soldiers?' asked Dr Hungerland. 'Too many of them, and the best ones at that. What will become of Germany's future now?'

'Leave it to this pair,' said Frau Magda in a sour voice. 'They'll have babies soon enough, can't wait to be at it.'

'You need something to sweeten your tongue,' said Effi, grinning. She got up and started bringing in the tinned peaches, the macaroons, condensed milk and tiny coffee cups to drink it out of, marrons glacés. This is the land of Cockaigne, she thought, like in the fairy tale, as much as you like to eat and drink and no need to do the dishes afterwards. Hanno had put his thin blue and white dinner-plate on the floor for the dog to lick, but Cornelius found better things to do. Barbara was holding a macaroon out to him.

Dr Hungerland started to talk. You'd think he was giving an after-dinner speech.

'The problem was,' he said, 'that while German men were dying in battle – and you must remember that we already had lost more good men than we could afford in the First Great War – we were keeping worthless specimens – no, dangerous specimens – alive in our own country. Idiots, for example, or those born blind and deaf. Clearly something had to be done. For one thing, if they had been left to breed freely Germany would soon have become a nation of defectives.'

'What?' asked Ida Rupf. She was angry all of a sudden. 'Defectives: does that mean innocent, sweet children who have to wear leg-irons?'

Dr Hungerland looked at her as if she'd no right to speak. This, thought Effi, is where the piano goes out of tune.

Ma Headscarf broke in as if she wanted to shut her mother up.

'We have some children left,' she said in a hurried voice, 'and when they're old enough they'll help build Germany up again.' She turned round to Hanno and smiled at him – she must really want to make a diversion if she was smiling at Hanno. 'What work would you like to do when you're grown up, boy?'

Hanno's cheeks burned, and he said: 'I want to be a sculptor.'

'A sculptor?' said Magda, disapproving in spite of herself.

Otto let out a harsh laugh. 'The only thing your conquerors will allow you to be is a peasant, boy. If the Russians don't drag you off to be their slave. You needn't bother with any ambitions. It's finished.' He bit his lip.

'No, it isn't,' said Effi. 'You can be a sculptor, Swing Boy, that's really cool. You'll be famous and you can come to America, you can have an exhibition in some big art gallery in Los Angeles and we'll go out on the town in my limo.'

Ma Headscarf tut-tutted. 'A limousine! The lies the girl tells.'

'Leave their dreams alone, Magda,' said old Ida sharply.

Dr Hungerland looked round them all, thought they'd finished their unnecessary interruptions, and resumed his speech. He was crazy, after all.

'I spent two years working in America after I qualified,' he said. 'Under Professor Baines.' He spoke the name reverently, he seemed to think they'd have heard of the Prof. 'He was undertaking a major programme to sterilize carriers of unworthy genetic stock. Individuals from criminal families as well as the physically and mentally unsound. He always said to me that I should carry his message back to Germany. And indeed, when the new government came, there were soon opportunities to transfer the policy to our own country. It was only during the war, as I have already said, that it became imperative to deal more radically with the situation behind the lines. It was costing more money than we had available to care for bad genetic stock while healthy children were going short of schoolbooks. These individuals were a burden that we had to get rid of. I was a major participant in the programme. It was a way in which I could fight for my Fatherland as if I was a soldier at the Front.'

Ida said, 'I *will* speak, Magda. Don't try to stop me. When I hear this fellow preening himself – Dr Hungerland, I had a little son. He was born much later than Magda. He had a weak leg, and had to wear an iron.

Such a good boy he was, he was slow to read, but he stuck at it and he managed in the end. He had the nicest smile, always cheerful, always brave. It used to make me so happy to have him put his arms round my neck. And he helped me with the hotel, he was anything but an idiot, it was only the reading he found hard. He didn't sleep very well, and he suffered terribly with his digestion. Dr Steinberg used to come out any time I was worried about him; he loved Hans too. He found out some exercises for him that helped him to move better. Then the Nazis came to power and they said our doctor couldn't attend to Hans any longer because he was a Jew. The doctor who replaced him wasn't so helpful – I thought he wasn't interested. But one day he came and said they could carry out an operation on Hans. It was a new operation, he said, and it might make all the difference to him. So I took him to the hospital. It was a long way away. In Brandenburg. I stayed in the town, but I wasn't allowed to visit him. They said he died during the operation, his heart was unsound, they said. Later, though, Cardinal Galen preached about how they were killing so many people in the hospitals, and I understood what they'd done to Hans.'

'Adults were selected for treatment as well as children,' said Hungerland, as if he was pleased to explain to her. 'But I participated only in the children's programme. We used luminal. It's a sedative. We administered it dissolved in a tea, or injected. There were some subjects who were so excitable that they had become tolerant of luminal, so we gave them an injection of morphine-scopolamine. I was aware that I was dealing with organisms who could feel fear and pain. I was compassionate in my proceedings. Unlike Pfannmüller, who starved them to death. I would never have done that to my subjects. We kept the programme going in secret, even after the Cardinal's ill-judged intervention. Of course the public was told it had been brought to a halt. It has to be said that I did not make the final decision. I filled in the forms and despatched them to the central authorities. If the names came back marked with a plus sign, that meant the subjects were to be put to sleep. Unfortunately, my nerves – it started with the occasional hallucination, but as soon as I left the hospital the eyes were with me all the time. But not here, not inside the train.'

'The eyes of the children you murdered?' asked Ida. She was shivering. Effi put her hand on hers and Ida gripped it hard. Effi felt cold, too. She thought of Claudia. Maybe Hungerland had filled in a form for her and it had come back with a plus sign.

'There was one girl,' said Hungerland. 'Bettina Grauss. She had black curly hair and black eyes like this girl.' He pointed to Effi as if she was an illustration for his lecture. 'She had gypsy blood on the mother's side. She was six, she would have been pretty if she hadn't been an idiot. She danced in the ward, the nurses permitted it. I admit it was pleasing to see her dancing. She called me Daddy. She seemed to like me. On the same evening that she was to be given her dose I picked her up and bounced her on my knee. I know now that I should never have done so. The nurses were amazed because I had never taken a personal interest in any of my subjects. The child laughed, she shrieked at me, "Go on, Daddy!" I didn't understand myself, but I continued. Then she had to go to bed and we carried out the procedure. In the morning I certified her death. In the evening I went to my room and I saw her eyes looking at me. Later, all the other eyes came to torment me. And they have made me suffer till this moment.'

Otto laughed bitterly. He stood up and went to the desk and picked up the picture of Hitler that Ida had laid on its face. 'We failed him,' he said. 'All of us. We hadn't the strength or the resolve to live up to his vision. We couldn't be hard enough. For all they had been outlawed, we still fell prey to ideas about humanity, compassion, the rights of the individual. But what about the right of a people to exist, what joy is there for any individual when the people is decaying from within? And we were undermined by sentimentality.'

'You mean mother-love,' said Ida, still holding Effi's hand tight.

'What you call mother-love is the perverted love of a perverted woman, a self-confessed Jew-lover. Admit it,' said Otto, 'when you couldn't corrupt German stock by producing wretched mongrel offspring, you tried to keep alive a monstrosity who should have been killed at birth. We should have killed so many more people. When the Führer came to power in 1933 we should have been ruthless.'

'What do you mean,' said Effi, 'you didn't kill enough people?' It was too late to be careful. 'I thought you killed plenty. And the Jews in Russia, and the Russians, how many of those did you kill?'

'Not enough to finish the job,' said Otto. He got his gun out and swung it round his finger by the trigger. She ought to be really scared now, and yet she wasn't. There was something going on that had to be finished. She was cold, that was all.

Old Ida took her hand out of Effi's and put it to her throat. 'Is it true, then, about those camps? Where thousands of Jews were gassed?'

'Of course it's true,' said Otto, impatiently, as if it

wasn't important. But it was important – they'd discussed it once, Pierre and Aunt Annelie and Effi, and Aunt Annelie had said, 'It has to be a rumour. Even the Nazis wouldn't do anything so horrible.'

Effi felt giddy and sick.

'My Felix,' said Ida. There was anguish in her voice. 'Did they gas him to death in Poland? I should have married him. We could have gone abroad together.'

'Mother?' asked Magda. 'I wouldn't have been born. Or Hans.'

'Oh, God,' said Ida, 'it's all so difficult.' She started to cry.

Effi passed her a damask napkin, but it was too hard. The old dame needed a soft handkerchief to comfort her. Or maybe nothing would comfort her. But supposing her boyfriend had gone abroad and been friendly with Mama and Papa?

'What was Felix's surname? Did he get famous?' she asked again.

Ida said, 'I don't know if he became famous. I never heard about it if he did.'

Otto broke in: 'We should have killed this boy's father.' He was staring at Hanno. 'All right, boy, you wanted to know this. In 1930 your father and I were both second lieutenants and I was the secretary of the Nazi Officers' Association. I invited your father to join us and work for our national renewal. He wouldn't. He belonged to a filthy leftist police union. The Schrader League it was called.' Otto bit his lip. 'Frisch laughed in my face – I hope you're right, boy, and he's really dead. Or else he'd be laughing again now. He said he couldn't understand how any policeman could be a National Socialist, I'd never get promotion *that* way, he said, the Nazis were a disorderly rabble, he'd treat them fairly if he had to break up one of their demonstrations, and that was all he'd do for the Nazis. That was when Prussia was ruled by the Social Democratic swine, so Frisch soon got promotion himself, to first lieutenant. That was how you got promotion in those days, by being a leftist. Then one evening I was out with some friends and we met Sternberg's deputy to the Reichstag. He was a filthy Social Democrat. We cornered him and kicked the living daylights out of him. Who should happen along but Frisch? He arrested me. I was demoted to sergeant – lucky to keep my job, the tribunal told me. Only three years later the Führer was in power. Suddenly I was the most important man in the Sternberg police station.'

'And making the most of it,' said old Ida. Her voice was harsh.

'Why not? Hadn't I suffered? But now the Schrader League had been disbanded. Frisch was out in the cold. The Party was passing a law to get politically unreliable people out of public service. So he thought he'd make himself safe by joining our Officers' Association after all. He got one of our members to put his name forward. I opposed it, but they overruled me, because your father, the rat, had a way of sneaking himself into his comrades' good graces.'

'You mean he was a good comrade,' said Hanno angrily.

'I denounced him. Leftists like him were a danger to the Reich and we prosecuted him under the new law.'

In the same harsh voice, old Ida said, 'Those were frightening days, lad. The storm troopers were coming round to get whoever they liked and killing them in their concentration camps. Most people said it was good to get rid of the Communists. Because of all the battles there'd been on the streets between the Communists and the Nazis. I wasn't sure it was a good thing to be left with the Nazis. But I kept my mouth shut.' She was shivering even more violently now. 'Because I was afraid. And we had a hotel to run and Party high-ups were coming to stay there. And I had two children to consider, dear God, I had two children. I never even asked where Dr Steinberg had gone.'

Otto said, 'They were good days. Frisch was found guilty. On good evidence, too. I was on the commission that judged him. We got information from one of the other filthy leftists.'

'What?' said Effi. She'd never have thought she'd feel sorry for a policeman. 'You denounced *and* judged him? And what did you do to the other man to get him to confess?'

Otto ignored her. 'Bernhard Frisch's career was on the scrapheap. And he was an ambitious rat, he'd thought he was really going somewhere, first lieutenant already at thirty-four. But the ruling on people like him was that they'd be put out to grass at some little village police station. They'd never get promotion.'

'But it would never have come to that,' said Effi. 'Would it? You'd have sent the storm troopers round to get him.'

'I wish I'd had the chance,' said Otto. 'Everything seemed to be pointing in that direction. I said to Frisch: 'If you want a widow's pension for your wife, the best thing you can do is go and shoot yourself.' I don't know if he ever got his gun out, probably he was too big a coward, because he sent your mother to go and bat her eyelashes at a bigwig who'd got connections in Berlin. Fontane, he was called. She was a pretty little thing, I've often wondered what favours she did Fontane to save your father. Half an hour's work on her back probably swung it.'

Hanno was white in the face. 'You swine,' he shouted. 'You swine!'

He launched himself at Otto. Oh, God, thought Effi. Otto's going to get his gun out and kill him.

Chapter Seventeen

Hanno wasn't thinking about the gun when he hit out at Otto; when he remembered it he was already hunched together, coming at Otto. It was too late to draw back.

Otto had hold of the gun's handle, his finger was closing on the trigger. Hanno brought his arm round, a good strong punch, and managed to send the gun flying. He didn't see what happened to it, because Otto put his fists up and started to fight in earnest.

He was bigger and stronger than Hanno, but drunk. Also it wasn't always bad to be smaller than your opponent. Angry though Hanno was, a cold, clear voice in his head reminded him of the upward jab he'd once used on big Willim in the playground. You pushed into the punch from your feet and legs. His fist went into Otto's chin from underneath.

Now Otto was furious because Hanno had hit him twice. Something made Hanno fake a punch to the right. Otto lashed out to protect himself and now Hanno got him in the belly on the left. No boxing rules here. Otto teetered, shouted; he was tearing at Hanno's hair. Hanno butted him. Otto had his arms round him. There was a crash of plates going flying. Hanno heard the old woman cry out as they hit the floor together, Otto's weight on top of him, Otto's quick breaths coming close and hot in his ears. And as he struggled underneath Otto Hanno knew, somehow, that Effi had the gun. But she mustn't use it, he thought. I don't want to be rescued. I want to fight him myself, to the end.

Otto's hands were coming round his neck, wanting to throttle him. There was all of Otto's weight on top of him, and his drunk breath in Hanno's face. Hanno pushed his hands into Otto's face, feeling the hardness of his cheek-bones, shoving his thumbs upwards into the eye sockets. He found Otto's eyeballs, and though he was fighting and retching for breath he dug into them as hard as he could. Otto shouted. His hands were off Hanno's throat, he was shoving against Hanno's hands. Hanno wriggled, reached out with his foot and found the edge of the desk. He pushed against it, using it as leverage to heave himself and Otto over. Otto's bloodshot eyes were staring into his, but his hands were on Hanno's face, he was trying the thumbs-in-eyes trick now. Hanno turned his mouth round and bit his hand. Hard. Otto yelped. He punched Hanno in the mouth with his other hand. Hanno had a mouth full of blood, but he kept struggling, down on the floor with Otto. Then Otto kneed him in the stomach, pushed him away, and was on his feet while Hanno's belly fought for breath. Otto kicked at Hanno: Hanno rolled away, only copping half the kick. The next minute he was up on one knee, then on his feet before Otto could take another step and kick him again. But he was tired and winded, he only had his anger to keep him going. He zigzagged away from Otto. 'Coward,' he said in what was meant to be a shout, but he didn't have the breath to shout, so it came out like a half-sob. 'You ran away from the fighting. Coward. Coward.'

Otto didn't answer, but came after Hanno with his fists clenched. Hanno ducked away from the punch. Otto's punch went into the air and he all but toppled. He got his balance back and came after Hanno again. Hanno went backwards. Then he felt the two walls behind his shoulders. Otto had him in a corner. I'm a fool, he thought, and, Where's Wolfgang? But he was fighting alone, Wolfgang couldn't come to back him up now.

The next second Otto was punching at him again: it was meant to get his stomach, but Hanno managed to dodge sideways and it caught his hip instead. Now Otto went for his head. Hanno just fought off the punch, and then the cold, clear voice was talking in his head again – use his own strength against him, it said. You did that to big Willim, too, remember? Keep your eyes on his fists.

The blow came: he saw the fist getting bigger as it hit towards him, but he seized hold of Otto's arm with both hands and pulled, twisting sideways as he did so. He felt all Otto's weight hurtle past him into the wall. Then Otto was crumpling – it seemed to take for ever.

Otto lay on the floor. He was out cold. Hanno wiped the blood off his mouth with his sleeve. He was out of breath and giddy, and now he noticed where he was hurting, his mouth, his hip, his hands, his belly and all the bruises from when he'd hit the floor. Any moment now, he thought, the women will be there wanting to clean me up. Scolding like mothers. He didn't want them. He wanted Wolfgang. Thumping him on the back, saying, That was some fight, big brother.

Dr Hungerland was there, kneeling down beside Otto, putting his hand to the pulse in his neck. 'He's alive,' he said. 'Thank God. We must take care of him. Restrain that boy. Throw him off the train.'

Effi said, 'Nix take care of him. Give me your tie.'

'No,' said Hungerland. 'I have to preserve a decent standard of appearance.'

'If you don't,' said Effi, 'I'll shoot you. I've got his gun.'

Hungerland shuddered. He took his tie off carefully, as if he was going to roll it up and put it in a drawer. He handed it to Effi.

'Now get away from him,' she said. She got down beside Otto. Ida Rupf came to help her. Together, the two women rolled the unconscious Otto onto his front and tied his hands together with the silk. 'We need something to do his legs,' said Effi. 'I know. Go into the third bedroom, you'll find a silk kimono there, with a belt.'

Frau Rupf went away. Hanno saw Frau Magda standing there, quite still, white in the face. She said, 'How can we find the train now?'

'There isn't a train,' said Effi shortly. 'There never was. It was a game I was playing with Hanno, this joker came along and it got too serious.' Ida Rupf came back holding something white. Effi tied Otto's legs together with the belt. It'd hold him, silk was strong.

Hanno said, 'He's got the diamonds in his pocket.'

'No, he hasn't,' said Effi. 'They tumbled out when you were scrapping. And the pearls. I've got them all here. Do you want the diamonds?'

'No,' he said. 'Hungerland can have them.'

'*Doctor* Hungerland,' the doctor corrected him, sitting up in the chair and wiping his face with his handkerchief.

Ida Rupf was ripping the kimono apart. 'We can truss him,' she said. 'Tie his arms and legs together.'

'Good,' said Effi. 'Don't get down. I can do it by myself. Hang on. Here are your pearls. Have your diamonds, doc.'

Dr Hungerland said, 'But they were my fare. I paid for the journey.' He paused, then went on, 'I shall give them to the conductor in the morning. Because I don't believe these tales of fraud.'

'Defeatist rumours?' asked Effi. 'Like the stories about the Russians reaching Berlin?'

Hungerland said, 'I intend to remain on this train till it moves.'

'Good luck to you,' said Effi. She was really making a parcel out of Otto's arms and legs. 'I'm moving on my own two feet in the morning.'

Frau Magda was crying.

'I'm sorry,' said Hanno. It wasn't enough, he knew that.

Ida Rupf said, 'At least we've been well fed, lad. Now we must get a couple of hours' sleep. We have to be out of here at first light.'

Hanno knew what she meant: if any Russian bombers saw the train, they'd target it.

'Clean yourself up,' said the old woman to Hanno – he was surprised it had taken her so long to say it. 'There's some champagne left, the alcohol will disinfect the cuts.'

'Cognac,' said Effi, getting up from Otto. 'It'll sting nicely, then you'll know it's good for you.'

Dr Hungerland said, 'I have grandchildren. I used to play with them. Perhaps that was why I played with the Grauss child. But my grandchildren all have blond hair.'

'Of course they do,' said Effi. 'Now shut up, will you?'

'I had to think about their future,' said the doctor.

'It didn't make any difference. Fighting Otto,' Hanno said. 'It felt as if it would.'

'Nothing will make any difference now,' said Ida Rupf, grimly, 'but maybe, when we've got some time, we can sit down and ask ourselves how we could allow all this to happen? The war, the Jews, the dead children. Or maybe we'll just decide it was someone else's fault.'

'Do you hate me, Mother?' asked Frau Magda.

'Of course I don't,' said the old woman. 'You're my daughter. Magda, I'm so weary, please have some pity on me tonight.'

'What was Felix's other name?' asked Effi.

'Dresner. Are you interested in poetry?'

Effi shook her head. 'I thought I might have heard what happened to him. I haven't. I'm sorry. Look, Swing Boy, don't lash yourself. It did make a difference, fighting Otto. God knows what he meant to do to all of us, you know what he's like. Anyway, fighting him was something you had to do. Are you going to get the cognac, or do I have to?'

It did sting, like iodine, and he was glad. He couldn't understand why.

One bedroom the doctor had bagged, one Frau Magda used with Barbara, old Frau Rupf had the third. Otto was lying trussed up on the salon floor, so Effi and Hanno could use the fourth. It was a nice bed, a metre wide, but they still had to cuddle up together. Hanno went in first, then Effi came. She lay down facing him: a moment later she had her head on his shoulder. He put his arm round her and stroked her back. Little flames of pleasure ran up and down her.

'You're nice,' she said. 'Swing Boy.'

He grinned at her. He was cute when he looked really happy. Then he kissed her face in an awkward, damp way. She kissed him back. A moment later they were kissing properly. It was good. It went on being good. Till the happiness drained out of him – she'd swear she could feel it go, it was like a greyness creeping over his body, which had been nice and rosy warm.

'I beat him – but my father's still dead. And Wolfgang.'

Jesus, he sounded just like a little kid. She understood, though.

'Swing Boy, we've all got dead people we'd like to bring back to life.'

'You've got your mother, of course, and that Frenchman, and your aunt. Effi, what Otto said, about my father –'

'You believe it, don't you?'

'I'm sure it's true. My sister told me once – she's two years older than me, she was four in 1933. She remembers Mother sitting there crying and crying. And Father was in the dining room and Mother went in to him and suddenly she shouted "No!" at him and something fell on the floor. Heide went in there and it was his gun. She never understood why he dropped his gun like that. Now it makes sense. He tried to shoot himself, and Mother told him not to. And there was that bad feeling about Otto. I told you. When I think about Father believing the only thing he could do was to go and shoot himself –'

Effi said, 'Did you hear what Otto said? They really were gassing all those Jews in Poland. Why didn't I want to believe it? I know enough about what they were capable of. There was a man who lived near us, he'd been in a camp. For being a trade union organizer. A bit like your father. Whatever it was they did to him, they made a wreck out of him. He wasn't allowed to talk about it, you know, they'd warned him they'd have him straight back in if he did. He used to drift into my aunt's bar like a ghost, order a glass of beer, drink half of it and sit staring at the other half for two hours. Only if anyone spoke to him he'd start shaking and then he'd get out of the bar as if someone was after him. I reckon they let people like him out to put the frighteners on everyone else. Your father knew that kind of thing was happening.'

'That finishes it all for me. I know it's finished anyway. But there's another way of things being finished, inside your head. Do you know what I mean?'

She stroked his hair.

'I do, Swing Boy.'

'You know, he'd never let Wolfgang and me grumble about the Hitler Youth, I thought it was because he believed in it; maybe it was because they still had an eye on him and it was dangerous for us to bunk off HY. But maybe he did start to believe in it, later on.'

'Maybe he didn't. You don't know. Maybe your mother does.'

'I told you, when we went for the walk that time, he said to my brother and me, "All I want to do is to forget." But he didn't do anything to stop it. Not like those people who tried to kill Hitler.'

She said, 'You had to know people. People you were sure were safe. Difficult in the police force. Maybe he thought things would get better – even Jews thought that at the beginning. Then he got so far in it was too late. Maybe all the time he was hating it. But *you* know what bastards they were, kid. That's what counts.'

Hesitantly, he asked, 'Do you think Otto was lying about my mother? You know, she didn't want my teacher to have me and Wolfgang in the Home Guard, and he said to her: "You won't move mountains this time."'

'Your mother knew the Brownshirts might come for your father. They both knew that all of you'd be destitute if that happened. I reckon your mother was a brave woman, she went like plenty of others to beg for his life. It was bad enough for them, having to beg and plead to those bastards; I never heard that any of them had to do anything like that. He was just trying to rile you.'

'How come you know so much? Were you really a criminal? If you were, why did you give the diamonds back, and the cigarette case? And why did you ask about Frau Rupf's Jewish lover?'

So she told him. All about Mama and Papa, about Uncle Max, and what Aunt Annelie and Pierre had been doing. About helping with hiding Jews and looting food for them, about how she'd taken messages and food back and forth, Little Red Riding Hood among the wolves. About Schulz. Now what was he going to say?

He didn't say anything. Was he only taking it all in?

At last: 'Did you want us to lose?'

'I wanted Hitler to go. I didn't want kids like your twin brother to cop it. But if losing was the only way for the Nazis to go – better a horrible ending than a horror that never ends. Do you hate me for that?'

Now suddenly she was crying – she'd thought she couldn't till she reached Papa, but she had to. And Hanno was stroking her hair, and his front was getting all wet with her tears, and she sobbed and sobbed, and it was OK, he kept on stroking her hair so lovingly.

The next thing she knew she was awake, there was daylight coming in through the blinds, and there was the noise of a plane. She could hear Otto bellowing in the salon. She and Hanno jumped up together.

Frau Magda, Barbara and Frau Rupf were up, running to the salon, and Hungerland opened the door of his bedroom and looked out. His feet were bare.

'We've got to get out!' yelled Effi.

'I shall remain here,' said the doctor. He started to slide the door shut again.

'Don't you realize that plane could bomb us?' Effi asked him.

'The eyes are outside,' said Hungerland. 'They can't look at me while I'm in here.'

'Please yourself,' said Effi.

In the salon Otto was still yelling. He wanted them to release him. But they picked up the cart and started to lift it out of the door. The dog came too, running up the bank. The women and Barbara were outside already, they'd even started to climb the bank. The cow was at the top, looking down at them.

'Otto,' said Hanno from the bottom step. 'What shall we do about him?'

'I've got his gun,' said Effi from the doorway. 'What say we let him go? I don't want to have killed him, soft of me, probably, Swing Boy, but I did tie him up.'

'He'd hate us to free him,' said Hanno. 'It'd humiliate him. OK, let's do it.'

'I'll hold the gun to keep him nicely-behaved.'

They got back into the carriage, lifting the cart up again. Hanno cut the white silk and Dr Hungerland's tie. Otto stood up, lurching with grogginess. She supposed he had a hangover as well as concussion.

'You can help with our cart,' said Effi, keeping him covered. 'To say thank you to us for saving your life.'

'I'm not leaving,' he said.

'Oh, God,' said Effi, 'another one. Why not?'

He took no notice, but stood up and went to the wall, did something with his hands, and a panel flew open. She saw a safe in there. He started to fiddle with the combination dial.

'You'll die,' said Effi, 'the Ivans will bomb this train.'

'Get out,' said Otto, staggering, but straightening up at once to go back to the safe. 'I'd have finished you last night if things hadn't got out of hand. Now at least I'm not sharing my haul with filthy Communist brats. You wait, I'll catch up with you yet.'

'Let's go,' said Hanno. He got the cart out and Effi almost fell out after him. She kept the gun handy in case Otto came out after all. The plane was still there, not directly overhead, though. At the top of the bank they were among the trees; that felt better.

'Hurry up,' said old Ida. 'What kept you?'

They didn't explain. No time. They ran on away from the cutting. And then the plane dived, coming in with a roar over their heads. Everyone fell flat on their bellies. There was an explosion. Effi heard a creaking and smashing of trees, but only twigs and pine cones came down on her head.

They were all getting up, coughing.

'I'm going back to see what's happened,' said Hanno.

Effi came with him, so did Cornelius. They left the cart.

The railway cutting had turned into a crater whose edges were made of sand, wood fragments, and twisted metal. Effi saw something lying half-buried in the sandy soil. It was the perfume flacon with its rubber bulb. And there was a champagne cork, and a battered tin of something with the label scorched off it. In the middle of the crater there was only empty earth.

'They must be dead,' said Hanno. 'Both of them. Unless they're buried.'

They climbed down with Cornelius, who went sniffing round. They didn't hear anyone calling for help, nor did the dog find anything.

'Dead *and* buried,' said Effi.

'Do you think Otto got the safe open?' Hanno asked. 'How did he find it anyway? Maybe there was a secret lever and he found it when he was tapping the walls last night.'

Effi stared at the wreckage.

'Maybe,' she said. 'I hope he didn't get in there, it was one thing for us not to kill him, but I don't want him to have died happy. Anyway, he's gone and good riddance. Let's go back and tell the others.'

Frau Rupf shook her head, then she said: 'What food did we bring? I took some black bread. And caviar, it's very nutritious.'

'You remind me of someone else I used to know,' said Effi.

'I've got condensed milk,' said Ma Headscarf.

Barbara fetched out half a bar of chocolate.

'I've got chocolate too,' said Effi. 'And tinned salmon.'

'Which way do we go?' asked Frau Rupf. 'We want to go to Frankfurt.'

'So do I,' said Hanno. 'South-west, that is.'

'South-west for me, too,' said Effi, 'if it's true the Amis are there.'

Chapter Eighteen

They walked. They didn't count the days. They noticed the dawn, when it was time to start out. At nightfall they had to stop walking and even though they were tired out, they were sorry to stop. They slept soundly, they were exhausted. Still, when the next day came they woke at once and felt such relief that they could walk again, you'd have thought they'd spent all night awake with their teeth rattling. They didn't talk much.

They stuck to forest tracks and paths. Sometimes the paths took them near roads and settlements and every so often they'd hear women screaming. Effi would look at little Barbara then. She'd gone back into her silence, as if she felt safer like that. She had a way of keeping herself still even when she was walking: Effi thought her self was a long long way inside her body, maybe with its arms wrapped protectively round her heart. Barbara's face was white and ugly because her self was so far withdrawn from it, only her eyes were huge and watchful, fixed on the path in front of her: pine needles and twigs, thought Effi, that's what she sees.

They did meet people in the woods: girls who'd been sent away by their mothers to hide, whole families who had left their homes in the neighbourhood, refugees who'd abandoned the westward trek and were waiting out the rest of the war there.

'Why are you going on?' these people asked. 'The Russians are everywhere now.'

Sometimes Effi thought old Ida would decide to stop walking and stay put with Barbara and Frau Magda. Ma Headscarf had been doing everything her mother said since she'd been proved wrong about the train (but that wouldn't last). But Ida was determined to get Barbara away from the Russians, so she went on with Hanno and Effi.

They went south-west, as best they could, but they were always getting onto paths that snaked and bent and took them off-course, or towards the fighting. When they came upon a road they checked carefully before they crossed it. Several times they had to wait for hours for Russian tanks to pass. Once they came upon a little house in the middle of the woods: there were chickens, geese and goats running around, but no people, and the furniture had been thrown all over the place and broken. Someone had been looting here. They caught a nanny goat who was bleating to be milked, but she butted at Effi and Frau Magda as they trapped her between them: Frau Magda held the horns, Effi the hind legs, and then old Ida milked her, because she knew how. They'd have liked to kill a chicken, too, but they couldn't catch any and the birds made too much noise.

They'd thrown Otto's gun away, so they couldn't use that to shoot a chicken. Ida said when the Russians had stopped them before there'd been a man who had a gun. He hadn't tried to use it against the Russians, though they'd taken his wife, but they'd taken it out of his pocket and blown his head apart with it. They got some eggs, though, and most of them were good. Cornelius found a few for himself, he didn't care whether they were good or bad. He just ate them all.

It was a good thing they'd milked the goat, because that was the day the cow's milk dried up. There'd been less and less of it, now there was nothing left in her udder. They left her on the farm. There was plenty of grass and she could recover from the journey. Effi was glad for her.

As they walked onwards, the skies cleared and the weather grew sunny and warm, it was the kind of weather you wanted for your holidays. There'd be the odd rainstorm, but then the sun came out again at once. The larches were breaking out in feathery new needles. The oak leaves turned green instead of red and grew larger, and the birch-tassels dangled longer and looser, powdering the air with their pollen. The birds sang. But always, in the middle of all this loveliness, there'd be an explosion somewhere and you'd see earth and debris flying up into the sky, or a squadron of bombers would fly overhead.

Once they met a group of British Tommies who the Russians had let out of their prisoner-of-war camp. They had news, the Amis were at the Elbe, they'd met up with the Russians in Torgau and they weren't coming any further. There was still fighting in Berlin, and Hitler was probably still alive. The British were heading for Torgau, too, but they were able to use the roads. One of them had a camera and some film that the Ivans had given him – looted of course – and he took a photograph of them all. That was crazy, tourist snaps in the woods when they were still supposed to be at war with the Tommies. But cool, too, in a way.

You got used to the weight of your bags on your shoulders, and the particular aches they gave you, the hurt in your arms and shoulders became part of you, the bags were like an outgrowth of you. The bags got lighter of course. So did the handcart, that Hanno insisted on pushing all the time, he wouldn't let Effi take a turn. They ate Ida Rupf's potatoes raw. They ate the good sausage from Silesia and Sperling's blue-stripe sausages too, small slice by small slice. The chocolate went quickly, because it'd have melted if they hadn't eaten it. They opened the tins of salmon and ate them, also the caviar. There were no more treats for Cornelius – he got the odd slice of raw potato but otherwise he had to fend for himself. As soon as they stopped every evening he'd disappear into the forest and come back licking his lips. He came back to Effi. He'd chosen her for his special person; he liked Hanno next best, then old Ida, then Barbara. He put up with Ma Headscarf; he knew she belonged to their party. He got upset if they spread out too far. He'd run round them then, trying to herd them together.

The odd thing was that he'd stopped barking. He didn't bark at the other refugees, he didn't bark at the Tommies. He seemed to know, all of a sudden, how much danger they were in. At night he'd sleep curled up against Effi's stomach, while she slept back to back with Hanno. Every night Hanno and Effi would kiss each other before they sank into dark, exhausted sleep, every morning they'd have a kiss because each of them was so pleased to see the other one was still there. Cornelius tried to get involved in the kisses, so half the time Effi would end up with Hanno kissing her lips and Cornelius kissing her ear, then he'd switch to Hanno. He made them laugh. That was good. Laughter kept you alive.

Then one day they came across an old woman gathering wood. She wasn't a refugee. She said she lived in a village nearby. Yes, the Russians had been there. She shook her head. She said she had a bakery, she was selling bread to the Russians now, and she'd supplied British and French prisoners-of-war on their way to the Elbe – they wanted to cross the river but the Russians weren't letting anyone across, not even the Franzis and the Tommies. The Germans had destroyed the Elbe bridge at Torgau, but the Russians had put a pontoon bridge across. American high-ups were allowed over it, she said. She said it was a good thing to have the bakery, word had got around and the Russians were leaving her in peace, because they wanted her good bread.

'How far does the forest go?' asked Hanno.

The old woman didn't ask why they wanted to stay in the forest. She said: 'You need to go a bit south-east from here. Towards Arzberg.' She put her bundle of wood down and pointed. 'You don't want to go to Torgau, it's full of Ivans. The Tommies and the Franzis go there, the Russians let them sleep in the old army lockup. The Ivans don't trouble *them.*' She gave a shrill, nasty laugh. 'If you want to cross the Elbe, you need to go away from the Ivans' head-quarters. It's about a kilometre from the edge of the woods to the river. Mind you, the Ivans patrol the bank. They won't let you across. They'll kill you first. I don't know what the world has come to, that we can't move freely in our own country and the barbarians come here to kill and torment us. I don't care. I just bake my bread.' She laughed again, just as nastily. Her eyes looked like mildewed blackcurrants and her lashes were clogged with flour. There was flour in her hair too, and Cornelius went and sniffed at the bits of dough that were clinging to her arms and the sleeves that were rolled halfway up her arms.

'Keep that dog away from my bakery,' she said. 'Or I'll get the Ivans to shoot it for stealing the bread.'

She's almost mad, thought Effi, only she's got her bakery – that keeps her sane. That's the way it goes, everyone needs something to hold onto.

She glanced at Hanno and saw the sun shining on his fair head. She wanted to put her hand there, his hair would be warm with the sun. She didn't like to, though, not with the old woman's bleary eyes on her.

They thanked the old woman and left. On through the woods and the good smells of spring. Almost there, thought Effi. It's going to be OK. It's got to be OK. But she didn't dare say it aloud.

The forest gave out in the end. They saw a meadow full of dog-daisies and a cobbled road bordered with trees. There was a wrecked Wehrmacht tank on the road, the cobbles must have been well laid because the fighting hadn't broken them up.

'We can't go out there,' said Hanno. 'It's far too open and the Ivans could come any time. Not now, anyway.'

'Yes,' said Ida. 'We've got to wait till dusk.'

So they went back a little way into the woods and sat eating cold potato. The sky darkened and it started to rain. It was a warm rain; Effi put her face into it and washed it clean, rubbing it with her hands.

'You're better off dirty,' said Ma Headscarf in her crossest voice.

'Maybe,' said Effi. 'But I'll get myself clean first. It feels so good.'

'It wouldn't make any difference to the Ivans,' said Ida.

She was brown now, they all were, and the brown was kind to the wrinkles on her face. You could see how pretty she'd been when her Felix had gone walking with her up in the Giants' Mountains. But her eyes were sunken deep into her face, which was too thin. She was forcing herself on even though she was almost deadbeat. Effi remembered what Otto had said about her dying on the road.

She thought: I don't want old Ida to die. She's cool. I want her to make it.

'Hey,' she said. 'Granny, get some sleep.' The old woman liked it when you called her Granny. She grinned, sighed, and did as Effi told her, lay down on the grass and let her eyes fall shut. She snored a bit, but not too loudly, not enough for the Ivans to hear. The rest of them sat and dozed too. The day wore on, sunshine and then another rainshower, and at last it started to grow dark.

'It's got to be dark enough for us not to be visible, but not too dark for us to see,' said Hanno in his 'I'm a boy, so I know' voice. But he did know, really, so she'd let him off.

'Isn't it dark enough yet?' asked Frau Magda after a while. 'We don't know how far it is to the Elbe.'

'The baker woman said a kilometre.'

'If we've got to the place she was talking about.'

Hanno said, 'If we go out too soon we might never find out how far it is. Anyway, the moon's still quite full. If we get to the river it'll give a bit of light. Too much, maybe.'

'How long before we start?' said old Ida.

'Not long,' said Hanno. 'Ten minutes maybe?' So they sat still till he nodded to himself, and said, 'Yes.'

Up they got, and went out through the meadow of sleeping dog-daisies. The trees were dark and straight against the deep-blue sky: it's a lovely colour, thought Effi, I wouldn't mind a dress that colour. When I'm in America, I'll have one. They walked alongside the road, on the other side of the ditch. Listening all the time. For an engine, or booted footsteps, or the quiet sound of bicycle wheels turning. She thought: How are we meant to get across the Elbe anyway? It's not just the old woman who's crazy.

Of course they were all crazy with hope. So was Hanno; maybe he was telling himself there'd be a boat with oars waiting for him when they got to the river bank. There wasn't, of course. There was a group of Russians, sitting by the river with a blazing fire. Two of them had guitars and they were singing. Effi wanted to stand still and listen all night, it was dreadful that she had to back off from music like that and creep past it. The music made her think of huge open spaces where the wind blew through long snowy winters, of enormous forests of birch, lovely white stem after white stem, birds flying between the branches, of huge rivers that froze up in winter and broke up, crashing and racing in the spring.

She puzzled for a moment over the Ivans. They were really good musicians, they'd come here to finish Hitler, she was grateful to them, really she was. But they were like some huge piece of machinery that produced what you wanted but kept catching people up in the cogs and mashing them to pieces.

They got about half a kilometre away from the Russians; if you listened carefully you could just still hear the singing, or maybe that was only because the music had got stuck in Effi's mind. They came past a bomb-crater and stopped by a big tree that must have been knocked sideways by the blast. It hung at a crazy angle over the river. Even without the half-moon the water gleamed pale grey as if it had collected all the light that was left in the sky. It was smooth water, and not flowing too fast.

'How are we going to get across?' Ida Rupf asked.

'I could swim,' said Hanno. 'I used to swim in the river.' With Wolfgang.

'But –'

'I couldn't,' said old Ida. 'You're quite right. And I'm not sure about Barbara. Magda can swim, she's a good strong swimmer. We had her taught when we used to go to the North Sea.'

'I'm a strong swimmer too,' said Effi. 'I used to swim a lot in the Wannsee.'

'It's too far,' said old Ida. 'And there must be currents and weeds. And the Ivans might hear the splashing.'

Suddenly Effi thought there must be a Russian in the bushes behind them, listening, waiting to jump out at them. She felt goose pimples start up all over her skin. And then it grew much darker. The clouds came over and the heavens opened. They all ran under the shelter of the leaning tree. It was a bit drier there, though the rain still dripped through the branches. Outside you could hear it hissing down onto the ground. Effi thought, The river's really going to be cold now.

The cloudburst eased off after about ten minutes. Now the rain was coming down only thinly, but they stayed under the tree, till there was a creaking sound, and the earth heaved underneath them.

'Get out!' shouted Hanno. He had hold of Effi's arm and dragged her away from the tree. The other three ran out after them. Cornelius was already clear. But they'd have had time to stroll out because the tree went over really slowly, groaning and creaking all the time, till it came to rest on the surface of the water. The river started to gurgle against it on the side where the current was. They could just see the fringe of roots that kept it moored to the edge of the bank.

'The rain must have done it,' said Hanno. 'The earth got soaked, and then it gave way.'

'We didn't bring the cart,' said Effi.

They went round searching for it, but it had vanished.

'It must be in the water,' said Hanno in the end.

'On its way to Hamburg by now,' said Effi. 'That's bad; we promised Sperling to look after it. At least we've still got Cornelius.'

Hanno said, 'Look at the tree. It's half of a bridge.'

'Not quite half,' said old Ida. 'It's further than it looks. And are we proposing to dance along the trunk like tightrope walkers?'

'We could hold onto it and float,' said Hanno. 'On the side the current washes against so that if we lost our grip we'd get washed against the tree.'

'I can help you,' said Frau Magda to her mother.

'You couldn't,' said Ida. 'You'd have to look after Barbara.'

There was a silence. Old Ida was the most likely person to drown, there was no getting round that. The tree shifted a little in the water, like a moored boat.

'It's a present from God,' said Ida suddenly. 'If we don't accept it, who knows what other chance there'll be? And I've had my life, and there are these young girls to think about. We'll go. No, don't waste time thanking me. We'll have to leave what we can behind. At least we've eaten most of the food.'

'We mustn't have too many clothes on either,' said Hanno. 'They'll weigh us down.'

Effi thought about the stuff she had in her bag. She'd take the fags, they'd get soaked, of course, and the paper would be ruined, but you could dry the tobacco out and use it for roll-ups. And she'd take the cotton reels: they'd dry. But she'd brought the silk pyjamas with her when she'd changed back into her ordinary clothes. She might as well leave those behind.

'I'll leave my fox-fur,' said old Ida. Effi could just see,

in the dark, how she stroked the heads one last time and then dropped the fur in the grass.

'And we'll have to take our shoes off,' said Hanno. 'We can hang them round our necks, though – we'll need them on the other side.'

Effi took off her jacket and strung the boots round her neck. Here goes, she thought. There were lots of spirituals about crossing the river – only that was the river of Jordan. You died and the other side was heaven. Well, she didn't need to die; it would be heaven to be with Papa.

Hanno went first, then old Ida with a bit more of a splash than he liked, then Frau Magda with Barbara, and Effi. Hanno thought it was better if the weaker swimmers had a strong swimmer either side of them. He didn't like to be so far away from Effi, but he reminded himself that Effi was tough and a good swimmer. Cornelius stayed on the bank for a moment, then jumped in after Effi and paddled – *he* made a splash, and they all held still, listening in case the Russians were coming with their guns. But there was no sound apart from the night-time quacking of ducks and the odd shrill noise from a coot.

The rain had left a layer of cold water at the surface, but there was warmer water down below that had held onto the warmth from the day's sunlight. The current tugged where it ran away under the tree-trunk. People had probably been taking branches off the tree for firewood lower down, because at first they had a nice smooth trunk to hold onto and everything went easily. They were quite a way out into the river when they came to the first branches. They came splaying out into the water, you couldn't climb over them because you'd splash into the water on the other side. They'd have to float out to the end of them.

I didn't think about this, thought Hanno. I should have done, though. And supposing the tree came away from the bank and started to float away? It might roll and push us underwater. Maybe this was a bad idea.

Then he thought about Mother. He had to reach the other bank of the river before he could get to her and to Heide: for a moment he had a vision of her lying in bed in Aunt Lisi's house, trying to imagine where he was, trying to protect him with her thoughts. They had to go on. Old Ida had said it, what other chance would they get?

So he stopped thinking. It was a nightmare getting round the branches. The twigs and leaves came in his face and scratched him: the tree didn't want him – or the others – there now, it wanted to be left alone in the water, maybe. The river ran faster out here, too, and eddied as it ran into the tree. He had to fight the current. The smaller branches bent and whipped around. Sometimes he took hold of dead wood and it snapped. And always he was listening out for old Ida behind him, calling as quietly as he could to her, encouraging her.

'I'm all right,' she called back. 'Save your breath.'

He thought her voice was wavering.

'Come closer to me. Keep a hold of my shirt, I'll hang on to the tree for both of us.'

She came, probably she'd have argued but she didn't want to waste time. Even a heavy person – which she wasn't – wouldn't be much weight to pull in the water. Sometimes the ends of the branches were close to one another, so he only had to let go of one and grasp another to pull them both forward, sometimes the current washed them back into the trunk and then he had to work his way right out to the end of the next branch. It was completely dark now, there were only a few stars in the sky, and he

had to do everything by feel. Once he was suddenly terri-
fied that Effi had been drowned, so he called back to Frau
Magda, who called behind her to Effi, and then told him
Effi was still there 'and the dog,' she said.

A jeep came along the road and the headlamps lit the
water just ahead of them. They tried to be still, though the
water moved them around in among the branches; there
was no helping that. Hanno's heart bumped fast – but the
beams swept away before they reached the floating tree.
Then the moon rose and gave them a little more light, but
that was a worry, because he saw that they were less than
ten metres from the bank, and if a Russian foot patrol
came, they might see them. A few minutes later they came
to a place where there weren't any more branches ahead,
and now the current was flowing really fast. Suddenly,
Hanno couldn't hold on any longer. Ida's grip tightened
on his shirt, and it tore. He reached out and managed to
grab her before she was pulled away from him. She'd
never survive on her own in this water.

'Lie on your back,' he shouted in her ear. She did as she
was told, coughing with the water she'd swallowed. He
got behind her, managed to hook under her arms with his
hands and started to kick out with his legs, hard. He'd
used to play drowning and lifesaving with Wolfgang, now
it was for real and it didn't matter about splashing any
longer. They had to stay afloat or die. Effi, he thought.
What's happening to Effi?

Effi saw the current tear Ma Headscarf and Barbara away
a moment before it reached her. Cornelius was swimming
beside her, but he whirled away faster than she did. Oh,
God, she thought, and the water was throwing her about,
shoving her along; it didn't care if it drowned her. And

then suddenly it was as if there were huge springs inside her arms and legs, as if someone else was using them to swim, someone hugely strong and powerful.

When at last the river stopped giving her a hard time and let her float easily, she'd forgotten which bank she was heading for, for all she knew she was on her way back to the Russians. Please God, no. And she thought about the others, what had happened to them? It was no good wondering, though, all she could do was get herself onto dry land.

She made herself think: the river was flowing north and she wanted the west bank. So she'd have to try and swim to the left. She kicked out, but the enormous battle with the river had taken all her strength, for all it had felt as if someone else was helping her. She couldn't fight any longer, the best she could do was to float for a while. She hung in the river and trod water, and then the faint moonlight showed her the left bank coming closer, there were willows hanging over the edge of the water, please, river, she thought, take me to the willows.

The river wasn't taking her to the willows, it was bearing her past them, just out of reach. She wanted to cry, but that'd be a stupid waste of energy. How far was she going to go, and how far would it be before she lost all her strength and just drowned? And then she felt something under her feet: the river had brought her to the shallows. She stood up in water that reached to her waist and waded towards the bank. About a metre from the nearest willow tree there was a deep pool, but the water was hardly moving there, so she splashed in and swam across. Then she scrambled to the shore under the splaying willow branches.

She tried to shake some of the water off her and ended up falling down in the grass. She sat there, dripping and shivering. In a moment she'd need to go looking for the others. But how could she ever find them? She might be walking one way along the river bank, and they might be walking the other. They might keep missing each other – and then the really bad thoughts came and this time she couldn't brush them away. It was so cold and quiet here on the other side of the river, it made her believe they were all dead. Hanno might be dead. Maybe even Papa had been killed on his way through Germany – he was in the army, after all. To make herself better she got her harmonica out of the bag, the poor thing was wet through, so she shook it before she tried to blow through it. At first it didn't make any sound, then it made a lost little note, and then another. It sounded so sad she put it away again. The wind blew.

And then someone *was* there. It was Cornelius.

He was wagging his whole self, not just his tail, he was licking her face all over and making little crying, barking noises. It was OK for him to make noises now, the Russians were on the opposite bank. She put her arms round him and felt his wriggling warmth, but he wouldn't be held still for very long. He got up and nudged her. He wanted her to come with him. So she stood up – that wasn't easy, she felt like an old woman – and he put his nose in the air and ran, looping back to make sure she was still following him, nudging her to get her to keep up. He brought her to Frau Magda and Barbara, who were standing staring out at the river. Effi shouted and they turned round. She'd never have thought she'd be so pleased to see Ma Headscarf. They kissed each other and hugged, and then Barbara spoke – she thought it was OK to talk on this side of the river, then. She said: 'My grandmother.'

Hanno, thought Effi. I want Hanno. And she was scared for him, so scared that the insect was crawling round and round her stomach the way it had done when they took her off to hospital after Mama died.

She wanted to shout his name out, but when she opened her mouth she couldn't; it was as if she'd got used to hiding and keeping quiet, it was hard to make a noise. She got the harmonica out again and tried to play it. It was a bit better than last time, but not much.

Then Cornelius started to bark. That was some solo, fit to wake the dead. No, she shouldn't have thought that. It was live people he was trying to reach.

Hanno was there. He was coming through the trees, he had his arm round old Ida, you could see she couldn't move without his help. But Effi ran towards him and put her arm round old Ida on the other side and then Frau Magda came up and put her arms round her mother, and they were all embracing and kissing, but the best thing was when she and Hanno were in each other's arms, that was heaven on earth, his wet front against hers, the warmth of his hard chest, the feel of his hands in her wet hair, the feel of his lips on hers.

'I love you,' she said to him.

'Remember you're not alone,' croaked old Ida, grinning.

'Exactly,' said Ma Headscarf; *she* didn't like the great love scene – well, that was her problem. Effi didn't care. She pulled away from Hanno but they kept on holding hands.

'So now we go on to Frankfurt,' said Frau Magda. 'Only what are we going to eat?'

Effi said, 'My father will help.'

'Your father?' asked Ma Headscarf. 'Where's he meant to be?'

'He's in the American army.'

'Not *more* lies,' said Ma Headscarf. 'You'll go to hell, my girl, if you don't mend your ways very soon.'

Chapter Nineteen

Bruno Mann, of the US Psychological Warfare Branch, stood in his office in Leipzig. He was about to start another day interviewing prisoners of war for information about the German army's plans. He'd liked it better when he'd been writing pamphlets urging the soldiers to stop fighting and recording announcements to be broadcast over to German troop placements: 'The war's as good as over! Why die now?'

Now they were here, coming into his office. They never seemed to expect a German in US uniform. They'd give him the information but resent him for being an émigré. Sometimes they'd get self-righteous with him: 'I never liked Hitler but I'd never have joined the enemy. I stayed and fought for my country.' Even when in the end the only thing they'd been fighting for was a place in the queue to surrender to the US Army.

It was pointless to interview them anyway, all he got was rumours and the business about never having liked Hitler. No German soldier had ever liked Hitler, it seemed, and yet they'd done plenty of mischief at his command. And now the Russians were in Berlin. Bruno had been hoping to go to Berlin – it was the real reason he'd joined the US Army – till the bad news came that they were stopping at the Elbe.

He'd been over to the other side. He'd gone with a

group of war correspondents – he was supposed to interpret so that they could interview the civilian population, but the journalists had been more interested in getting together with the Russians to drink vodka and confiscated German booze. He'd taken the jeep and driven out into the countryside alone. He'd found Germans then. Women mostly, women with hollow eyes, one with half her hair torn out. When they'd seen the US Army jeep they'd thrown themselves at it, they'd hardly bothered to wonder that it was a German inside the foreign uniform. They'd all talked at once.

'The Russians caught us up on the road. They took us away and – please tell the other Amis, they ought to know what's happening.' Or: 'We took shelter in a farmhouse, in the middle of the night the Russians were suddenly there. My daughter, yes, four of them. Please help us to get to the Amis.'

All he could do was to urge them to find a doctor. He turned the jeep round and drove as fast as he could, back to the war correspondents' party. He drove them back over the bridge and went back to his lodgings where he drank half a bottle of American whiskey all alone. It didn't drown his fear. The war correspondents were all writing that the Russians were being decent to the German population – that was what the folks at home wanted to hear. Bruno imagined the Russians in Berlin, going into the bar where Effi and Annelie cowered, grabbing them – he threw the rest of the bottle of whiskey onto the floor. The smash of the glass was no consolation. It only made him think of the Russians wrecking the bar. And worse thoughts came. Effi and Annelie might be dead. A bomb or a shell might have got them.

If only Annelie and her lover had been able to send Effi out! They knew how to do it. They'd been part of the network that had smuggled Jews out of Germany. They'd had their routes and their couriers. Schulz had stopped them. Bruno had gathered that from the carefully coded messages in Annelie's letters.

Our friend has made up a list of guests for his party in Prince's Street. He hasn't yet told his wife about the party. That meant Prince Albrecht Street, the Gestapo's headquarters. The list of friends meant a list of Annelie's contacts that Schulz had got together – but he hadn't shared them with the Gestapo. *The date is not fixed yet, but he has assured us that when our little Effi goes on her holidays he'll send out the invitations.*

Annelie had told him how Schulz had wanted to adopt Effi. She was the image of Leni, and Schulz had wanted to marry Leni. Effi wouldn't let herself be adopted, and Schulz didn't want to force her, because then she'd hate him. So he'd let her go to Annelie, but because he'd wanted to keep her near him, he'd black-mailed Annelie. If Effi left Germany, he'd tell the Gestapo what he knew and more people than she would have lost their lives.

Annelie had never told Effi about Schulz's game. She was an intelligent little thing, but she had to be innocent with Schulz when he came visiting. She had to be friendly. That was their only guarantee of safety. If she'd refused to see Schulz he might have lost patience and shopped them after all.

'I should have gone myself,' said Bruno aloud. But he knew he couldn't have done. Even if he hadn't been arrested himself, once he took Effi away Schulz would have taken his revenge.

Now – as he did almost every day – he was remembering the horrible arguments with Leni, when she'd said she wanted to go back to her mother in Germany. How she'd shouted at him that she'd given up everything just to come with him and stay in this miserable flat in this horrible country, and she'd spent years being lonely and bored all the time the child was at school. And he'd asked her if she'd rather have stayed in Germany and made films for Hitler.

She'd turned away from him and said, 'I'm my mother's only child and she's dying.'

I should have been kinder to her, he thought. I was a brute.

Then one day she'd told him she was going. That she'd bought the tickets. And he'd said, 'You're not taking the child into that hellhole?'

He thought he remembered every word of that shouting match, he could play it in his head like a film.

'You're so busy,' said Leni. Angrily. 'You hardly have time for us now, how could you look after her on your own?'

He hadn't considered her loneliness in England – he'd had plenty of time to do that since.

'I'm working myself stupid,' he'd said, 'just to keep you and the child.' He'd said it self-righteously, he'd remembered the schlocky popular songs he had to write, he'd felt sorry for himself because the world wanted those instead of his symphonies; he'd even, God help him, been afraid that now his working-class origins were catching up with him, clawing him back. Fine Communist he'd been.

'We could have stayed,' Leni had said. 'Other people got by, they adjusted.'

'Turned into Nazis, you mean? Do you remember the Brownshirts were coming for me? Do you remember what they did to Max? The trouble with you is you grew up with too much money, you never had to face reality.'

Leni shut her mouth tight for a moment. Then she said, 'Schulz will look after me. He'd have made it all right for you, too.'

He was furious. 'So you've been writing to Schulz? As well as sneaking off and getting the tickets behind my back?'

'Schulz will make sure I get in and out all right.'

He screamed: 'Go on, then! Go to Schulz! Marry him if you like! Just leave me the child!'

'No,' said Leni.

They caught the evening boat train. He refused to go to Victoria Station to see them off. It was raining and they stood outside the house getting wet and not saying anything while the taxicab waited for them.

Leni said, 'Are you hoping we'll miss the train?'

'No,' he said angrily. 'You've given yourself plenty of time.'

'Bruno,' she said, 'we'll be back soon.'

She'd wanted to kiss and be friends. But he wouldn't. He'd kissed Effi. He'd said to her, 'Remember I love you.' He'd given Leni a quick unfriendly kiss on the cheek and gone back into the house. He'd slammed the door. And she'd gone to Germany and that was the last time he ever saw her. Oh, they'd made it up in letters. But he'd never held her in his arms again.

If Effi's dead, he thought – and he'd thought that more often than once a day – my life won't be worth living and I'll throw my useless body in the Elbe.

His phone rang.

'Lieutenant Mann? My name's Kline, Lieutenant Kline. I'm a medical officer in Torgau. I've got a German girl here, speaks English, claims to be your daughter. You don't have a daughter in Germany, do you? I'd have gotten rid of her right away, but she won't leave me alone. She's with a little bunch of bedraggled refugees and a comic dog, they swam the Elbe last night, she says, flagged down my jeep on the road – pretty little thing, mind you –'

Bruno said, 'What does she look like?'

'Black curly hair, black eyes.'

'I'm coming.'

He ran outside and got into his jeep. He didn't care about the prisoners he had to interview. He drove to Torgau. He had to drive more slowly than he wanted to because suddenly his life was worth something after all. He kept having to stop for tanks or for queues of prisoners being marched off to camp, for civilians going God knew where. It took him two and a half hours. Towards the end of the journey he started to worry that the girl wasn't Effi after all. That she was just some crazy girl who'd got hold of one of his records and liked the song, so had decided to be his daughter. Maybe he should have had Kline bring her to the phone and asked her a few questions to make sure the journey was worthwhile?

He found Lieutenant Kline in a big old house that had been turned into a temporary hospital, and asked him if he could see the girl where she couldn't see him.

'Sure,' said Kline. 'I'll get her in the yard here, you can look out through the window from my office.' He put his head on one side. 'So you do have a daughter in Germany? What's the story? OK, OK, I won't hang around.'

He stood by the window, another US officer in uniform. He looked out into the yard. There was an arched gateway at the back of it. Kline came back with the dog he'd been talking about – and Effi. He knew her at once. She looked just like Leni when they'd first met. He ran into the yard, almost tripping over his own feet, clumsy with joy. Effi saw him. Her eyes opened wide. She recognized him. After all these years she recognized him. She was running towards him. A moment later she was in his arms.

Chapter Twenty

Even then, it wasn't easy. The Americans weren't supposed to be 'fraternizing' with the German population. This didn't stop the GIs going to bed with German girls – nor did it stop Papa squeezing all five of them, and the dog, into the jeep and driving them back to Leipzig, but it did make it strictly illegal for him to keep Effi and Hanno in his apartment. The dog wasn't a problem. Papa could keep as many dogs as he liked.

What Papa did was to have Effi tell her story to the Colonel. In English. By the time she'd finished the Colonel was in tears.

'Just forget about the rules,' he said. 'After all, we're making them now.'

That was crazy because the Amis had made the non-fraternization rule, but it didn't matter. You did what you could get away with, Effi had known that for years. It wasn't going to be any different in peacetime. Now Papa was getting the Americans in Frankfurt to look for Hanno's mother and his sister; when they'd done that, he said, he'd wangle a trip to Frankfurt, so that he could take Hanno in his jeep.

Effi didn't want Hanno's mother and his big sister to be dead, but she wanted it to be a while before the Amis found them.

Frau Rupf, Frau Magda and Barbara went on to

Frankfurt anyway. They'd thought they might stay in Leipzig for a while, but Papa warned them that the Americans were likely to withdraw a long way behind their present lines. The Russians would almost certainly be coming to Leipzig.

He gave them a good meal and a supply of tinned rations, and he got hold of a little cart and a pony for them – that cost a lot of American cigarettes – so that they could ride to Frankfurt in comfort. They left on the day that the news came about Hitler's death. Effi was truly sorry to say goodbye to old Ida and little, damaged Barbara, who was talking again and had discovered chewing gum. She was almost sad to say goodbye to Ma Headscarf. She gave them all the dried-out tobacco, and the cotton reels. She didn't need either now and they'd be able to sell them. She just kept one cotton reel for herself in memory of Aunt Annelie.

It hadn't been easy, telling Papa Aunt Annelie was dead. Except at least there was someone else who minded that as much as she did.

Effi and Hanno hardly noticed the final ending of the war in Europe. The war had ended for them when they got out of the Elbe. There was a time for them to try and forget about what they'd been through, just to be relieved that there were no more air raids, there was no more fighting, no more hiding from the Russians, and that they were alive. They slept a lot in comfortable beds. The sun shone every day and there was plenty to eat, water to wash with. Papa managed to find clothes for them. He gave them books to read, chewing gum and candy. And there was music, Papa had a gramophone and records, too many symphonies and operas, but there was a Louis

Armstrong record. Effi and Hanno played it till Papa complained he'd never be able to write any more of his own music again, he said all he could hear was 'Pennies from Heaven'.

Every morning Effi woke up and said to herself: 'I'm with Papa, and Hanno's here too.' She didn't really want to see anyone else. All the time Papa was working she wanted to be with Hanno. Dancing with him to the new jazz records Papa got hold of – 'So at least,' he said, 'I have more than two jazz tracks in my head.'

Papa saying that, grinning, and then coming over to hug Effi. Hanno in the daytime, hanging out in the apartment with her, drawing on paper Papa got, drawing Effi – especially her feet, which made her giggle – drawing jugs, bottles, flowers, the furniture – anything he could see around him, whittling at a few bits of wood, though Papa thought most of the wood should be left behind for the people to burn. Papa listening to her sing, singing with her, telling her things. Hanno listening.

When Papa was free he'd drive them out into the countryside in the jeep. Hanno and Papa talking, talking, about Hanno's father, about Papa's past.

'We Communists were partly to blame,' he said, taking his hands off the steering wheel to wave them about and having to quickly put them back on again. 'Would Hitler have come to power if people hadn't been frightened of the street battles between the Nazis and the Communists? We thought the Republic was rotten, we hoped for a violent revolution as much as the Nazis did. We thought we'd break the old order and make heaven on earth. We were so keen on our own ideology, we wouldn't co-operate with anyone else on the left, let alone the conservatives. So there was no proper opposition to Hitler. We should have made friends with the conservatives, the way people like my sister had to later on, to try and kill Hitler. Only then it was too late. It was because we wouldn't compromise that other people ended up compromising their integrity. People like your father. There are a few people who are fanatics – like that Otto or your mad doctor – but any ordinary person can do horrible things if society demands it of them. And only a few people – like my sister – are in a position to say no, let alone having the strength to do so. It'll be different now, anyway. Now we will make a better world.' A glance and a smile at Effi.

'Are you still a Communist?' asked Hanno.

'No. I've heard things about Russia. I don't like them. But I still believe in social justice.'

Hanno, hesitantly: 'Do you think I could really become a sculptor?'

'Do you feel like one inside?'

Hanno understood. 'Yes. I have the feeling inside. But I know how much I've got to learn. Who's going to teach me? I don't know any artists.'

'You know me. And I have a friend in Frankfurt. He's still alive, I know. He was a painter, not a sculptor. He's had to paint secretly for years – watercolours so that when the Gestapo came to search the house they wouldn't smell the oil paint. He kept his work in a hiding place under the floorboards. He could teach you to draw, if he likes your work. I'll take you to see him when we go to Frankfurt. Listen, Hanno, I was just a working-class kid who loved music, and our doctor's wife encouraged me. She was an artist, a printmaker and sculptor. You wouldn't have heard of her, she's been in disgrace under the Nazis too. Käthe Kollwitz. Anyway, she showed me how to get the training I needed before and after the war.'

'Did you fight in the First World War, then?'

'Just for a year. I was lucky. I survived.'

'I ran away from the fighting.'

'That was a courageous thing to do. You turned your back on the propaganda, you did what was right. You're needed for the future, lad. And the peace will be a challenge, believe me.'

There was a German maid in the apartment – 'chaperoning you,' said Papa, but they didn't really need that. They'd dance together, they'd give each other little kisses, but it was almost as if they both wanted to be much younger than they were for a while. As if now each wanted the other to protect them from any excitement, from anything else happening. Sometimes they'd just sit quiet with their arms round each other. They'd find out how many tricks Cornelius could do and try to teach him new ones.

Then the news came about Hanno's mother and sister. They were alive, living with his aunt in the bottom floor of her house, which was all that was left standing. It was an American padre who'd found them, and he'd broken the news to Frau Frisch about Wolfgang's death. She sent her best love to Hanno, and said she couldn't wait to see him again.

So there he was, sitting in the jeep with Bruno and Effi, on his way back to the Germany of ruins he'd been sheltered from for – how long was it? A month? This was the real test, Bruno was right. The peace was going to be far harder than the war and there'd be no running away from it. And he'd be with Mother and Heide, but without Wolfgang or Effi. Or Bruno.

He looked out of the jeep and saw the people walking as he and Effi had walked. He saw the buildings in ruins. Little kids begging from the Ami soldier. Bruno always had a pocketful of sweets and cigarettes to throw them. All these things had been there when Bruno used to drive them out to the countryside, but Hanno hadn't focused his eyes on them then. Not properly. And hour by hour they got closer to Frankfurt. It took them three days. They stayed in American quarters at night – he was still insulated from Germany.

He looked at Bruno, whose eyes were on the road. He was tall and blond and as honest and kind as Otto had been vicious. Effi sat beside him. On the seat behind them Cornelius sat and breathed damp warmth down the backs of their necks. It seemed unbelievable that they were going to leave him behind in Frankfurt. Of course he wanted to see Mother and Heide, but Bruno and Effi – and Cornelius – felt like his family, he wanted them too. Only he couldn't have them. And he'd have to forget about the chewing-gum boy, the jazz-dancing boy. He'd have to be the German boy, running errands and slogging again. He'd have to help mend things and go hungry.

They got into Frankfurt, along roads cleared through the broken buildings. He'd seen this before in Leipzig but these were going to be *his* ruins, the ruins he'd live in. Dusty, dangerous, sprouting fireweed.

'We'll write,' said Effi. 'We'll keep in touch.'

He saw that she was crying. He put his arm round her and comforted her, it helped him pretend he didn't want to cry himself. And too soon they were in the street, looking at a one-storey house huddling in the ruins of a big one. And there was a girl on the street, she was Heide, and she screamed 'Mother! Mother!'

And he was in Mother's arms and they were both crying, and then hugging Heide, he was so glad to see them, and ashamed of himself for what he'd felt before. And Aunt

Lisi was standing there, waiting to hug him too, saying 'Thank God you were spared, thank God.'

It got bad then, because though Mother was crying and thanking Bruno for bringing her son back to her, she was talking to him as if he was a stranger – it was clear she didn't want to invite him into the house. Hanno saw that she didn't like Bruno being in American uniform when he was German. And when Effi spoke to her, she smiled at her, but her face said, 'Listen to this girl talking, she's really common.' She looked afraid when the dog jumped down from the jeep, relieved because he wasn't going to stay with them. And too soon Hanno was hugging Bruno and Effi to say good-bye to them, and Mother saw Effi in tears and her whole body said, 'What have *you* got to cry about?'

At least they came back the next day. They took Hanno to see Michael Hildebrand, the artist, whose house was about half an hour's walk away. He was a shy man with dark, greying hair, and dark eyes. He showed Hanno a painting he'd started since the Americans had come. Hanno couldn't quite understand it, but he was interested. He showed Herr Hildebrand his drawings and small carvings. The artist lingered on the knot of wood that Hanno had carved in the forest. He turned it over and over in his hands.

'Yes,' he said. 'I like this.' Then he gave it back to Hanno. 'You could come here tomorrow,' he said, smiling carefully, as if he wasn't sure about smiling. 'And once a week, maybe?'

'Yes, please,' said Hanno.

Then Bruno drove him back towards the ruined street in the jeep but he stopped a block away and said, 'I'm going to stand over there and turn my back on you.'

*

Hanno said: 'I can't believe it's time to say goodbye.'

'But you want to be with your mother, don't you? And your sister?'

Effi was crying. He put his arms round her and kissed her wet face. And then he was crying, too, and he wasn't ashamed of himself. They weren't little-boy tears.

'I want you too.'

'I know. But listen, Swing Boy, we'll write. And we'll get together again. Maybe Papa will come back to Germany and I'll come with him, don't you worry. And you'll come to America. You'll have an exhibition or something, and I'll be living in Hollywood.'

'With your lion and your pink limo.'

'The lion's going to be so kind and friendly. Like Cornelius. He'll rub himself against you and purr. No – lions don't purr, do they? Anyway, you'll be able to stroke his mane and then we'll go out for a walk with him and the dog. And everyone will say, Who's that stunner with Effi Mann? After the journey we've just done, getting to America in peacetime will be nothing. You've got to believe in the future, Hanno. I won't forget you. I love you.'

He kissed her again, they held on as if they'd never let go. He was saying: 'I love you too, I do, Effi.'

Now Bruno was coming back. He drove them round the corner. Hanno got out. He saw Effi's hand waving good-bye out of the jeep and Cornelius peering anxiously, as if he couldn't understand why Hanno had to stay behind.

He stood in the street with the tears running round his face, and then someone touched him on the arm. It was Heide. He stopped crying and let her take him back to Mother.

Bruno had left food for them – he'd said it was the least he could do when Hanno had taken such good care of his daughter, so Mother had accepted it. Now they were going to have tinned meat for dinner, but she sent Hanno out to look for nettles to go with them. They'd make the Ami food go a long way.

He was lucky, that first day. He found a clump of dusty nettles growing out from under a pile of rubble only a block away. It made him remember how he'd got nettles for Effi at the ruined farm. And he thought: She didn't like me at first. Supposing she forgets about me?

But he'd never forget her. Maybe he'd go to America, as she'd said. He'd go to her dressing room after a show. He'd knock, and her dresser, or whatever you called them, would let him in. She'd turn round and look at him as if she was about to say she had a gun and would shoot him if he wasn't careful. And then she'd recognize him. Her face would soften. They'd start getting to know each other all over again. Would she have the lion in the dressing room? And Cornelius?

A nettle stung him all over his palm, but he started to laugh.